BOOKS BY PHIL EDWARDS

Jake Russo Mysteries
Retirement Can Be Murder
Death By Gumbo
Dead Air Can Kill You
The Show Must Go Wrong
Lights! Camera! Murder!

Thrillers
Cloud Crash: A Technothriller

Humor
Fake Science 101: A Less-Than-Factual Guide to Our Amazing World
Dumbemployed: Hilariously Dumb And Sad But True Stories About Jobs Like Yours
Snooki In Wonderland

Learn more and connect with the author at PhilEdwardsInc.com.

Copyright Information

This book is a work of fiction. Names, characters, places and incidents are products of the author's imagination or are used fictitiously. Any resemblance to actual events or locales or persons, living or dead, is entirely coincidental.

Copyright © 2011 by Phil Edwards

Published by Harrison-Mills Media

All rights reserved, including the right to reproduce this book or portions thereof in any form whatsoever.

This book is a premium edition 2011.

Created and designed in the United States of America

For more information about the author, visit PhilEdwardsInc.com.

Retirement Can Be Murder

A JAKE RUSSO MYSTERY

PHIL EDWARDS

Harrison-Mills Media

CHAPTER 1:

It was a warm day at Sunset Cove. Of course it was warm. They both had a thin film of sweat on their foreheads, but they weren't hot enough to wipe it off. Jake didn't mind sweating in khakis. Mel was wearing a skirt and she looked good. She wore her waist high like someone older, but she was young enough. She'd been talking for a while.

"And on this patch of grass here, we're going to have the new garden. I'm told that we'll have some flowers that are particularly rare in Sarasota."

"What are the flowers called?"

"Oh, I don't know what they are." She gestured again. "I just know they're rare."

He started writing in his notebook, but she stopped him.

"Don't write that down!"

"Why not?"

"Please Jake!"

"Why not?"

"It's embarrassing." She bit her lip. "I'll find out what the flowers are called."

"Don't worry. All I wrote down is that the flowers would be rare, whatever they are called."

She still got nervous around him. He didn't like it—she should be comfortable by now. This month he'd stopped by twice a week, whether he needed to or not. Really he could come by every day, if he wanted to. It wasn't like his beat had a lot of structure to it. He could always find something to write about, dress it up in fancy words, and send it to New York. Mel bit her lip again.

"Did your editor like the last piece?"

"The one about the movie room?"

"Yes."

"I think it went all right. You know, instead of running the picture of Sunset Cove, we had to go with the one at the Palmstead Homes. Sorry. They had stadium seating. We had to use that, since Gary got a good shot."

"Oh that's fine." She had a bit of an accent—sounds stuck in the back of her cheeks.

"But I'll write about your new garden in the landscaping piece. I'll say something about what it will look like once you finish."

"Thank you Jake." She touched his arm. He patted down his hair. The humidity down here, it made it flop up instead of staying combed back. She let go.

"You know, I still can't believe New Yorkers would actually want to read about us."

"Well, they do. I mean, once they retire from the city, this is where they're moving. Right? Half the people in Sunset Cove are former New Yorkers, aren't they?"

"I suppose."

"And the people who are still in the city want to know what to expect when they move down here. Trends. Outlooks. Prospects. After all, they want the best years of their lives to be well planned."

She laughed.

"I suppose. It just seems funny. I'd rather read about things up there, if I were them."

"Well..." he said and trailed off. They both looked to the right. Someone went by in a vehicle that was larger than a wheelchair, but smaller than a golf cart.

"Are you from New York originally Jake?"

"Yup. I had a nice condo in Long Island City too."

"You hated the weather?"

"Not really."

"Then why did you come down here?"

"Just shuffling at the desk. What our readers wanted."

He knew he should be asking her out. That way he wouldn't have to come back again and think up another story that could include Sunset Cove. But he kept looking around. Took his notebook, wrote something short and quick. She smiled again. She had nice lips that looked soft. It was times like these he thought his boss might have been right. Maybe he really wasn't aggressive enough for this job. When his boss had said it, Jake had yelled at him, shouted about professionalism and decorum. But maybe Thompson had been right to move him down here to this humid beat. There were four syllables in the word "Sarasota." That was probably the most interesting thing about it.

"I'll be back tomorrow," he said, finally.

"Yes?"

"Yeah. For a follow up. You have to find out what type of flowers you're getting. And why they're so rare."

"That's right," she said and smiled. She shook his hand and held it before walking back to her office. He started walking down the path. Another trip back home with nothing to report.

Palm trees, green grass, giant bugs—they all lost their novelty after a while. They were just part of the local color, but nothing to notice anymore. Still, he always tried to mention them in his articles. Except for the giant bugs. He walked on the path and was careful not to step on the grass. He was doing an article about landscaping after all. It didn't seem right to mess things up.

He was getting closer to the parking lot when he heard it. A high sound, like wind hitting the side of a building. He reached in his pocket for the keys to his car. Got them. Then he heard the noise again. He looked back and then down.

The old woman's head came up to his chest and not any higher. She was leaning over a walker, and the angle of her back was almost ninety degrees to her legs. Her body was a corner. She had long gray hair. Thin. Blew out in the wind. He'd never seen her before in his life. Of course he'd never seen most of the residents before. She was wearing a blue jean dress with long sleeves. It must have been hot as hell under there.

"Wait," she cried. That was the sound. She'd been yelling to him.

"I'm waiting mam."

"Sir, are you the reporter?"

"Yeah."

"You are?"

"Yes mam." More polite. "I'm Jake. How are you doing today?"

"I'm fine, thank you. Why are you here?"

"I was just working on a piece about your community's landscaping. I heard each of the Rothschild condos is updating and expanding. All across the state. What do you think about it?"

He got out his notebook and pen. She stayed cornered over the walker and whispered something. He asked her to repeat it louder.

"I said that I have a story for your paper."

"Yes mam? About the landscaping?"

"No." She looked him in the eye. "I have a real story."

He backed away a couple of steps. She was leaning in close and he could hear her tiny breaths. She looked up again—pale skin for such a hot place.

"You'll come to my building," she said. "I'm Room 112 in Building B."

"Room 112 in Building B?"

"Yes. Please do meet with me. It's very important. When will you be by?"

He rested his pen on the paper. He'd already written down her room number. It was like a contract.

"Well, I'm coming back tomorrow around nine. But I can't be sure I'll have time—"

"Stop by then."

She started to wheel the walker away. He didn't chase after her. It wasn't worth it, really. He'd stop by. She'd tell him something about aliens, or World War Two, or her son. A "real story". It would be a normal morning. Hopefully he'd have gotten a date with Mel by then. He didn't know what they'd do. Maybe they'd drive somewhere far away, where they couldn't be interrupted. He imagined looking out at the water with her and whispering something nice about the waves.

CHAPTER 2:

He took a long run around the neighborhood when he got home. A warm day turned hot. He was sweating through his t-shirt and he climbed up his apartment stairs slowly. Tired. Seven miles was his longest yet. He let his watch beep and went inside to take a shower. After he took one, he'd finish up work for the day.

The apartment still looked new. It was small and the closet door was open. Most of the clothes were new—he'd had to buy new ones. The carpet on the floor was thick and blue. He kept his socks on, so he wouldn't make sweat marks with his toes, and checked the cell phone quickly. Two calls—one from Gary and one from Thompson. Great. When he got out of the shower, he knew who he'd call first.

"Russo!" Thompson screamed. "What the hell have you been doing?"

He sighed and combed his wet hair with his free hand.

"I just took a shower after my run. You know what the hours are like here. The business day ends around dinner. 4PM."

"A run! I'm your editor, Jake, I know when you're full of it. We don't pay you to run. If I wanted a runner, I'd pay somebody who could run. You think I believe that you could run?"

"I ran seven miles today."

"I'd pay a Kenyan if I wanted somebody to run. At least I'd believe they were telling…telling the truth."

Thompson always sounded like he had something stuck in his throat. Maybe a whole nest was in there. He repeated words sometimes, but he wasn't stuttering. He seemed to be doing it for emphasis. It was best to ignore him.

"I really did run seven miles."

"Russo, what are you eating right now? Just…just tell me. I want to imagine it. We miss you here. You know what?"

"What?"

"We still call the weekly donut day 'Jake's Day.' We really still do it."

"That's great. You know, you should change the name. I've cut out all the junk food since I got here. I don't know how much weight I've lost. It's more than seventy five pounds. Maybe a hundred."

"Sure you have. Carla...Carla come here," Thompson yelled. The phone went dead and he heard Thompson and his assistant Carla laughing. "See Russo—Carla agrees with me. Stop it Carla, you do agree. Every day I bring in donuts, people still call it 'Jake's Day.' 'Thank God it's "Jake's Day,"' they say. 'I didn't think I was going to make it to "Jake's Day,"' they tell me."

"All right. Really. I've changed since then, but that's fine. Did you have something to talk about?"

"Last week, oh boy." Thompson laughed but didn't cough. "Last week, a new guy, Jason Edelman came up to me. He...he says, 'Sir, I was wondering—could we push "Jake's Day" forward? I won't be able to write up this fire in the Bronx without a little sugar in my system.'"

Jake's hair was dry by now. He hung up the towel and poured a glass of filtered water.

"Can you believe it?" Thompson said, screaming now. "Jason Edelman. Do you remember him?"

"No, I don't."

"Exactly! Exactly! He didn't start until after I sent you to Florida! Can you believe it? This little dork never even knew you, and he still says it's 'Jake's Day' when I bring in the donuts!"

"That's fantastic sir."

"He's got glasses, ties, the whole thing. Harvard or something."

"Wonderful."

"And this kid was practically crying for 'Jake's Day!'"

Jake didn't say anything. He just finished the water and looked at his watch. He had run seven miles. He had looked it up on the computer and measured it out, step by step, and his time wasn't bad either. Not great, but not bad. He had stopped sweating and took off his socks one at a time.

"Ah Russo," Thompson laughed. "You're a great guy. You don't have to tell me what you're eating. It's fine."

"Thank you sir. Is there something we need to go over?"

"Right...right. I'm afraid there is. I got your latest article about the...what do you call it?"

"The entertainment centers piece? About trends in condo movie nights?"

"Right. I'm just a little disappointed in it."

"Why? What's wrong with it?"

Jake picked up his notebook and pen. Thompson answered after a pause.

"Where...where are the palm trees?"

He put his pen down.

"The palm trees?"

"For God's sake, Jake. Your article is about all these movie theatres and TVs or whatever. Jake. We've got TVs here in New York. Big TVs, tiny TVs, medium TVs, pink TVs, black TVs, white TVs. I don't know why I'm talking about TVs. I hate them—all colors. But the point is, our people don't want to read about TVs. They want to read about the things they don't have. They want palm trees, and beaches, and motor boats. And palm trees, Jake. They want palm trees. We sent you to Sarasota for palm trees."

"But the piece was about the new spending on entertainment centers. A good part of condo community spending is going to build these things. And most seniors love them. I thought the readers would want—"

"Listen. I know you think you know what the readers want. That's why I'm the editor and you're sweating and eating fried Snickers bars in Sarasota. OK? Just listen—palm trees. Sound nice, don't they?"

"I can't put palm trees in every article."

"What about celebrities?"

Thompson said something off the phone. Someone laughed. Jake sighed.

"Sir, there aren't any celebrities in Sarasota."

"Then find some. There must be some stars down there. Our readers love that."

"I can't promise it." Jake doodled in his notebook. "I'll try for the palm trees."

"Both!"

"Do people really want that?"

Thompson laughed.

"Right. Again, that's why I'm the editor and you're having your third ice cream cone by 9AM."

"I told you that I've been on a strict diet—"

"So that's it. More palm trees, please."

He sighed and wrote it in the notebook, next to the doodles. He penned in his mileage for the day next to that. He had run that far. His thighs ached. He wanted to stretch. But he had to ask now.

"Wait a second, sir. I have just one other thing."

"Yes? What is it?"

Sometimes, Thompson pretended he liked questions. Not this time.

"It's about Gary."

"Who's that?"

"My photo guy. I'm just wondering if there's anything in the budget to get somebody a little more…"

"More…more what? Spit it out!"

"Just more…a lot of things."

"Gary, huh. Listen, Russo, his shot of the movie theatre was the best thing about your article. He's staying. Our photographer there has been our man for 45 years this June. He's getting a plaque."

"Exactly—45 years. Almost half a century. There's no way we could get someone a little…"

"Tell Gary to shoot more palm trees though. You…you both could use more palm trees."

Thompson hung up. He still did that. Jake held the phone in his hand for a few seconds then put it down. That's how it was. He hadn't even gotten to argue his case. But he hadn't had time, had he? He stretched a little and looked around. The kitchen was in view. He'd promised himself he wouldn't do this. But it had been a hell of a day. He walked to the kitchen and opened the cabinet.

He took out the shot glass. "Queens NYC" it said. A memento. He opened the refrigerator. He'd sworn he wouldn't do it. He was going to turn over a new leaf. He'd bought the bottle on a dark day a few weeks ago and kept it there. He'd never opened it and he knew he should throw it out. But he couldn't. He went in the fridge, pushed aside the jugs of mineral water and the containers of Diet Vegetable Juice, and there it was. He felt his hand wrap around the label.

He set the bottle beside the shot glass. It was just a sip. And this small of an amount didn't matter, right? It couldn't matter. It was trivial. He ran his hand through his hair and combed it back again. He'd burned off all the calories during his run. It was fine. And since he'd bought the bottle, it would be wasteful not to use it. Sixteen ounces had 252 calories and 65.7 grams of sugar. 65.7. But when you poured cream soda, you could smell it and see it sparkle. He used to drink a bottle a day. He deserved a taste.

He started twisting the cap, the little white ridges lining up with his fingerprints. Right when he'd almost broken the seal, the phone rang. He screamed and put down the bottle. His heart was beating faster than when he'd been running. He put it back in the fridge—if he didn't answer the phone now, Gary would keep calling back.

"Hi Gary."

He tried to forget what had almost happened.

"Hello Jacob!" Gary usually shouted on the phone. "Jacob, I was talking to Meryl. I have an idea for a new story for you, one that will really knock socks off. People, they'll be in the streets, running, their toes bare, yelling about this."

Gary shouted something to his wife and Jake sat down and leaned back in his chair, waiting. Gary had a lingering accent from Eastern Europe. Jake didn't know the country, but he assumed its name had changed a few times since Gary left. He wheezed into the phone.

"Wait. I think I pressed a button. Can you hear me on this thing?"

"I can hear you fine Gary."

"Jacob—testing, testing. Can you hear me?"

"I can hear you Gary. Do you want to talk?"

"Jacob. I am going to test if you can hear me. This is a test."

"What is it?"

Meryl yelled something on the other end, and Jake heard a beep.

"Jacob, I'm here. It's me, Gary!"

"Great Gary. I can hear you."

"Jacob?"

"Yes?"

"I think I forgot my idea."

"That's OK, Gary. I understand."

"It was such a good idea!"

"I know. I know. I'm sure it was a great idea."

"Well, that's the way things will go. Do you need any photographs in the near future?"

"I should be fine." The air conditioning had finally cooled him down. He put on an old sweatshirt he'd brought down with him. It hardly fit. "Thanks for calling, Gary. But I just have a little thing tomorrow with Mel. Then I'm talking to some lady and doing research at the library."

"An interview with a lady? I'll come out."

"No, she's nothing. Not a story—just a crazy woman. Don't bother."

"Where is it? Sunset Cove?"

"Well, yes. But really, we won't run anything about her. It doesn't have to do with the landscape piece. She just approached me randomly."

"I'll meet you at Sunset Cove. What time? Meryl, get me a writer."

"Really, Gary, don't bother. I'm going over around nine, but you don't—"

"I've got a pen. 9 AM. Sunset Cove. Will we be needing my new special lens?"

"Gary, it's not necessary."

"No special lens?"

"No."

"Anywhere particular in the Cove?"

"I'm serious." He didn't want to say it, but he needed to this time. "We won't pay you for it."

He waited for Gary to respond. He heard him breathing.

"No problem!" Gary shouted. "I'll practice with my new lens. It'll be perfect. And you wanted me to test it out. So 9AM, Sunset Cove. What's the room?"

It wasn't worth fighting.

"Fine. Room 112, Building B. I might be a few minutes later than nine though, so—"

"I'm there. And if I remember my idea, I'll write it down this time."

"Thanks Gary. All right. I should go."

"Jacob?" He repeated it louder. "Jacob? Can you hear me?"

"I can hear you Gary."

"Jacob. Can. You. Hear. Me."

"Yes, I can hear you."

"Jacob?"

"Yes?"

"Good night."

Gary hung up and left Jake holding the phone, shaking his head. At least he hadn't had the cream soda.

CHAPTER 3:

Things started so early in Sarasota. He got up near sunrise and took care of some work. Cleaned up an article about the best "New York" diners in the Sarasota area. None of them were very good, especially when you were on a permanent diet. He went for another run since he didn't know if he'd have time when he got back. It went longer than he thought—by the time he'd showered, had breakfast, and gotten dressed, he was running late. When he got to Sunset Cove, it was already almost nine.

Mel had dressed up for him. He could tell. When he showed up that morning, she had on a red dress. The waist high, again, with a white flower print on the dress, scattered. She looked good. Maybe too good. Her hair looked wavier and a little darker than it had before. He knew he needed to be confident, so he asked her if the pattern on her dress showed the rare flowers she'd forgotten. She liked it. Then she told him she hadn't learned the name of the flowers yet.

"So that's all you came by for?"

"I just had to check that fact."

"Oh, OK."

He wasn't aggressive enough for this job.

"Is there anything else that I should know?"

"I don't think so. I'm sorry that we can't get the landscaping people to talk to you. But I don't think your readers know Spanish."

She laughed a little loudly. He did too.

"Well, thanks again. Mel."

"Any time." She looked around and clasped her hands. "I like your shirt."

"It's just a collared shirt."

"You don't see those enough these days."

"True." He rubbed his hands together. "That's a really nice dress."

"Really?"

"Really. It is."

More aggressive.

They walked from the patch of grass where the garden would be into her office. Mel's room just had a desk, a phone, and a flat screen TV showing ads for various Rothschild properties. They looked at it a bit and listened to the music in the background. She walked to her desk and brought him a piece of paper.

"Did you see this article about us?"

"Of course."

"Very exciting, isn't it? And they ranked all our properties not just for size, but for quality too. It's so flattering."

"That's true." Jake handed it back to her. "I've done a few of those "Best of" surveys. Worked on them. Mine covered different subjects than retirement communities, of course, but I can still get an idea of things. I get the impression that this one's on the up and up."

"Aren't all of them?"

"You'd hope." They listened to the music again. He picked out a melody but couldn't match it to a song.

"I should be going." Be aggressive.

"Home?"

"Not quite. Some woman here wanted me to talk to her. I agreed. So I'm going to go make a house call."

"Who was it?"

"I don't know actually. I just got her number."

Mel blushed. She sat on her desk and crossed her legs at the knees. Her toenails were painted red.

"Oh really, Jake? 'Just got her number.' Are you dating one of our residents?"

They laughed. She shook her hair back and touched his arm. He blushed the color of her dress.

"I wish. I'm not that lucky."

"Aren't you?"

"Nope." Be aggressive.

"I'm sure you could find a date."

"Maybe. We'll see."

"You know you could."

"Well then. Have a good day."

He was sweating even in the air conditioning. The muzak was stuck in his head and he kept repeating the melody over and over. Then he repeated the command. Be aggressive. He was different now, he could pull it off. But he kept walking away. He felt the rush of air as he opened the door and a little bell rang. Now he had to talk to an old lady. It fit. The door started to shut behind him.

"Jake, wait."

He turned back. She slid off the desk and stood up.

"I was wondering..."

"Yeah?"

"Since you aren't dating any of our residents, I was wondering what you were doing tomorrow night."

"I'm not sure." He knew he was doing nothing. "Why do you ask?"

"Mr. Rothschild is having a banquet tomorrow. It's to celebrate his various charitable donations. Of course, really it's to celebrate him. A lot of people from the company and the community will be there."

"Sure." He got out his notebook. "If you think I should report on it…"

"No." She clasped her hands again. "I was hoping you'd take me. Not as a reporter though."

"Really?"

"I'm sorry. It's probably unprofessional. A conflict of interest. I shouldn't have—"

"No. I'd love it."

"You would?"

"Of course. And not as a reporter. As a person." He was sweating again. She laughed.

"Can you pick me up here sometime tomorrow night?"

"What time would be good?"

"7 PM. Fortunately, Mr. Rothschild doesn't eat dinner as

early as most of our residents."

"No, that's great." He felt his neck turning red. The blush moved down his body.

"Great. It's a date."

"I'll see you then."

"Oh, and it's semi-formal dress. So I'll be better dressed than this."

She looked great. He wanted to tell her. Be aggressive. But he'd done well enough. He gave her a wave goodbye and the bell dinged again as he opened the door. He could feel himself smiling, even though he couldn't see it. Outside, everything looked beautiful. It wasn't even hot yet, even though it was…

He looked at his watch.

He was late. It was already 9:10. The old woman probably didn't have anything to do, but he still didn't like to keep people waiting. And he hadn't been in any of the residences before. That was something to look forward to. He might even be able to work a detail or two into one of his pieces. "Residents in some condo communities put out welcome mats in the hallway, even though they are indoors." A white haired woman walked by, dragging a dog along a leash. That welcome mat thing seemed like something she would do.

He walked briskly down the winding path. He knew where Building B was, but he wished he knew the woman's name. At least he had the number: 112. As he reached the bottom of the path, he looked at his watch again. 9:13. He'd apologize to the woman before she started her little story.

But when he rounded the corner, he didn't see the door to the building. He saw something else. Something he didn't expect. The door to the complex was being held open by a rock. And two men in white clothes were going in and out. An ambulance was parked on the curb next to the building and the back doors were open. He ran around and looked in the ambulance's cab. No one was inside yet.

He ran to the propped open door and grabbed one of the men on the shoulder, a short Hispanic kid who smelled like aftershave.

"What happened here? Is everything OK?"

"Sorry sir, we're very busy."

"I know, just tell me what happened."

"An accident." A walkie talkie buzzed but the kid ignored it.

"What kind of accident?"

The kid strained to hear his walkie talkie. Someone came out of the building—an elderly man wearing a red-brimmed hat. Jake turned away from the kid and caught the man.

"Sir, what's going on? What happened here?"

"Oh, they wouldn't let me look in. But this always happens. Happens every few days. A sad thing though."

The man shook his head.

"What? What happened?"

He tipped his hat and started walking away.

"Sir," Jake said. "Can you tell me what room this happened in?"

"Charlotte's room." He turned back. "She's in room 112."

The old man walked off and Jake ran his hands through his hair. Room 112 in Building B. He looked at the ambulance idling by the curb. He could imagine the siren spinning around, glinting red when it took her body away. Bright bright red. The same color as Mel's dress.

CHAPTER 4:

The Hispanic kid was more talkative when he wasn't distracted by his walkie talkie. While he sat in the passenger seat of the ambulance, Jake talked to him. The driver finished paperwork for the call.

"Does this sort of thing happen a lot?" Jake asked. He stood on the curb, still breathing heavily. The kid leaned out the window.

"Oh yeah, all the time."

"Do you get used to it?"

"I wouldn't want to." He squinted. Might have been thinking. Or it could have been the sun.

"Why don't you want to get used to it?"

Jake got out his notebook and pen. He started writing it down.

"It's good to stay nervous. It keeps you on top of your game."

"That's great."

The driver said something to the kid. Jake waited and the kid buckled his seatbelt.

"We have to go. Call at the Palmstead. Nothing urgent."

"Sometimes you just drive a loop from here to there, I bet."

"Sometimes."

"So is there anything else?"

"Just make sure he stays off his feet for a bit. And don't let him exert himself again. He needs rest. But otherwise he should be fine."

The ambulance drove away slowly. They didn't have to turn on the siren.

As soon as the man in the red-brimmed hat told him about room 112, Jake had started running. He couldn't stand outside any longer. He'd run into the hallway and looked left as the numbers slipped down. 118, 116, 114. When he got to 112, he stopped—the old woman was outside the door, leaning over her walker.

"If you're here," he asked, "who's in there?"

"A gentleman showed up at my door. He was wheezing. And he had a heavy case around his neck, a type of case with a strap."

"And what happened?"

"Well, the case seemed to have shifted while he was walking. I think the strap was strangling him. His face was almost purple."

"The strap was strangling him?" He looked inside but couldn't see past the half-shut door.

"The case was too heavy, with the strap wrapped around his neck like that. He fainted right in front of me."

Jake pushed past the door and saw the kid and the ambulance driver crowded around a large recliner. The camera case was on the floor and Gary Novak was passed out in the chair with an attendant on each arm.

He was still sitting there when Jake came back in the building after the ambulance left. Now that he knew everyone was OK, he could look for details. None of the doors in the hall had welcome mats. But Charlotte's condo looked like he'd expected. The living room had pictures of family members on the walls and the whole space smelled like cinnamon. It was a little dark because the blinds were closed. Charlotte was slowly wheeling her walker over to Gary's chair while she tried to balance a glass of water on a tray. She needed help.

"Charlotte, let me get that."

She turned and stopped.

"How did you know my name?"

"Sorry. A man outside told me."

He stopped for a moment.

"You see, I thought the ambulance was here for you."

She started wheeling closer to Gary. Jake pointed at him.

"Let me introduce the man passed out on your chair. That gentleman is Gary Novak."

"You know this man?"

She handed Gary the water. He took it and rested it on the

19

arm of the chair. He stared down at his stomach and glared angrily at the camera case. Jake shrugged.

"He's my photographer. I'm sorry."

"Don't be sorry. I'm glad he survived."

Suddenly, Gary looked up. His white hair fluffed around his ears like ripped cotton balls, and the top of his bald head was shining with sweat.

"Jacob! I saw the white light, I am thinking! I saw that big flash bulb in the sky. The bright light!"

Charlotte eyed the water as Gary waved around his arms. With each move the water almost spilled. He reached his hand out to Jake, spreading his fingers wide.

"I saw it for a second, I think. It was after I fainted. I felt death pulling at me. It was gripping at my neck."

"Gary, I think that was the strap on your camera case."

"Death was gripping also. And then a tiny pin prickling of light. Then I woke up. This woman, she was slapping me in the face."

Charlotte sat down in a wooden chair next to Gary. She leaned forward as she sat and looked like she was about to pick up a penny off the floor.

"I had to slap him," she whispered. "That's how we woke him up."

"I wasn't complaining. You saved my life!" He looked at the camera case angrily another time.

"So how did this happen?"

"Jacob, I am glad you asked." He sipped from the water glass and rested it on the arm of the chair again. "I was here at 8:58 sharp. Two minutes earlier than you asked me to be here! But I've always been prompt. As a boy, sometimes the other children called me prompt. They had a nickname for it. I forget what it was."

Charlotte coughed. Jake stood up.

"Can I get you anything?"

"I'm fine. Where is he from?"

"I don't think he remembers."

"Anyway," Gary continued, "I knew I didn't have time for two trips. No time! I couldn't let down my reporter. But in addition to my camera, I had the special lens you said I had to bring. So I put the camera case around my neck and then held the lens with my left hand. I use my right hand for my cane."

Charlotte looked at Jake. She was wearing a purple dress with frills around the neck. She folded her arms across her knees, like she was cold, and Gary picked up his cane.

"Have you seen my cane?"

He held it out and she looked at it.

"It's from Ethiopia! My son had it especially made for me. My height. The tribes there love to make canes. My son, he bought it from a store in LA."

"Anyway, Gary, you were walking..."

"And I felt the camera case start to swing around. So I lifted up my shoulder." He jerked it up to demonstrate and the water nearly spilled. "And then I had to do the other one to balance it out."

He jerked the other shoulder. Charlotte reached for the water glass but stopped. Gary sipped again and finished it. They all exhaled.

"But then," he continued, "I had to keep switching my shoulders, because as soon as I relocated one I dislocated the other. So then, Jacob, I realized that each time I did it I was pulling the camera strap around my neck. By the time I reached the door of this young lady, I was being choked by it!"

Charlotte smiled and took the water glass away.

"Do you remember what happened next?"

"All I remember is everything becoming extraordinarily dizzy. Then, kaput. I was out. But I wasn't ready to go to the light. Not yet Jacob! Not yet!"

Charlotte started to lean toward her walker. Jake stood up again.

"Can I get you something?"

"I'm fine." She reached her walker and took the glass over to the sink. She dropped it in and slowly wheeled back to them.

"Well, I'm glad you're ok."

"It was all for you, Jacob. I risk my life for you. For this job."

It wasn't worth fighting.

"Yes, yes you do."

Charlotte pushed the walker aside and sat down again. She seemed calm now and looked at both of them. She had her hair down. It was long, and though it was gray, it made her look like a girl the way it outlined her pale face. She sat with her legs crossed at the ankles. She was waiting for an introduction.

"Charlotte, do you have something to say?"

"I do."

"Let's hear it."

She pursed her lips and spoke.

"Now Mr. Russo, I have a story for you. It's why I wanted to speak with you today."

"How did you know my last name?"

"I looked you up. I know your work."

"He's a real writer," Gary said. He seemed resuscitated—he was talking enough. "Jacob can take sentences and spin them into gold. Or at least newspapers."

She kept going.

"Mr. Russo, I have a story. But you'll have to promise confidentiality. Or that I'll be protected until it's published."

He almost laughed. But she looked serious sitting there, her hair falling down.

"I'm sure that won't be a problem Charlotte. But I can promise you that I won't tell anyone anything. And if I write an article, I'll ask your consent. That goes for Gary and his photos, too."

"Thank you."

Gary looked at Jake and arched his eyebrows. Theatrically. Jake didn't respond. He did it again. Jake tried to nod a bit, but it wasn't enough. Gary kept going and Charlotte looked over.

"Sir, what are you doing?"

"I'm sorry. It must be a spasm from my near death experience."

She waited until he stopped.

"Well, Mr. Russo, I'd like to tell you my story now."

Suddenly, Gary sat up straight.

"Remember, I died for this story!"

Jake and Charlotte looked over. She looked back at Jake and leaned forward further in her chair. Her hair fell down past her knees.

"I think this story could change conditions in every building in Sunset Cove. I know that some people don't want me to talk about it. But I will talk about it, whether they like it or not. And Mr. Russo, I'm not going to be silent any longer."

Gary stopped raising his eyebrows. Jake looked at Charlotte. She was serious. Her eyelids were wrinkled but her eyes were bright. Shining. She didn't blink. He got out his notebook and pen again. He was ready to write. All they could hear was their own breathing and the air conditioner.

Then Gary shouted and almost fell out of his chair.

Someone was at the door.

They knocked three times. And they knocked harder each time.

CHAPTER 5:

"Jake, what are you doing here?"

Mel stood at the door with her hands on her hips. Her hair was mussed and she had a folder in her arms. They stared at each other for a moment and then he let her by.

"I was here to speak with Charlotte. We met the other day."

"She's the resident you're interviewing?"

Charlotte nodded.

"Hello Melissa. How are you?"

"I'm good."

Jake looked at Charlotte. She didn't seem nervous or upset. She carried the same posture she'd had before. Then Mel turned right and saw Gary.

"Oh. You're here. How are you, Gary?"

"I have a new lease on life!"

"OK. Well...that's good." She looked left again. "Charlotte, I'm sorry—I just got here. I didn't even realize an ambulance had shown up until a few minutes ago. Usually, Eddie calls me when he arrives, but this time he called me once he left. What happened? He said everyone was all right. Did you fall?"

She was speaking quickly and breathing heavily. Jake wanted to go to her and comfort her, to touch her bare arm and feel the goose bumps. He stood still.

"I'm fine," Charlotte said. "Actually, nothing happened to me. This man, Gary, fainted."

"Oh. That makes a lot of sense."

Gary looked up.

"Melissa, I never asked you if your ankle healed. Are you doing well? Such a nice young lady shouldn't have any handicaps."

"What happened?" Charlotte asked. Jake sighed.

"Gary was taking a photo for the paper. He kept telling Mel to take a step back. She took a few steps too many and ended up falling into a five-foot ditch."

Mel looked at her leg.

"I've healed up well, Gary. I haven't been able to run. I, uh, was growing tired of it anyway."

"Wonderful!"

"You run?" Jake asked.

"Yes, I did."

"So do I. I run."

They smiled. Charlotte and Gary looked at each other. Gary started arching his eyebrows again, and Mel took it as her cue to leave. She said goodbye and walked out the door. Gary seemed pleased.

"I'm glad her ankle's better."

Charlotte frowned.

"That was interesting timing, wasn't it?"

"What do you mean?"

Jake opened his notebook again.

"It was interesting that she would choose to burst in at that moment, exactly when I was going to reveal my story. I think she is a well-intentioned girl. But she isn't beyond stopping a woman like me from telling the truth."

"I'm sure it was a coincidence."

"You're compromised."

"What do you mean?"

"I saw you two smile. You're on her side. I don't know if I can trust you."

"Of course you can."

"Can I?"

"Yes."

"Then check if she is outside."

He sighed. Gary swallowed and Jake could see his Adam's apple rise and fall from across the room. He heard the air conditioner humming as he got up and walked to the door. Right before he looked in the peephole, he realized something. He wasn't sure what he would see.

He saw nothing.

Nobody.

25

"It's fine. No one's there."

"Good. Perhaps I was being overly suspicious."

"When I was on the other side, in heaven," Gary announced, "they told me not to hold grudges. They said I should trust in my fellow man."

Jake tried not to laugh.

"You think you went to heaven?"

"Yes."

"I didn't realize you'd had time for conversations."

"Many."

"So you really think you died?"

"If I didn't, then how would I have known to trust my fellow man? Logic, Jacob. Wisdom."

Charlotte coughed again and Jake looked at his empty notebook. She focused her eyes on his.

"Trust is good. But sometimes, certain parties have interests that are more important than trust. Like money. Power. Jealousy. Those are all the things I've encountered in the past month."

"I see."

"Are you willing to be a part of this?"

"I'll do my best."

"So will I," Gary said. "By the way, do you have any cookies?"

"Cookies?"

"Yes, Or crackers. Anything will do. You see, I am a diabetic."

"Oh." She looked toward her kitchen. "I can check if I have anything."

"He's not a diabetic," Jake said. "He just says that when he's hungry."

"No, I will find you something."

When she used her walker it changed her. She seemed alive when she was sitting, leaning forward. But her back didn't straighten when she stood. It was stuck that way. When she stood she looked as old as she was, and the effort made her seem tired. Jake wanted her to keep sitting.

"Don't worry about him. Tell us your story."

She complied and breathed in. She looked scared but started talking.

"Recently, Sheryl Goldfein hasn't invited me to play bridge. I've played bridge with them for the past five years, every single week. Now they won't let me play with them anymore. It's an outrage."

Jake sighed. He rested his pen on his notebook, but she just sped up.

"I have gotten better, if anything." She was excited. "And they just got an extra day each week to use the common building. It's unfair. I don't know why she did it, but quite a few things I've found are suspicious."

"I see." Jake closed the notebook. "Gary, what do you think?"

"This is the story I died for?"

Charlotte sniffed.

"I think you should write a story about this Mr. Russo. It has betrayal. All of a sudden, everyone hates me. It's Shakespearian."

"Everyone hates you?"

"Yes."

"Well, I'm sorry." He stood up. "I should probably be going."

He was too busy to be nice. He had to be aggressive. He couldn't waste the day listening to stories about bridge games.

"I don't understand." She was shaking. "I'm making waves in this community, and nobody else here likes it. Your readers should know."

"Right, I'm sure." Being tough was as hard as he remembered. "Gary, I can get your stuff."

"Thank you Jacob."

Charlotte stayed seated, leaning forward. She held her arm out one last time.

"There's more."

Her eyes were shinier now. It seemed like she might cry.
"Yes?"
"I received a threat on my life."
He put down Gary's camera case and sat down in the chair. This was worth getting out his notebook.

CHAPTER 6:

Charlotte waited until he was ready. She spoke in a whisper.

"It all began a week ago. I was about to go to sleep. Before I go to bed, I always close the blinds for the night. A week ago, I was closing the blinds when the telephone rang."

He wrote it down in shorthand.

"I answered the telephone and I heard a clicking noise. My hearing has stayed sharp over the past few years, and I remember hearing that noise. The next thing I heard was a very deep voice."

Her own voice shook a little and her eyes shone. Jake reached out to her.

"What did it say?"

"I...I can't....repeat it. I wrote down what he said."

A white note emerged from the purple fabric of her dress. She handed it to Jake. It was folded at least four times, and he uncreased it slowly so he wouldn't rip it. He read it silently.

I see you closing your blinds. If you want us to stop watching you, then you have to stop watching us. Or else.

She was shaking. Jake folded up the piece of paper and looked at her. He recorded the words in his notebook.

"What does it say?" Gary asked.

"Gary, please. It's sensitive."

"What does it say?"

"Here."

Charlotte was still shaking. He slipped Gary the piece of paper.

"I'm sorry about him. He's just curious."

"The voice hung up after that." She seemed calm again. "I haven't heard anything since."

"Jacob!" Gary shouted.

"What Gary?"

"I don't have my reading glasses."

He was rotating the paper in his hands.

"Jacob, I can't read this note without them."

29

"Charlotte, let's get back to your story."
Gary was holding the note up to the light. Upside down.
"What does it say? Just tell me."
"Later."
"It won't make sense if it's later."
"Not now."
"Why won't you tell me?"

Charlotte looked worried again. Jake stood up and Gary followed. Jake cupped his hands over Gary's ear and whispered. Gary shouted back.

"Why are you whispering?"
"Come here." He led him to the hallway. Jake closed the door and told Gary what the note said. When they walked back in, Gary began arching his eyebrows uncontrollably.

"Some note, Charlotte. That's very scary stuff!"
"It was very frightening," she continued. "I've been fine since then. But I haven't…"
"What?"
"I used to like sunlight in the daytime."

She looked down at the floor and Jake looked up at the shut blinds. That's why they were closed. She didn't want the man who called to see her again.

"I'm so sorry. Do you want me to open them?"
"No. It's fine."
"Did you tell Mel?"
"No, I haven't told anyone. I don't know who I can trust."

Her hair fell in front of her face, gray lines like a pencil sketch. Gary touched her shoulder and whispered that she'd be OK. Jake tapped his notebook with his pen.

"Well, I think you will be fine. One prank call can't mean anything. Let's try to figure out who made it."

She looked up.
"How will we do that?"
"We have to figure out what's really happening. If we don't do that, then we'll just be scared."
"I don't know who the voice was."

"Right. But who might it have been?"

"I don't know." She crossed her arms over her knees again.

"You think this started because of bridge?"

"Yes, I know it."

"Well, why would they be upset if they kicked you out?"

"I suppose I've been making trouble since then. I've made some noise about starting my own game, and I've also been making some investigations. Private investigations. I admit it."

"I see. And who would be upset about that?"

"Everyone. Everyone plays bridge."

"I play bridge," Gary said proudly. He swallowed. "Oh, but I'm not mad at you."

"Thank you." She smiled faintly. "I just know it must have to do with bridge. I've started getting very, very good. But then when I came home one day, I received a call from Sheryl."

"Who is that?" He wrote down the name.

"Sheryl Goldfein. I had already changed my dress for the night's game, but then she called and said that they had filled up for bridge that night. I know they always have room for more people in bridge. She thinks that just because she heads up the council she can do anything."

He tapped his pen on the side of his notebook. Gary's head nodded back and then he snapped awake.

"Charlotte, what is this council you've mentioned?"

"Oh." She blushed, her pale cheeks spotted red. "We all make decisions about the community. There are eight of us and Sheryl is the chair. She's very bossy, and I'm sure that's why she was able to kick me out of bridge."

"Right. So what do you do on the council?"

"For one of our recent projects, we helped decide where our new garden would be."

He smiled.

"I saw that spot. Mel showed me."

"Yes. It will be lovely. We chose relatively rare flowers. They will be an interesting mix."

"Do you remember the name?"

"I don't remember right now."

"That's fine." He wanted Mel to tell him anyway. "Does the council work on anything else?"

"We have many projects." She was getting excited again. "I've always ensured Sheryl doesn't roll over everyone else. She can do that."

"How so?"

"The worst thing happened a month ago. We eventually passed the motion, although I tried to stop it."

"What happened?"

"Well," she began, "every year, we make a donation to a local charity. It has been a tradition for years."

"Did she try to stop the donation?"

"No. However, she pushed very hard for her charity to receive the money. Every year since I have lived here, we have donated to a charity called Ducks Unlimited."

"What do they do?"

"They preserve wetlands. I just know that it has been a tradition here. Sheryl, however, decided that we should change to a different charity this year."

"Did you mind?"

"I wouldn't have minded. Though I do love ducks."

She pointed to the left side of the room. A small painted wooden duck sat against the wall. It was swimming in the blue carpet.

"Isn't he cute?" She sounded happy again.

"I can see you like them."

"My husband made me that one."

"He made that?"

"He was very handy." She touched her face, letting her hand linger on the side of her cheek. "He could carve a piece of wood easily. He carved pumpkins for Halloween. He could hollow them out in a few minutes. The skin would be so thin you could see the candle."

"I can't imagine Halloween in this weather."

"Oh yes. We used to live in the North. He made the pumpkin as thin as paper. Our daughter made the designs."

"You love ducks." He looked at the green wooden one again. "Did you like that charity?"

"Honestly, I'm not particularly attached to the one we've used in the past. There are so many good causes. Still, Sheryl nearly forced us to donate to the Saving Tomorrow Initiative."

"What is that?"

"None of us knew. It was very vague. Eventually, she told us it was an educational charity to help save the wetlands. I believe the wetlands are important, but I had not heard of the Initiative. I didn't see why we had to switch from the ducks."

"I see." He looked at his notebook. A full page. He hadn't had that in a while. Then he looked at Gary, who was gently snoring in the chair. Charlotte didn't notice.

"I challenged Sheryl at the meeting, in front of everyone. I told her that I would be willing to switch, but I needed evidence of the group's quality. Almost all of them voted against me, except for Abram. She's unstoppable."

"That's odd. No one wanted to know?"

"None except Abram and I." She threw up her hands in frustration.

"And so you're still having problems with Sheryl?"

She smiled and narrowed her eyes.

"After Sheryl kicked me out of the bridge games, I started to do research on everything about her. I don't have anything to do at night, since Sheryl won't let me play. They have two games a week now, too. But apparently not enough space for me."

"I see."

Charlotte looked down again.

"I'm starting to discover some very interesting things in the course of my investigations. I'm closer than ever. She'll regret what she did."

"I see."

Her hair nearly covered her face. He stood up and touched

her back. Bones. Hard, bent over bones. She looked up and smiled weakly.

"That sounded cruel, didn't it? I'm so dramatic these days."

"No, you aren't."

"I know I am," she said and laughed. "All this for a game. If my daughter saw me…"

"Where is she?"

"Pennsylvania."

"I see."

"And now I'm causing all this commotion over what you say is a prank call. I'm like a child. I said I wouldn't cry…" She trailed off. Then she turned her head, her back holding still. She looked at the closed blinds. Jake stood up quickly.

"You know what? Let's fix something."

He walked over and opened the blinds. Light entered the room and thick beams of it made everything bright. The duck's bill turned from black to orange, and the walls seemed cleaner. Gary snapped awake and looked around in shock.

"The white light! Am I dead again?"

"Gary, let's get a picture."

Charlotte looked worried.

"A picture for publication?"

"Of course not. Just for you."

She stayed seated in her chair, the walker at her side. Jake helped Gary set up the camera. It was heavier than he thought. Then Gary smiled as he screwed on his special lens. Charlotte touched her hair and pulled it back and up. She sat up as straight as she could. The light smoothed out her face. It was a pale plane, but a pretty one. Around it, her hair looked like rising smoke. Gary adjusted the angle and clicked. He didn't even need to use the flash because the room was so bright.

CHAPTER 7:

It wasn't until 3PM the next day that Jake realized his problem. When he came home and went inside, he realized it as soon as he looked at his open closet. He had a semi-formal dinner date. His first date with a beautiful woman. But he didn't have a suit that fit. He'd brought two suits down to Sarasota, but both of them had been made for a different man. Black and navy blue, and both for someone 75 pounds heavier. He couldn't tell Mel, but he didn't want to cancel.

He tried to do all his other work first. He filed his dispatch to Thompson as quickly as he could and hoped he wouldn't call. He went in the bathroom and took a shower. Razor. Deodorant. Toothbrush. But it was all stalling from trying to solve the problem of his suit.

He put on underwear and a white shirt. That one was new and tailored. Then he walked slowly to the closet. He picked out the black suit. Black was slimming, he'd heard. He'd heard it when he was 75 pounds heavier. And he was sure that black only made the person look thinner. It didn't work for the suit.

He held it up and looked in the mirror. It looked fine then. But he knew that it fit differently on your body than it did held in front of it, like a paper doll. Even his ties seemed fat now. He didn't know why he'd kept the suits. Maybe it was supposed to be motivational, a reminder to eat carefully. Now he didn't know if he'd be able to go to dinner.

He'd have to cancel. He picked up the phone and scrolled to "M." It was the way it had to be. Her name flashed, but he didn't press send. No, it would be fine. It was just a suit. People didn't notice what men wore anyway—he couldn't cancel over that. The women were the show. He admired the crisp outline of his shirt. Then he put on the jacket and pants.

It looked like he'd snuck into his fathers' clothes. It wasn't just baggier, it seemed longer. His bulk had taken up length, not just width. The sleeves went down through his wrists and the pant legs covered his feet. He didn't know he'd been shrunk. Around his waist, the belt bunched so much cloth it looked like he was wearing frills. He stood in front of the mirror. Then he jumped. Someone was standing outside the window behind him.

He didn't have time to change into something else. Now they were knocking at the door. He never had visitors. Why would he have them now, of all times? He opened the door and stuck out his head.

The woman standing there was short. She wore a tight green t-shirt that looked soft and she had short, pixie hair that was red or brown. He couldn't tell in the light. She wore tight jeans and was barefoot, not even wearing flip-flops. When he opened the door a little wider she leaned toward him.

"Is this a bad time?" Her smooth voice, a little nasal, made it sound like she'd just told a joke.

"It kind of is."

"I just wanted to introduce myself."

"Hello," he said. She tilted her head to the side.

"Can I come in?"

He let her in. She walked in like she owned the apartment, taking wide steps over his carpet.

"Your suit's too big."

"I know." He pulled his pants up further. "That's why I didn't want you to come in."

"I live next door. I just moved in. I'm Kaylie."

"Kaylie?"

"Yes. And you are?"

"Jake." He sat on the bed. His suit jacket was like a blanket. "Jake Russo."

She pulled his desk chair out and sat across from him.

"How long have you lived here?"

"Uh, a couple of months. You?"

She put her hands on his chair like it was hers. She stretched.

"I've lived in Sarasota for a few years. I just moved into this building. Hence the introducing myself. Why is your suit so big?"

"What's that?"

"Why," she repeated, "is your suit so big?"

"Is it that noticeable?"

"Yes."

"Damn."

"Why is it?"

"I should go." He stood up but she stayed seated. She scanned the room. The short sleeves of her shirt ran up her arm and caught around her shoulder.

"You can't go anywhere in that."

"I can't?"

"Nope."

"I know."

"Go to the store."

"I have to be somewhere tonight. It was nice to meet you though, Kaylie."

"What's going on tonight?"

"Something."

She tilted her head and walked out of the apartment without saying anything. He started to follow, but when he looked out the door, he didn't see her in either direction. She came out of the door on the right.

"Here." She handed him a piece of paper. Hotel stationary. She'd written an address in block letters.

"What is it?"

"Directions. You probably don't know where the Men's Wearhouse is."

"I didn't."

"Then there you go. You can buy a new suit."

"Thank you."

They went back in the apartment.

"So, what do you do?" She sat on the bed this time and tested it with her hands. He sat in the chair.

"I'm a reporter."

"Here?"

"Yes, right in Sarasota." He told her his beat and she

sighed. He changed the subject.
"Well, what do you do?"
"I'm between jobs."
"I see."
"That means I was fired."
"I see."
She laughed.
"Do you smoke?"
"No. Do you?"
"No, I was just asking for fun." She tilted her head to the side and laughed. She took a single cigarette out from behind her ear. He hadn't seen it. She didn't light it. Good.
"What are you looking at?"
"Nothing."
"If you have a date tonight, you need to go."
"I have to change. And buy a suit. Thanks for the directions."
"Go ahead."
"It was nice meeting you."
She stayed seated.
"Yeah. Come over sometime."
She stood near him and then put out her arms. She took the cloth from his jacket and pulled it taut. He walked closer to her. They were a foot apart. Then half a foot. She looked at his side and pressed the jacket buttons against his stomach.
"You have lost a lot of weight, Jake."
"How do you know I've lost weight?"
"Because men don't buy suits this large for no reason."
"Right."
"Don't be embarrassed." She pulled it tighter and he stepped closer. Four inches between them. "You don't need to be embarrassed now."
"Good." Then she let him go. The fabric flopped around him, loose as a sheet. She turned a little and started walking to the door.
"Go on! Change already. We can catch up later."

"It was nice to meet you."

She'd already shut the door behind her. He took off the jacket and gathered it in his arms. He couldn't believe he'd worn it. He smiled. This was how things were now. This was how it felt to need a new jacket.

CHAPTER 8:

"I like your suit," Mel said.

"I like your dress. A lot."

It was blue and shiny and ran down to her calves. She was wearing heels and they made her almost as tall as him. Her shoulders looked tanner than he thought they would. She must have sun bathed at home.

They walked to his car from her office. They were already in the car when he realized his mistake.

"Damn."

"What?"

"I forgot. You're supposed to open the door for the woman."

She laughed and looked at him.

"You're such a gentleman."

"It's because I've never driven."

"Jake, should you be telling me you've never driven?"

"No, no. I've driven. But I didn't have a car in New York. And then I came down here and had to get one. So I've never driven as an adult."

"You've driven here as an adult, haven't you?"

"I meant..." He looked at her and waved his right arm. "I meant I've never driven on a date."

He could feel himself blushing and thought she would too. She started laughing.

"Jake, do you have a tag on your sleeve?"

He thought he'd removed all of them. He was wrong.

"Do I?"

"Yes, right here," she said and grabbed it. He lifted his hand off the wheel.

"It must be from the dry-cleaners."

"No, it looks new."

"Right." They were on the highway. He tried to make it seem like he needed to pay attention. It didn't work.

"Is this a new suit?"

"Yeah."
"It is?"
"Yes, it is."
"Just for this?"
"Well, that depends."
"On what?"
"On how you look at it."
"What do you mean?"
"I got it today. But I've needed one for a while."

She let go of the tag and put her hand around his wrist. She squeezed it and let go. The smell of her perfume mixed with the air freshener's pine. It smelled like a season they didn't have in Sarasota.

The drive was only a few minutes long. Rothschild's headquarters was nearby, almost equidistant between all of its developments in the Sarasota area. Sunset Cove was the second largest community in the county. The competition had the biggest one. They passed it on the highway. Palmstead. Jake and Gary had gone there more than a few times. It was bigger than Sunset Cove, but for the most part the places were the same.

They weren't actually going to the headquarters, but to a banquet hall nearby. It was a big poured building, a product of too much concrete. Palm trees surrounded the drive as they went to the parking lot in back, a half empty grid with cars clustered at the front. The building stood next to an office supplies store and it was a few hundred feet from a place that sold pool supplies.

"Do you have a pool?" Jake asked.
"My building does."
"I'm envious."
"Doesn't yours?"
"No, I wish."
"It's nice. I swim a lot."

"I saw your tan," he said and touched her shoulder. It was warm, like she'd just been in the sun.

"Look." She pointed to a sign. Right beneath the name of the place, Giordano's, block letters were spread out. "Congratulations to Simeon Rothschild."

"That's him."

A waitress stood in the reception area, which had linoleum floors and potted plants. She wore a green vest and could have been working a casino.

"Names?"

"Melissa Tyllis. And this is my guest, Jake Russo."

The waitress didn't bother to check anything off, and she told them to go ahead.

The room itself was better than the reception area. All the concrete in the roof had been covered by dark wood. It was a wide-open space and almost twenty round tables were spread across the floor, like coasters on a coffee table. Rothschild was a popular guy. A band sat in the corner and most of the members had tiny plates in their hands. One middle aged man, the youngest in the group, struggled with a shrimp.

"Where is Mr. Rothschild?" Jake asked.

She scanned.

"I don't see him yet."

"I've never gotten a chance to talk to him."

"You haven't? Well, he's very busy. I'm surprised though. He's very good at being open about projects. You'll meet him tonight."

"Is he as good at PR as you are?"

"What do you mean?"

"Well, how could I not give you a good report?"

She laughed, a little loudly.

"I didn't want that to be a problem." She grabbed his arm. "I asked you, remember."

"I remember."

"And it isn't a conflict of interest?"

"I think that I'll still be able to write puff pieces about 'Sunny Sarasota' without a conflict of interest."

Mel introduced him to the people who came around. He

handed out and received business cards. There were a lot of them: a director of public relations; a business development director; an architect; a strategic planner.

"How many people work here?" His suit pockets were full of thick-stock business cards.

"We're growing very quickly." She held a martini and didn't look like she was worried about spilling. He liked that. "In fact, we're growing a little faster than Palmstead, I've heard."

"Is that true?"

"That's just what I've heard."

"Who told you?"

"Oh, you just see it in e-mails. I don't know how they know really."

"Well, Rothschild won't catch up to Palmstead just yet, right?"

Mel stood silent. She was looking over his shoulder.

The man standing behind Jake had short white hair, disheveled intentionally. He was wearing a tuxedo with a tight knot at the tie and a wide cummerbund. He stood taller than Jake but it might have been because of his heels. The veins in his face drew little marker lines on his skin. His chin jutted out a little and he looked like he was tilting his head a few extra degrees.

"We'll catch up to Palmstead soon enough."

The most noticeable thing were the eyes. They were black, surrounding a deeper black in the pupil.

"Hello Simeon," Mel said. "We were just talking about you."

"Hi, Mr. Rothschild," Jake said quickly. "I'm Jake Russo. I don't think we've met."

"Did you say Mr. Rothschild?" He looked around the room. "That's my father. I don't see him here. Please call me Simeon."

"Certainly—"

"I'll tell you something." His face moved while his eyes

stayed steady. "That's one reason we're already catching up to Palmstead. They have such an antiquated approach to things. I'm sure that everyone there is calling Jerry 'sir,' or 'Mr. Rubenstein,' or something formal like that. His staff is busy bringing his puppies caviar instead of scoping new sites. Does he still have that dog?"

"Well, when I interviewed him, there was a dog in the room..."

"Jake," Mel said, "I told Simeon I'd be bringing you. And he's read your work, of course. So he knows you've met Mr. Rubenstein."

"He and I play golf sometimes," Rothschild said, flicking his wrist. "Well, we did. Now things have gotten a little more serious."

"I see."

"And that's off the record. Mel, make sure he doesn't write too much."

"Don't worry. I mostly talk about the good things. It's just about trends. Lifestyles. Pretty soft focus."

"That's good." He waved at someone. "I have to duck off. It was nice to meet you. And remember, we will catch up."

He walked away, his chin raised. He moved quickly and stood behind someone else. Jake saw a man turn and start laughing.

"So that was him?"

Mel smiled and nodded.

"Yes, that was him."

"He snuck up on me."

"He gets involved in a conversation," she said, "whether you know it or not."

CHAPTER 9:

It always started with the rolls.

The way people passed around the basket. The little pads of butter, slipping inside their foil wrappers. People looked disappointed if you didn't take a roll and spread it thick with butter. It was like an insult. What they didn't realize was that if you took one roll, there was no reason not to take another. He passed the basket on to Mel and hoped nobody would notice.

There were eight people at the table, including Jake and Mel. Three of the others were developers for Rothschild, and the other three were unaffiliated. They'd all decided that Jake's job was the most interesting and they asked him questions about it. They eventually asked if he needed a roll.

"I'm fine," he insisted.

That was the problem with fancy meals. Even if he ordered chicken for the main course, they always found ways to surround it with other food that he'd never asked for. Turtle soup seemed to spontaneously condense, thick with chunks of meat and swimming with fat. Someone at the table requested shrimp and it arrived surrounded by bowls of butter. Little pools to drown it in, so it dripped a yellow trail on the tablecloth. Mel had one, but she didn't spill.

He gave them the usual speech about his job. Most of it was true. How he'd wanted to be a reporter since he was a boy. He'd been editor of the high school paper, huddled in rooms cutting and pasting articles for the Xerox machine. Then he'd gone on to write in college. He was lucky enough to get a job straight out and earn a chance to work his way up. A decade's worth. They asked him where he'd been when one event or another happened in New York and he told them.

"And so why did you come here?" a middle-aged man asked before he sucked on a shrimp tail.

Jake brushed his hair back. That was where the editing came in. He had a different reason sometimes, but never told them Thompson's reason. The real one. He said he wanted a change of pace. He wanted to see more of the country. He wanted to do a different type of writing. He couldn't tell if they'd bought it or were just being polite. The two things looked the same.

"But enough about me," he said. "I bore myself."

"Well, not us," a woman said, and her husband nodded. He was one of the Rothschild employees. Jake decided to distract them.

"So what do you do for Rothschild?"

"I'm on the construction end of things. I make sure these communities get built. But nothing like this building," he said and laughed. "God awful, isn't it?"

"Just the outside."

"I guess. I'll be on a site tomorrow though, supervising a new project. I make sure things get done."

"That must be satisfying."

"It is," the man said. "You watch something really come full circle. It starts out just a patch of land and then ends up as a place where people live. My wife's heard this a million times."

"I haven't heard it lately," she muttered.

"Well...it's just a phase."

Jake wanted to get out his notebook, but he hadn't brought it. The entire night was supposed to be off the record. More importantly, the notebook didn't fit in his new suit's pocket. Especially with all the thick-stock business cards he'd gotten.

"What's just a phase?" he asked. He'd have to use his memory—never optimal.

"Just the usual stuff."

"What's that?"

He could feel Mel looking at him. He didn't look back.

"You know—just regulations."

"Oh. Union stuff? About when you work?"

"No. You have to go through a lot with wetlands preservation. So we're dealing with that. And you've got these environmentalist people. It's the usual."

"Do you have to deal with that though? Shouldn't it all be taken care of by the time you've started building?"

"I wish," he said and grunted. He took another roll. "They still protest, even after you've done all the legal work. It's crazy, but they do it. That's what happens when those people have all day free without real jobs."

"I guess so." Jake looked at the rolls but left them on the table. The man grunted again and started eating his in big bites. Eventually, a waitress collected the plates. Jake wiped the sweat off his forehead as the couples split up into conversations of their own.

"Why didn't you have a roll?" Mel asked.

"I want to save my appetite."

"For chicken?"

"There's nothing like it."

"Everything's like it."

"Did I get you in trouble before?" he asked under his breath. Change the subject. Even if the new subject was more dangerous.

"What do you mean?"

"With Mr. Rothschild. I had no idea that he was behind me when I said that about never catching up to Palmstead."

"I wouldn't worry about it. He puts on a show, but he doesn't mean it."

"Did he..." Jake started. He touched the prongs on his salad fork and waited.

"Did he what?"

"Well, did he tell you anything? About me?"

"What do you mean?"

"I don't want to bring it up. But is this date just to, you know, try to get me to write something? Did he tell you to take me out tonight?"

She looked down at the white napkin on her lap.

"If you think that Jake, really..."

He frowned, but she smiled.

"Case closed," she said and touched his arm with her hand.

"Besides, Gary's already sprained my ankle. Mr. Rothschild knows your paper won't be easy on me, even if I do wine and dine you."

He reached for her hand as they laughed. But then they heard the sound of shattered glass. Mel grabbed him, her nails scraping his skin.

"What's happening?" More glass broke. It echoed across the room.

A man was standing on the table next to the band. He wore blue jeans and a white tank top. He had a long beard that went down to his chest. A message on the tank top read "Stop The Development." It was written in dripping crimson paint.

"Everybody listen to me!" His words were slurred and it sounded like he was drunk. He picked up another glass and held it by its flute. He tossed it up, nearly hitting the wooden ceiling. Half the people stood up at their tables and the other half ducked under them. The glass crashed to the floor.

"I want to talk to you about what's happening. You people are endangering the most precious resource we have." His voice was hoarse. Jake held Mel close. "Why are people more important than animals? Why you are risking the wetlands for this? For people! For your company's developments!"

He flailed his arms around. He didn't hold a weapon. He continued to talk, though it quickly became impossible to tell what he was saying. Jake and Mel watched as a man crept up behind the table. Jake hadn't noticed him before. He wore all black and had thick red hair running to his collarbone. He had long arms and wide shoulders. After touching an earpiece with his hand, he nodded and jumped on the table in a single leap.

Both men fell on the floor and more glass shattered.

Then it was quiet again. The red haired man got up and held the bearded man's hands behind his back. He walked him to the back of the room and then out the door. People started clapping and everyone sat down again. Rothschild was sitting in front and he stood up and walked to the podium.

"Well," he said and adjusted his tie. "That certainly seems

like a cue for the next course."

Everyone laughed. A moment later, waiters started circulating with the meal. They stepped around the busboys, who were busy cleaning up the broken glass.

CHAPTER 10:

"Are you sure I can have this?" Mel asked.

"Go for it." Jake pushed the rest of his strawberry cheesecake toward her.

After the bearded man was escorted out, the night had gone more smoothly. They'd eaten and talked as a table, then the conversation split into couples again. He'd learned more about her. The college she'd gone to. The one she'd wanted to go to instead. She didn't like filling in Sudoku puzzles—she liked writing her own on Saturday mornings, while she drank orange juice and listened to the radio. He learned that when she said "cabinet," for some reason she drew out the "i" long enough that you could hear it. When her ice cream melted, she caught the liquid in her spoon and raised it to her lips.

Rothschild approached the podium while the waiters and waitresses served coffee. A man from Rothschild's table tapped a glass with his spoon. Sound pinged against the walls and Rothschild took the mic from the podium.

"Just for the record, I didn't want to come up here."

A few people laughed too loudly. Mel set her spoon against her dish. Then the man from Rothschild's table stood up. He teetered a bit. Mel whispered to Jake.

"Eliot Walters. He's a development VP." He was a short bald man whose face had blushed red.

"He likes a drink or two?"

"More than two."

"Before you speak," the man said and pointed at Rothschild, "I want everybody to stand up."

Chairs squeaked against the floor.

"We have got to give a toast to our hero!"

Rothschild brought the mic to his lips.

"Just don't hit the glasses as hard as our environmentalist friend did earlier this evening."

When the laughter died down, the VP continued.

"He's too modest to say it, but what Simeon does, the

amount of money he gives...it's a beautiful thing. If that doesn't deserve a toast, well, I don't know what does. So, a toast to generosity in all its forms. That's why we're here."

They raised their glasses and hit them together. Gently. They drank.

"That's very kind of you, Eliot," Rothschild said into the mic. "It's true that I'm modest. I'm one of the most modest people in the state."

The crowd laughed and he waited it out. He held the mic with one hand and let the other hand settle in his jacket pocket. From far away he looked different—the veins were smoothed by distance, and the dark eyes were just spots to center the audience's focus. Jake wished he had his notebook. He listened instead.

"It's great to have so many old and new friends here today. All of you are important to this company and what we are trying to do for Florida. We are trying to build high quality spaces for a range of residents with a range of needs."

He switched mic hands and walked to another part of the room. He was a politician, hitting every corner.

"Just the other day, I met someone who told me that our work helped them to afford their first home. And the next day, I met someone who said that our work helped them finally reach the luxury they deserved. They didn't put it quite like that, of course. But it was gratifying to hear people embrace Rothschild."

He crossed the room again and picked up a glass. Not water. Champagne bubbles rose to the top.

"As you know, we have our fair share of opponents. Tonight we saw that. The environmentalists are a violent and extreme group. Many of them have great principles, but far too many don't. If Conrad hadn't tackled that man, who knows what he would have done? Who knows what might have happened? Sadly, a lot of the environmentalists are like our bearded friend tonight. They are violent. Concerned only with personal gain. They aren't the people we listen to though, are they? We listen to the people who want to live in Rothschild units, whomever they may be."

People began applauding. He put down the champagne and waved them off.

"Those whackos aren't what we're here for tonight. We're here to talk about charity. We have been building the Rothschild foundation for years, and we aren't going to stop growing."

Jake touched Mel's arm.

"This is why we're here?"

"It's the tenth anniversary."

"Seeing how our efforts have grown," Rothschild said, "has been an amazing process. Still, I know we can do better. That's why I'm announcing that I'll be increasing my personal donation this year. We can do more for the great communities around us. That's what this foundation has always been about.

"Part of the reason we're doing it is to expand our mission. As you know, we've always dealt with a wide range of issues and concerns in this area. We won't stop. We support a wide range of causes. With my donations, and your help, we can add depth to our breadth."

Everyone clapped again. Rothschild didn't bow or acknowledge it. He just stood waiting. He'd heard all the applause before.

He circulated the tables again, never sitting down. The band played a slow song and people began to file out of the room. The waiters and waitresses circulated, asking the guests if they needed anything else. No one did. Jake was talking to Mel when he felt a hand on his shoulder. He turned and black eyes stared back.

"Quite a night, wasn't it, Mr. Russo?"

"It was, Mr....Simeon. Quite a night."

"Did you see that madman? He must have a personal vendetta against glassware."

"He must."

"Mel," Rothschild said, "I'm going to make you tackle him

next time."

"He teases me," she told Jake.

"I'd ask the same of you, Mr. Russo. Hopefully we didn't make a poor impression."

"It wasn't your fault."

"Good." He raised his chin and looked across the room. He placed his fingertips at the top of his cummerbund. "I'd hate to make a poor impression. It was a good thing we had Conrad, wasn't it?"

"Was he the gentleman who tackled the man?"

"That's correct. He's a very genial man. But when he needs to act otherwise…"

He laughed and Jake and Mel laughed with him. He stopped suddenly.

"But enough of madmen. When will we be speaking?"

"Sir?"

"An interview. I want to tell you about our plans. Your readers would love to know more about me."

"Well, if you'd like to schedule a time, I'd be happy."

"Here." He handed Jake another business card, made of thick stock. "This has my information."

"I'll give you a call."

"No. It's to write down the time. I'm free the fourteenth. Lunch. We'll have it."

"I'm not sure—"

But he was already walking away. Mel pulled at Jake's sleeve as they got up to leave.

"That's the thing about Simeon Rothschild. He not only starts conversations when he wants to." She shrugged. "He also ends them when he wants to."

CHAPTER 11:

At night the heat made sense. During the day, he couldn't understand the weather. But at night it all changed. The humidity seemed to thin out in the breeze. The moon took over the sun's shift. The roads were finally dark again, instead of being glossed up with mirage. Things made sense at night, especially with a woman in the passenger's seat.

She looked over at him.

"Where now?"

"Your car's still at Sunset Cove, right?"

"Yes, I guess that's where we can go." She looked back at the banquet building.

He started driving. He'd gotten the door for her that time. Heard the seatbelt buckle click. They didn't turn the radio on. All they heard was the road rushing, because Jake liked the windows open. Mel spoke over the wind.

"How was your interview with Charlotte?"

"That? Interesting. She has some interesting theories about things to be sure. A little obsessed with bridge."

She laughed.

"They all are."

"Are they?"

"Definitely. I know—I'm the one who schedules the common room for bridge games. It gets intense."

"It sounds that way."

The wind blew loudly into the car as they accelerated. Mel smiled.

"Can you hear it?"

"What?"

"The Gulf."

He went on the ramp.

"You can hear the ocean from here?"

"Yes," she said and laughed. "And it's the Gulf of Mexico. Not an ocean."

He looked over quick. Her tan paled in moonlight. She

smiled and her teeth shone.

"You learn to hear the water when you live here all your life."

"I'd think you'd notice it less."

"Most people do. But I always appreciate it."

He glanced at the road and then looked back at her. She still smiled.

"I was talking to Javier, and he said that he could hear it too."

"Who's Javier?"

The inevitable boyfriend? He waited for the answer.

"Oh, he's our maintenance person. Like our super."

It was a good answer.

"He's from Cuba, originally. And he says that no matter where he is, he always knows if he's near the water. Of course, he's never been very far from it."

"It sounds wonderful."

She ran her nails against the grain of the dashboard.

"It's not perfect. You know, I didn't exactly want the job. That's a whole other thing though..."

They passed Palmstead on the right. The tennis courts were still lit, though they'd probably been empty since five. The pool shone from the moonlight. He didn't ask her for directions to Sunset Cove. They pulled off the ramp and the wind slowed down.

"I guess I didn't imagine I'd be doing paperwork so much. I'd rather get to know the residents better."

He looked over and she smiled and tugged her ear. He could see Sunset Cove, rising up. Be aggressive. He swallowed.

"There are some things I'd like to know better."

"So would I," she said. "Though that was a pretty bad line."

He smiled.

"I know."

"But the sentiment was good."

They pulled up next to her car and they both got out. They

stood on opposite sides of it and then walked to the front. She looked at the hood of his car and Jake hopped onto it. It made a hollow sound and he grunted.

"I've always seen that in movies." It was a little warm from the drive. She sat beside him on the hood.

"What else can we teach you about the world of automobiles, Jake Russo?"

"I don't know. What else is there?"

"Drag racing?"

"That's certainly something to do."

"Driving around with your friends."

"I often drive around by myself," he said.

"That's close enough."

He leaned back a little and tested his weight on the windshield. It held. He leaned back and looked up, Mel's shape just a silhouette.

"Why didn't you want this job?"

She looked at the windshield and leaned back on it.

"Are we off the record?"

"Mel, of course."

"It's a good job. I like it. I like meeting the residents. Simeon can be…interesting. But he's a fair boss."

"But why didn't you want it?"

She paused. Her dress was shining.

"I guess, I don't know. I just don't enjoy all the bad parts."

"Like what?"

"The paperwork. Collecting fees. Scheduling common spaces. Being an enforcer."

"Why not?"

"It's just not my personality. I get emotional about it."

"You can't help that."

"I wish I could."

She sighed.

"I really just thought I'd find something with less paperwork by now. But I haven't yet."

"Yet. There's a lot of time."

"Like you. You just decided to come down here. You picked up and moved. I don't think I could do that."

He looked over at her. She was staring at the sky, shaking her head slowly, barely. He touched her arm.

"I don't know if it's like that."

"How do you mean?"

"I would have stayed, if I could have."

"If you could have?"

"I was told to come here. I was sent here by my boss."

"Oh."

"I'm just saying that…I understand."

"I know." She sat up. The back of her dress had stayed totally clean. He sat up beside her and realized he'd probably wrinkled his new suit. He clapped his hands together.

"Well."

"Well."

"So," he said. "It was nice, again."

"It was." They stood up. This was it. This was the time. She had asked him to dinner for a reason. He knew it wasn't a risk to ask her to stay with him longer. Just a little. She spoke first.

"What are you doing now, for the rest of the night?"

"I don't know."

"I could use a drink—it was like being at work with Simeon around."

Just ask her. She touched her hair. Smiled. She wanted him to.

"Well," he said and tugged at his sleeve. "I should probably get going."

"You should?"

"Just tonight." Thompson was right. He couldn't push it when he needed to. And now he was stuck. Too late to change the story.

"I have a deadline. And my editor, he's just—"

"I understand."

"I did have a nice time."

"So did I."

"I'll see you. Soon, I guess."

"Of course."

This was it. He turned around. Then he turned back. But she was already walking to her car. He let her drive out first and then he followed behind her.

He had to watch her from his car, fifteen feet away. The road to leave Sunset Cove was a long one, but it eventually turned. His headlights followed and at the foot of the driveway she stopped. She signaled and waved at him. He waved back and she turned left.

He turned the other way. Again.

CHAPTER 12:

He waited until he got home to eat it. He'd driven to the convenience store on the way back to the apartment. Picked it up, paid, and left. And when he got home, as soon as his feet were through the doorway he unwrapped it. A simple Hershey's bar. Nothing special.

He peeled away the plastic wrapper and set the chocolate on his desk. Be aggressive. He grunted. Right. It had been a long drive home. Each turn he rethought what he should have done. He could have asked her to have a drink. He needed to do it. But he saw her there. Heard her voice. It didn't seem like she could want him. How could someone like her…

He broke off a rectangle and smelled it as he tried to take off his tie. Trying just made the knot tighter. He put the rectangle on his tongue and let it sit. It wasn't melting yet. His fingerprints had a brown dust on them. He licked the tips of his fingers and waited for the chocolate to dissolve. He'd have to make it last. He felt it drip off the sides of his tongue. Water over a dam's edge. It flowed to the back of his cheeks and stayed there, a singed sweetness. He broke off another square. Then another. Then two more after that.

When it was done, he looked in the mirror. He had chocolate on the corners of his mouth. It made it look like he was smiling. He wasn't. He pulled the buttons of his suit jacket close to his stomach and stood in profile. Then he faced the mirror again. Why hadn't he asked her to have a drink? What had stopped him?

He sat down at the computer and decided to get to work. Two e-mails. One from Gary and one from Thompson. He draped his jacket on the chair and started reading Gary's e-mail first.

Dear Jacob,

I was going through some old things today and I saw something wonderful. A pair of 3-D glasses! And I was thinking, why not have the newspaper give out 3-D glasses?

We could show the pictures of Sarasota in one more dimension than we do now! Three Dimensions! I was thinking that you could—

He wished he had another candy bar. He stopped reading and clicked on Thompson's message.

Russo—what's next? Remember our talk. I want to hear about something good. A really strong story.

The time stamp was from only a minute or two before. He was at the office late. Jake typed back frantically.

Sorry—had a late night. Went to banquet at a big local place. Have a great story. You wouldn't believe it—a mad environmentalist stormed the stage. Threatened local developer, would like to do piece on tension between two parties. Condos: March of progress? Or environmental destruction? Violence or dissent? Freedom of speech, or chaos? Etc…great stuff.

He clicked send and went to the bathroom. When he came back, Thompson had already replied.

I like it.

Jake was surprised. Then he read on.

Good idea. People love banquet spaces. Bar mitzvahs, anniversaries. All that crap—give me a write up on the top places where retirees can throw a party. And get some good pictures, too. If possible, find a party with a celebrity host.

He wasn't surprised anymore. He made the window disappear and went to the refrigerator for the two-liter bottle. He didn't bother with the shot glass. He got out a mug.

The cream soda almost tasted sour. His body wasn't used to the carbonation and the bubbles. He started burping. He took off his suit pants and put on a pair of shorts. As long as he was indulging, he might as well keep going. He went back to the computer.

He hadn't done it in a while. He'd had self-control. But he pulled up the site now without thinking about it. All the old feelings rushed back. The excitement, the simple comforts. Relaxing and engaging at the same time. He signed in and looked over his shoulder, as if someone might see what he was doing.

It was like riding a bike. He went to a thread about an episode in season three and corrected a classic troll's interpretation. Why had he been hiding it? No one understood Buffy The Vampire Slayer like he did. None of them could grasp the nuance or understand the hidden meanings. He belonged on the message boards, writing fan fiction and summarizing episodes.

He fixed a quote about Oz. His eyes glazed and he was almost calm again. He asked for a citation for a statement about season two. He argued that a character on the television show didn't deserve their own biography. He felt full again and leaned back in his chair while he looked at the windows and exhaled.

Then he saw himself in the mirror, sitting there with his shirt and tie on, wearing shorts, the chocolate still staining the corners of his mouth. And the Buffy message boards open. He'd sworn he wouldn't do it again. Any of it. And there he was. It was late, but he wouldn't be going to bed soon. He could tell.

Why had it been so hard? Why couldn't he ask her to have a drink? He looked in the mirror and had the answer. It was because of this. This was who he was. He wasn't the person in the new suit, a person who deserved Mel. He was still this guy. Answering e-mails late at night. Eating chocolate. Drinking cream soda. Debating the impossible. He put his head against his arms.

Then the phone rang. It was her. He picked it up and started talking as quickly as he could.

"Mel! I'm so glad you called. I had been meaning to call you and I just didn't feel like I could. But about tonight, I just wanted to say—"

"Jake," she said. He stopped. Her voice sounded deeper and quieter.

"Yes?"

"I'm back at Sunset Cove. I drove home and got a call to come here. I thought you should know."

"What is it?" Here it was. The boyfriend. He wiped the corners of his lips. "Is there…someone else I should know about?"

"Yes," she said, almost whispering.

"What? Who?"

"Jake, I just can't say it."

He waited. She spoke again.

"I got the call and drove back here. It was a pair of teenagers. They were walking along our beach, by the concession building. They aren't supposed to be here. They aren't…"

"Are you OK?"

"The teens sneak on to the beach though. They can kiss behind the building. You can't blame them. They were the ones who found her there. They thought she was asleep at first. But then she didn't wake up."

"Who? Who didn't wake up?" He closed the laptop and looked into the mirror, waiting.

"It looks like it was peaceful. No convulsions. It was just her time."

"What happened?"

"They found your friend Charlotte on the beach tonight."

"My Charlotte?"

"Yes." She exhaled into the receiver. "Charlotte's passed away."

CHAPTER 13:

He'd thought the heat made sense at night. But now the cool seemed cruel. All the shadows were jagged and the water seemed too large. Near the beach, the winds were too strong. All of it was loud. How could he think that the heat made sense? Nothing made sense. Not now. He felt his feet sink into the sand. He'd be walking for a while.

He'd hung up after telling Mel he'd drive by in the morning. But he knew better than that. Everything would be changed in the morning. At night, he might have some idea of what the beach looked like when Charlotte had died. He'd put on a pair of jeans and started driving out to Sunset Cove. He stopped a full mile from the concession building where they found Charlotte. He hadn't told Mel that he was coming. But Mel didn't know that Charlotte had received a threat.

He walked quickly, first near the road and then closer to the shore where the sand was firm and wet. Ruined tennis shoes didn't matter now. As he started to splash through the sand, he tried to trace everything in his head. When had it happened? And how had Charlotte died?

He ran past a sign to his left. The beach officially closed at 7:00, and he knew they flattened the sand at the end of the day. From the tracks he ran past, he could tell that a few people had walked along the beach since 7:00. One of them had been Charlotte. Except she never left.

So she had died at some point after seven, but before Mel had called him. Judging by the time of her phone call, it had happened before 10:00 PM. Somewhere in that three hour interval, Charlotte had died. Now he needed to know why and how it had happened. Had Charlotte actually been right? He tripped in the sand and almost fell down. He'd have to find out.

As he approached the concession building, he slowed his pace to a walk. Sand had stuck on the soles of his shoes, and his prints were just sloppy ovals in the sand. He pulled out the digital camera he'd brought and kept his notebook in his pocket. He could see it in the distance—the concession building where two teenagers found her body.

It was a concrete rectangle with an overhang. Two large windows were closed up with metal shutters. An old printed sign said "Snacks" on it, but the way the light hit it, only the last two letters showed. The k sliced up the s. No one else was on the beach. Or at least he couldn't see them.

He walked closer slowly, moving carefully in the dark. The waves were at his back. They crashed loudly and then softened as he walked further up the beach, gradually muting to help him focus. He crouched down and looked at the ground. There were too many prints to be useful—more people than the teenagers had walked by. He took a picture, even though all the footprints meant nothing meshed together in a grid.

But he could see that it had happened near there. Big tire tracks came in from one side, sunk in, and then led off in the other direction. He guessed it was the ambulance they'd picked up her body in. He took another picture. So it had been here.

It was dark by the concession building. The perfect place to hide. He took a picture of it. Even at night, the structure cast a shadow. He started to shiver from the wind. If there'd been any other artifacts, the police or workers would have found them. Or they would have disappeared before anyone arrived. He'd have to ask Mel.

He was starting to shiver when he heard a noise behind him. A hollow noise, like when he'd sat on his car hood. He stopped and didn't move. It happened again. It was coming from the shutters on the other side of the building. Again. The metal sound died out quickly. There was no echo in a space like this. Just a thump and a pause, abrupt as a challenge.

He turned around slowly and stared at the wall. The door to the building was on the right side, where he was standing. He looked around and only saw the beach stretching out. No one was around to see what happened to him. He got out his keys and put them in his left hand, arranging them in a star between his fingers. It was all he had—his only defense was a trick he'd seen on an old TV show. He put his other hand around the doorknob and started to turn. He gripped tightly on the cold metal.

It was locked.

He breathed out and relaxed his grip. The keys loosened. Then he heard it again. Thump. No echo. Just the sound of something hitting metal. He'd have to walk to the front of the concession building, the side with the shutters. He crept against the wall, staring at the water. He pressed his fingers to the concrete, pocked with tiny holes, and turned the corner.

Seagulls. They'd found a piece of bread stuck on the ledge. He saw one fly into the shutter while trying to retrieve it. Thump. He walked forward and they scattered.

"Stupidest birds on the planet," he whispered and threw the bread to them. They all gathered around it gratefully. He laughed that they'd scared him. But then he remembered Charlotte.

He leaned against the shutters and thought about it. It didn't make sense—why had this happened now, to Charlotte? He hadn't believed she was in danger. She was just a harmless old woman, afraid of her shadow. But maybe she had actually taken a wrong turn. Maybe something had gone sour. And then one night, tonight, she took a walk and didn't come back. He was supposed to be aggressive, but when she died, he'd been drinking cream soda.

He looked around again. The empty beach was large and dark. She'd been crazy. She thought the threats were all about a bridge game. If she'd told him aliens wanted to abduct her, would he have believed that too? She was a good woman. A kind woman. It was like she'd died in her sleep. To think that he was scared, that he still had his keys splayed out in his hand. He laughed to himself.

He decided to take the street back to his car. He put his head down and turned the corner. More seagulls. Then he looked up. Someone was at the edge of the beach, a silhouette

with their hands raised to their eyes.
　"Hey!" Jake yelled. "Can you help me?"
　Silence.
　"Do you know what happened here?"
　The shadow ran away. It didn't look back.

CHAPTER 14:

He was glad Mel didn't look good the next morning. Her hair was pulled back in a ponytail and she was wearing a tank top and faded jeans. She had bags under her eyes and her skin looked dry. He couldn't have handled beauty, and she didn't hide her grief.

"It's not that this doesn't ever happen. People die. But to have a few teenagers find her body on the beach. And to have it be so sudden. It's just…"

He nodded. She'd taken him to the concession building once he drove in that morning. All the footprints he'd seen the night before were gone. He was glad he'd gone. Near the water, a couple walked hand in hand, their canes pressing periods into the sand. They didn't even know what had happened a few feet up shore. He reached forward and touched Mel's shoulder.

"You've done a good job."

"No I haven't. I just answered the call."

"That's all you could do."

"I know." She turned around. "Still."

They started walking along the beach in the direction of Sunset Cove.

"Do you know if they found anything else back there? Any other possessions or evidence?"

"Jake." She stopped and looked at him. Her eyes still looked pretty, even when they were inside dark circles.

"What is it?"

"I don't know if I should."

"Should what?"

"I don't know if I should be giving you material like this. I just know that Simeon will come around and tell me that I should be talking about our managed care options. Instead of our deaths."

She held her hands to her eyes. He pulled them away.

"Mel, I'm still a reporter. But I'm asking about Charlotte as her friend."

She looked up.

"I just imagine you writing something gloomy about how we should have had a nurse with her, so she wouldn't have gone walking alone."

"I won't."

"I wish we had." They walked up wooden steps off of the sand and toward Mel's office.

"You couldn't have known her condition."

"I know," she said. "I know."

"So did they find anything else?"

"No, I remember that." She'd collected herself. Dried her eyes. "I remember that the teenagers just saw Charlotte there, lying down. And then they couldn't wake her up. That's what they told the police, too."

"What about in her home?"

"We can't go in there. Each resident uses different terms. Charlotte set hers so that only her daughter could enter the apartment. I told Charlotte's daughter what happened before you got here. She seemed better off than me."

"OK." He wrote it down—they'd only found Charlotte's body on the beach. He looked at her face. He wanted to stop, but he couldn't. It wouldn't be fair to Charlotte. "Did the hospital say anything?"

"Well, they are sure it was natural, guessing from her history. Charlotte had so many different conditions. I remember once I stopped by to ask her something and I had to use the restroom. She had even more medication than most of our other residents. Some of it was for the back pain. But some of it was for more serious conditions."

Mel had been speaking normally, but now she started looking down again as they entered the office. Then she started crying.

"Are you OK?"

"I don't know why I'm crying."

"What do you mean?"

"I didn't even know her. I don't know any of them."

On the flat screen television, a commercial played above her head.

"You knew her some."

"I don't know her." She took a tissue and wiped it against her nose.

"And it's OK. It's normal."

"The worst part is that I think she knew. She must have known that it was her time. So she took one last walk..."

She stopped and shook her head. Her forehead was wrinkled and she bit her lower lip. He wanted to kiss it.

"What else Mel?"

"She always loved the beach, you know. It reminded her of her husband."

"Why?"

"He used to take driftwood. She told me this once. And he'd carve something for her from it. It sounded nice. I'm sure that's why..."

"Why what?"

"I think she walked out there to die."

She swallowed and then stood up. She went around her desk and started taking files and straightening them out. She took the papers on her desk and filed them, but she couldn't keep it up. She walked over to him and put her head on his shoulder. He patted her on the back and thought about what Charlotte had told him.

"I should get going," he whispered.

"I'm sorry."

"Don't be sorry."

"I really don't know why." She walked away and messed with the papers again. "I should be used to it by now."

"It's good you aren't." He walked out the door.

From the top of the hill, he could see the edge of the beach and then the water beyond it. The police hadn't found anything. If they had, they probably couldn't tell him. It made sense that Charlotte would walk out. Maybe the fear had gotten to her. Maybe she had just given up and gone into the night. They said that losing the will to live could be enough. He'd been eating chocolate when it happened.

He started walking to his car and looked down the hill one last time. Then, he looked again, closer. A large woman with thick gray hair was yelling at a man. It was the man with the red-brimmed hat, the one he'd seen outside Building B. The woman waved her arms around and yelled again. She looked like she was about to hit his hat off of his head. The man walked away quickly in Jake's direction.

He walked with his head turned down to the ground, the top of the hat facing toward Jake. Jake couldn't see the man's face, only his stooped shoulders and carefully polished shoes. When he reached the top of the hill, he looked at Jake and seemed to swallow. He looked back at the woman, who was pulling a weed out of the sidewalk. Then he tried to walk past.

"Sir," Jake said. "How are you? I met you earlier outside Building B. We'd thought there had been an accident in Charlotte's room. Do you remember?"

"I do," he said and started to walk.

"It was my photographer, Gary. He was locked in a battle with his camera strap."

"I see. And you are?"

"Jake Russo. What's your name?"

"I have to be going."

Jake pulled out his notebook.

"Did you know Charlotte well?"

"I suppose so. Why?"

"So you heard what happened to her?"

"What?"

"That she died last night, walking on the beach."

"I didn't know," he said and brought his hand to his chest.

"You didn't know she'd died? Then why didn't you say something when I asked if you had known Charlotte well."

"What do you mean?" He swallowed.

"When I asked, I used the past tense, Mr…"

"Samuels," the man said. "I'm sorry. I heard about it this morning."

"Did you know her well?"

"Yes, I knew her. I was sorry to hear what happened."

"Were you surprised?" He pressed the pen point on the paper.

"I should go. Please. Please let me go."

Jake looked past the man for a moment. The gray haired woman was holding a weed in her hand, staring up at them. She looked away when Jake's eyes met hers. The red brim on Samuels's hat seemed to darken, like he was sweating through it.

"It just seemed unusual," Jake said. "So sudden."

"We're all mourning." He tipped the hat. "It was good to meet you."

He ducked down and started walking again, surprisingly quickly. Jake looked back to see the gray haired woman halfway down the hill. She dropped the weed from her hand and bent down to pull another. Jake looked toward his car. Then he got out his notebook and started walking toward the woman instead.

CHAPTER 15:

She started talking before he even said hello.

"You should know a few things about that man. Abram Samuels likes to put up a front." She had a voice like a cough. Brooklyn, old Brooklyn. "Did you know his son is a hairdresser for a living? Abram will be happy to tell you about himself, but his son is living somewhere in New Jersey giving women perms for a living. Abram is a very handsome man of course. But his son is pretty."

When she stopped he told her his name.

"Ech," she said. "I'm Sheryl Goldfein."

Sheryl Goldfein. He remembered what Charlotte had said about Sheryl. She'd roll over you. He wasn't sure what had happened to Charlotte, but he could say he agreed with her judgment of character. Sheryl didn't wait for him to write down her name.

"Where you from?"

"Me?"

"No, the palm tree."

"I live here in Sarasota. Before I came down, I was living in Long Island City—"

"You had a place?"

"Yeah."

"Why didn't you live in Manhattan? While you're young?"

"Well, I'm from Queens, and the salary is a little—"

"Ech." She dropped another weed from her hand. He hadn't realized she was still holding one. "So why are you here?"

"Did you hear about Charlotte?"

"That she kicked it?"

"I wouldn't put it like that."

She shrugged.

"I don't have enough fingers to count the relatives I'm missing. Let alone friends like Charlotte. She missed her husband anyway. Now him, he was all right."

"So you heard that she died?"

"I heard. I'm sad." She shrugged and scratched her head. "She was our fourth for a long time. We played bridge a good deal. She was always there, always very dependable. Do you put grease in your hair?"

"I'm sorry, what?"

"Your hair. It looks like a grease trap."

"I don't follow."

"You know how you fold a slice of pizza, and all the grease drips off? It looks like you stood under a piece of pizza this morning."

"I use some product," he said and touched his hair. Baked in the sun. Hardened.

"I can tell."

"That's not the point." He looked back at his notebook. He'd written down "hair" unconsciously. "I don't understand."

"What?"

"You just said that Charlotte was your fourth in bridge. I thought you'd stopped playing bridge with her. You kicked her out."

She snorted and pushed her glasses up the bridge of her nose.

"This month we stopped playing, of course. But she knew why."

"Why?"

"It's a long story."

"I have time."

She started walking toward a bench further down the path. She shifted side to side as she walked, giving each side of the sidewalk equal pressure. He couldn't see where she'd been finding weeds. The whole sidewalk seemed perfectly clean. But somehow she had found them. They walked toward a white bench underneath a palm tree. Sheryl talked loudly even though she seemed taxed by the effort.

"Charlotte was an arrogant woman. She was my friend, but she could be arrogant."

"What do you mean?"

"Do you not know the word arrogant?"
He ignored her.
"She told me that things between you two went sour."
She muttered something he couldn't hear.
"What did you say?"
"I said that she knew why."
"Why then?"
She ignored it and fired back at him.
"Do you play bridge?"
"No, I don't."
"Of course not. You play videogames."
"I'm a little old for that."
"But you don't play bridge?"
"What did you mean when you said 'she knew why?'"
She ignored his question.
"Charlotte was arrogant. Last winter, she says her daughter is a doctor. We find out she was a podiatrist!"
"They're doctors."
"Ech. Charlotte took everything she could. Even when other people needed it more…"
She wiped her forehead.
"Why didn't I move to Arizona? A place with a dry heat."
"Please, continue." They finally sat down on the white bench and looked at the buildings below. Jake knew he could see Charlotte's window from there, but he wasn't sure which one it was. Sheryl looked out to the water.
"Once we stopped playing bridge with Charlotte, she couldn't accept it. Things always have to be her way. That's the reason she started protesting the community, going off on wild investigations, and trying to ruin me."
"She told me about that. She said you were switching the charities and that you didn't have any information about the new one you were choosing."
"After the meeting," Sheryl continued, "she went over to Abram Samuels. Abram was a gentleman, of course. But she says, 'I'm thinking about starting my own bridge group.' It

was horrible!"

"But you wouldn't let her play bridge with you, right?"

"Do you use mouthwash?"

"What?"

"You should consider it." She pulled at her collar. "It's this time of day that it gets the hottest. And what am I doing? Talking to someone from Queens."

"Sheryl," he said. "You stopped letting Charlotte play bridge with you, right?"

"True. But it lacked class for her to start rumors and bother everybody. It wasn't the right thing to do."

"So you kept her out? Why did you do it?"

"Of course we kept her out. The way she acted...she was always immature. Always selfish. "

He looked at Building B again. Maybe that was Charlotte's window, the one in the center. The sun glinted off it and made the blinds and inside invisible.

"Sheryl, do you wish you hadn't done it?"

"Done what?"

"Banned her from bridge. After what's happened to her?"

She paused then caught herself.

"I wish certain things had been different."

Then she looked down where Jake had been looking, at Building B. She seemed to slow down. She wiped sweat from her face again, right at her cheeks, and looked out a little longer.

"I don't think that we caused it. Whatever happened." Her voice had softened, from a saw to sandpaper. "I think she knew that. She knew that it was getting to be the time to go."

"I don't think she did."

"And you knew her how long? A day?"

"I knew her."

"Ech," she said. Hard again. "It's too normal of a thing. You'd get used to it. It's the way things are. There's nothing you can do."

"I don't feel that way."

She shrugged and patted out the wrinkles in her pants. She stood up, slowly.

"I think you'll be OK."

"This isn't about me."

"Then why are you asking these questions?"

"Why don't you answer my questions?"

"I never heard about you."

"I'll tell you about Charlotte."

The pages had started sticking together, but he leafed through it all quickly. What would Thompson do? Be aggressive. Put it out there. He read over the notes. Charlotte's threat. The end of the bridge games. The suspicious timing on the beach. The silhouette, running away. Charlotte had seemed paranoid, but there had to be something there.

"Sheryl, I don't think that Charlotte simply died. I think that she was murdered."

She sighed and barely reacted. She swallowed and looked down at Building B, where the reflected light shone back up. She breathed out slow, like she was exhaling cigarette smoke.

"Do you know what I did?" she asked. "When I was working?"

"No, how would I know that?"

"I was a nurse. My husband was a cop, not a chief. A guy on the street. So I had to make money too. For a long time. I worked before we had our kids, and then when they turned twelve I went back to it. You're from Queens?"

He looked at the palm tree above them, its leaves drooping.

"Yeah."

"Well, then you know what I saw in Brooklyn. When I was working a long time ago, it wasn't like it is now. It was different. I saw all the kids who were shot up, all the junkies, you know, all that."

"OK." He wasn't writing, just listening.

"And you know, some black kid would get shot. And he dies. And then the mother would come in. Some of them were quiet. But a lot of them, they come in yelling about the doctor killing their babies. Or about malpractice, if they knew what malpractice was."

"What did you do?"

"That doesn't matter," she snapped. "It got fixed. But I always noticed that those people were the ones who were the angriest. They were the ones looking for somebody to blame for their children getting shot or overdosing. The other patients' families—a lot of them poor, too—they never yelled about that. It was always the parents of kids in gangs, or junkies."

"Right."

"They thought they could make up for what they had let their kids do. They thought they could make up for being a bad parent by yelling about malpractice or a bad doctor. But they couldn't."

"I guess not."

"They couldn't. The kid was gone. But these people couldn't understand that the kid was just gone. That was it. You can't earn extra points."

She looked at him and waited. He had to be aggressive.

"Sheryl, this is different than your patients. I may not have known Charlotte." He thought for a second. "But I can still believe in Charlotte. And I'm not stopping. Your story isn't going to trick me into quitting. Maybe I'll find nothing. But I'm going to look—even if you won't help me."

"Have it how you want it."

She rose and began walking down the hill. She walked slowly, spreading her stride across the sidewalk, scanning in between the cracks. Then she bent down. The sidewalk had appeared perfectly maintained. But she found a weed and pulled it out.

CHAPTER 16:

The next day, Kaylie knocked at his door. This time he was wearing pants that fit.

He'd been trying to learn more about Sunset Cove. At the same time, he had to schedule times to see different banquet spaces—he made an appointment for the next day with Jerry Rubenstein at the Palmstead. He'd write a little about good times and good friends. Maybe pad it with some stats about social gatherings and cardiac health. The daily grind.

He answered the door and Kaylie was smiling. It was neighborly. She had on the same outfit as before, but different colors. A blue t-shirt and shorts, still barefoot. She walked past him and inside.

"I've come for the proverbial cup of sugar." She had a measuring cup and a smirk.

"How are you?"

"Do you have any?"

"I try not to use sugar."

"Oh." She cringed. "Your little diet."

"I just don't cook."

"Right. I was also wondering if you knew when our rent is due."

"Two days ago."

"Oh. Well. I wanted sugar too."

"Sorry. I'm sure the building manager will understand."

She sat down on the bed and crossed her legs. She pointed her toes at the floor.

"Were you working?"

"I was. Would you like water?"

"I'm fine."

He came in from the kitchen with a glass for himself.

"I'm sorry, I checked. I don't have sugar."

"What about flour?" she said and tilted her head.

"What are you making?"

"I'm just trying to squeeze you dry."

"I see."

"What were you working on?"

"Just this thing."

"That's descriptive. You really must be a writer." She yawned and stretched. He looked at his water glass instead of her.

"My editor wants me to write something about banquet spaces."

"Oh, how exciting."

"It's OK. It won't be a hard job, necessarily."

She got up and walked over to his window. She looked out. He couldn't tell if they were the same shorts as before. But he wasn't looking at his water glass.

"I used to work at banquets," she said and turned around. "I was a caterer."

"You were?"

"I was. The pay was terrible and so were the people. Will that go in your article?"

"I don't know," he said and laughed. When she walked, she kept her feet slightly—barely—arched. She moved to his desk and picked up his notebook. He walked forward and reached for it, but she turned around and held it.

"What's all this? I was expecting descriptions of appetizers and sound systems. Not all these drawings of the beach. And what's this? Rumors?"

He grabbed it from her. She held onto the end and looked at him.

"That's nothing," he said. "Just doodles."

"I see." She leaned against his desk and ran her finger across it. Slow.

"You're clean."

"I like a clean place."

"You like control."

"I think you dropped your measuring cup," he told her.

"Will you find it for me?"

"I should get back to work."

She stepped closer and looked him up and down.

"This fits better."

"It does."

"Did you get a suit?"

"I did."

"Can I see it?"

He started laughing.

"Do you act like this with all your neighbors, Kaylie? How many times have I met you? Once?"

"No, Jake, I don't act like this with all my neighbors."

She sat back on the bed. He got the suit and changed in the bathroom. Felt his hair. It was hard. Hers, that red brown color, seemed like it would be soft. He knotted the tie with both hands and splashed water on his face. She deserved to see the suit, he thought. She had told him about it.

When he came out of the room, he buttoned his jacket and looked up. She was holding a Hershey wrapper with two fingers, like it was soiled.

"Kaylie, where did you get that?"

"Tsk, tsk." She shook her head. "A moment of weakness?"

"Were you digging through my garbage?"

"I threw away my gum and saw this. I'm disappointed in you."

"You can't just burst in and do that. I don't even know you."

"It looks good, by the way."

"The suit?"

"Yes."

"I'm glad I got it. I wouldn't have known where that place was."

She dropped the wrapper on his desk and wiped her hands on her shorts.

"So what caused your moment of weakness?"

He sat down on the bed. He didn't care if the suit wrinkled. He unbuttoned his jacket and let it fall loose around him.

"Nothing."

"Come on. There must have been something that pushed you over the edge. I know that the guy you are now didn't lose all that weight by relapsing."

She tilted her head to the side. Strands of hair fell out from behind her ears.

"It's nothing."

"What happened?"

"Just something with work."

"Banquet spaces?"

"No. I had a friend pass away."

She sat down beside him, a half foot away. He could see the lines on her lips. No lipstick.

"I'm sorry."

"It's fine. It's stupid. I shouldn't have eaten the Hershey bar."

"Not about that. I'm sorry about your friend."

"I hardly knew her."

"Oh."

"But it was very sudden."

"I see. Well, that's enough."

"And..." he started then stopped. She leaned forward and nodded.

"And what? What is it?"

"I'm not sure what happened. There's just a lot going on that I don't understand. I'm not sure if she was crazy or right. Or maybe both. It makes it difficult to know what to do."

Kaylie looked at the wrapper on the desk and then back at him. He leaned forward and the jacket covered his knees. He put his head in his hands. She rubbed his shoulders.

"It's OK."

"No, it's not."

"It is."

"Anyway, I'm sorry. I'm telling this to a stranger."

"I think," she said quietly, "you should come out with me and some friends. Sometime this week. We'll have drinks. You can forget about all of this, right?"

"I don't want to forget about all of this. I don't think I know what happened yet."

"Your friend—what happened to them?"

"Well, fine." He sighed. "She was old. And she went for a walk on the beach. I admit that she seemed a little crazy when I met her. Scared. She didn't know what she was doing. She had weird theories. But she was worried something would happen to her."

"And what happened?"

"Sometime that night…two nights ago, I guess. It seems like it was years ago. But sometime that night she passed away on the beach. And I just didn't think that she could go like that. So quickly. The police don't suspect anything, but I know it must have happened for a reason."

She leaned in closer.

"I don't know what happened." She shrugged and smiled. "But I think it's just a part of your job you aren't used to yet. This is what it's like. You have to get used to that. It's natural. It's something that just…happens."

"You think so?"

"You can't fix it by reporting on her. Right?"

"No."

She walked forward to his desk and picked up the wrapper.

"You have to deal with this in other ways. Ones with less fat content." She tilted her head and laughed a little. It sounded different than he'd expected. It rang more. "I know what you should do. You should come out and have fun. Just have a few drinks, take it easy. It's the neighborly thing to do."

"I've never known any of my neighbors before you."

"Then that's your problem."

"Right."

"So just don't worry about it. Right?"

"Right."

She crossed the room and he watched her from the bed. She walked like she was testing out her hips. They worked. She found the measuring cup she'd dropped on the floor and picked it up. She put the handle in her front pocket, the cup sticking out.

"I'll talk to you later."

Before she walked toward the door, she stopped in front of him and crouched down. She leaned in close and took the knot of his tie in her hands. She took the back tail with one hand and the front in the other. She pulled on them hard and whispered to him.

"I'm good at knots."

She walked out the door and shut it behind her. He stood in front of the mirror. The tie was almost strangling him. This was what it was like to have a new jacket. He took it and threw it on the floor. He loosened the tie enough to pull it straight over his head. He didn't even bother to untie it.

CHAPTER 17:

"Jacob, did you receive my letter on the e-mail? The one about 3-D newspapers? I think I might have sent it wrong."

Lying to Gary was hard. Jake shifted the camera and all the gear over his shoulder: the lenses, the tripod, the case, and the camera. It was heavy. But Gary wasn't allowed to carry it after his accident. He looked up at Jake, nodding his head like they'd already reached an agreement. They hadn't.

"I didn't get that e-mail. It's just with everything that happened, it's been a really busy time. So I didn't get a chance to reply about the 3-D glasses."

He'd told Gary about Charlotte before he picked him up. On the phone, Gary had been quiet. He seemed silenced by the idea of Charlotte passing away so quickly, and he remained quiet as they drove to the Palmstead to shoot its banquet space. But once they parked, he wasn't quiet anymore.

"Well, Jacob, I understand with busy times, but it's something you should think about. 3-D, Jacob. People are always saying this and that about bringing newspapers into the digital age. This would be perfect! A 3-D newspaper. Comics, Sports, Lifestyles—all in 3-D! Technology!"

"Slow down," Jake said. Gary breathed.

"It's perfect though, isn't it?"

They reached the entry to the banquet space. Jake adjusted the gear and found a free hand. Somehow. He opened the heavy door.

"Gary, I think that when people say newspapers should use technology, they're talking about the internet."

"When you come over to see the photos I developed, I'll show you my old 3-D glasses. Can you do 3-D pictures on the internet?"

He didn't answer. Jerry Rubenstein was gesturing to them from the corner of the room. It was a large space with wood detailing on the wall, and a formal stage with rich curtains stood in front. Jerry seemed like another decoration.

Luxurious. The inside of a portrait, he was Palmstead's portly king. He needed a drumstick in his hand. Instead he had a leash. The dog barked as they walked closer.

"Jake," Jerry shouted, "Coconut remembers you!"

Gary whispered.

"That dog's name is Coconut?"

They stepped over the hardwood floor, their shoes squeaking and clicking. The space was nicer than Giordano's—both on the outside and inside. It was obvious that the only reason Rothschild hadn't rented it for his own banquet was because the room belonged to the competition. The hall was full of extras. Extra lighting. Extra windows. And Rubenstein had extra chins. They reached him and Jake shook his hand. Coconut stayed calm.

"Jerry," Jake said, "this is Gary Novak. He's my photographer. He'll be taking some shots of the space."

"It's wonderful to meet you."

"It's a beautiful space!" Gary shouted. "And this dog. It's a Labrador?"

"No, he is actually a Schnoodle."

"Are the two similar?"

"Not really." He shook Gary's hand. "No, not at all."

Jake got out his notebook.

"What's a Schnoodle?"

"Ah, it is a wonderful breed. A delicate cross between a schnauzer and a poodle. Very easy to train. And very nice, aren't we?"

Coconut barked on cue. Gary seemed to consider leaning down to pet her, but instead he pushed his cane forward slowly. The dog approached it tentatively before stepping away.

"I should have dipped it in bacon!" Gary said. "I bet they do that in Ethiopia, for hunting."

"I'm sure," Jake said and unloaded the camera. "This is our room to shoot. I might ask Mr. Rubenstein a few questions about the space."

He set the rest of the gear in front of Gary and led Jerry to another side of the room. While he walked, Jerry held his arm out halfway, letting the dog lead him on the leash. Jake leaned in closely.

"Gary's a good photographer. He obviously doesn't have dogs. And apparently he's never even seen a Labrador."

"I can't hold that against a man like him. I wish I could photograph so well."

"Have you seen his work?"

"Marvelous shots of palm trees."

"I see."

Jake looked around the room and listened as the smallest sounds echoed.

"This is a great space. Aged beautifully. I was at Giordano's the other night and it was fine on the inside. But this is beautiful on the inside and out."

"So, you were at Giordano's were you? I'm guessing Simeon Rothschild invited you."

"Yes." He didn't want Jerry to know that he'd been on a date with Mel. He might think she had compromised his reporting. Jerry didn't seem to care either way.

"Funny that. Simeon used to invite me. I noticed because this year was the first I didn't receive an invitation to celebrate 'his life and charity.' I can't say I was offended. Or that I was surprised. He's beginning to think he'll never overtake Palmstead."

"Is that so?"

"Yes. He's been trying to march past us for years. But he hasn't had luck. Has he Coconut?"

The dog sniffed Jake's shoes excitedly.

"I see," Jake said. He wrote it all down. "Well, you missed a hell of an event. I couldn't believe it. Halfway through, some environmentalist maniac jumped on a table. He held a protest during the banquet. We thought he might have a gun, or a bomb or something. He left peacefully, but it was quite a show."

"It makes sense." Jerry tugged Coconut closer. "The Development Proposition is coming to a vote so soon. The environmentalists are targeting Simeon every chance they get. They think he's first in line to benefit. If people vote 'Yes' on the Proposition and allow development in the wetlands, he'll jump on it. He's had his eye on it for a long time."

"Do you think he'd develop there?"

"I have no doubt he'd love to. It's a real fight."

Jake looked around the banquet room. Thick walls here. Gary was taking pictures of the wide stage and its rich curtains. Jake turned to Jerry and drew a dash in his notebook.

"Would you develop there, on the wetlands?"

"We can't. We don't have it planned into our budget. And we'd feel uncomfortable doing it, even if the Development Proposition passed."

"I see." He wrote it all down. The competition was supposed to be over between Palmstead and Rothschild. But the Development Proposition might change the story. Any space for new communities could change the game in Rothschild's favor.

"Enough of that," Jake said, only after he'd written it all down. "Let's learn about the space."

Jerry told him about the banquet hall and Jake dutifully recorded all of it. It would be turned into a neat paragraph, one with tailored sentences and close-cropped clauses. He watched as Gary polished off a roll of film. Rothschild hadn't mentioned the upcoming vote on the Development Proposition. That meant something.

"You'd love to put a Palmstead building on that land, wouldn't you?"

"We would," Jerry admitted. "But it just doesn't make sense. Development costs are high, the community would be upset. Too many risks. And we don't need it that badly. We're already able to have our brochures say we're the biggest developers in the Sarasota area."

"Does that really matter?"

"You know your readers," Jerry said and smiled. "Don't you think they want the biggest and the best for what's probably their last major purchase? We don't do a lot of market research, but what we have done shows it makes a big difference. Our buyers are naturally competitive people. They're New Yorkers."

"I guess so."

Gary walked up to them. The tripod was still set up across the room, but he held the camera in his free hand.

"Mr. Rubenstein, let's get a shot of you by those curtains. And we'll get Coco by there too."

"Coconut, Mr. Novak. Please do be careful. Coconut is a tremendously sensitive animal."

The dog started barking and running in circles. He did little hops around Jerry's leg and circled it like a cone. Jerry walked over toward the stage and stretched out his arms. Jake stood next to Gary and whispered.

"Something's up."

"What?" Gary yelled.

"Nothing. I'll tell you later."

"Tell me what later?" Gary said. Loudly. Jerry looked up and Jake pulled at Gary's arm.

"Later. Just take the picture."

"Are you sure you don't want to tell me now?"

"Gary—take it."

He snapped and Jake exhaled.

"You developed the pictures from Charlotte's place, right?"

Gary nodded as Jerry walked over, pulling along Coconut, who seemed to be distracted by a dust ball near the stage. Jake grabbed Gary's shoulder.

"Good. I want to see what the photographs show."

Rubenstein stopped in front of them. He breathed heavily from the exertion of his fifteen-foot walk.

"Do remember, Jake, Palmstead has the largest banquet space in the area."

"I've got it." But he was busy underlining key sections in

his notebook. He wanted to go to Gary's as quickly as possible. He needed to see the photographs of Charlotte's condo. He had a feeling something was there. Something had to be there. He just didn't know what.

CHAPTER 18:

Jake took the gear out of the trunk: the lenses, the tripod, the case, and the camera. Gary walked to his mailbox and pulled out a flier before heading in the direction of his garage.

"Jacob, you'll finally see my darkroom!"

Jake breathed heavily, already sore from carrying the gear.

"Can you open the garage?"

"There's one problem. We don't have one of the doodads."

"What doodad?"

"You know," he said and gestured. "A remote control."

"You mean a garage opener? Just go inside and open it then."

"We don't have one inside either. It's a manual door. The doctor says the exertion of opening a door wouldn't be good for me, in my damaged condition."

Jake put down the lenses, the tripod, the case, and the camera and lifted open the garage door. He noticed the windows were taped up with black paper.

"This is your darkroom, isn't it? Your garage."

"Meryl didn't want me to use the bathroom anymore. Once I switched the developing solution and shampoo."

"What happened?"

"Oh, everything grew back in a month or two."

They walked inside. Gary had hung notable photographs on the wall, attached with electrical tape. A cruise ship leaving a harbor. Sunset on a beach. And palm trees. Lots of palm trees.

"Do you like my gallery?"

"I actually do."

Someone yelled through the closed door from inside the house, their voice totally muffled by the wood.

"Meryl, I know!" Gary yelled back. "We'll put it out tomorrow!"

"Wait, you could hear that?"

"Of course not. But we've been married long enough that I can guess."

Jake went back outside, dragged all the equipment in, and pulled down the garage door. Gary turned on the light so it wasn't totally dark. Jake noticed the different stations, perfectly organized. Everything was labeled in glow in the dark pen, which made the labels shine softly in the light.

"So you got some good shots today?"

"Definitely. Do you want to shoot any other banquet halls for this story?"

"I'm going to interview some people, but I won't bother asking you to photograph them. To be honest, the Palmstead's as good as it gets. And Thompson just wants a good picture. He doesn't care if it's comprehensive."

"That's good."

Jake sighed. He took a quick look at his notebook and then put it away. He was ready to talk about Charlotte.

"The real reason I wanted to come here today is that we have more important work to do. Gary, it's a little beyond what I'm supposed to be writing. A little beyond my job description. But it's the right thing."

"I see."

"I want you to help me. We need everything we have to try and make this work. Are we on the same page?"

"Of course!" he shouted. His cane was propped against the wall and he kicked it up to his hand. "I'll be right back. I know just what we need to get started."

He opened the door to the house and Jake smelled a mixture of garlic and Febreeze. He looked around the dark room. Large, but practical. A whole wall full of different cameras and film. Different types and vintages. A collage of Polaroids, arranged in a circle, each image overlapping the next. It was a nice room. He shrugged. Maybe the man knew what he was doing.

Gary opened the door.

"Jacob, I'm ready to begin."

He was wearing his 3-D glasses. He waved his arms and whistled.

"Gary, that's not what I was talking about."

He was already walking around the room, pitching his head forward and backward at different photographs.

"Jacob!" he screamed. "This palm tree looked like it was grabbing me!"

"Don't they have to be 3-D images?"

"I don't think so," he mumbled. He brought a picture of a vintage car close to his face and then let it fall to the ground. Jake reached forward and took the glasses off his head. Gary's voice pitched high like a child's.

"Hey, what are you doing?"

"Gary, when I said all that, I was talking about Charlotte. I think something happened to her."

"Right. You said she died."

"No, I mean that I don't think that she died of natural causes. And I want to find out what happened."

"Oh."

"I know that we can figure it out."

"I don't think the 3-D glasses will help with that."

"I know. We're done with them."

"Then why did you take them from me?"

"Gary, focus." He put the glasses in his pocket. "Now I don't know how to find out what really happened to Charlotte. But I think a good starting point is to go with what we have. I went to the beach and took photographs there. Can you get the ones you took of her apartment?"

Jake took his digital camera out and put it on the table. He turned it on and set the viewfinder upright. It showed the footprints on the beach, dark and random indentations. Gary came back with three different photographs in his hand, printed on large floppy sheets.

"It was a good experiment."

"Why do they look like this?"

Each photograph was printed in brilliant color. The yellows looked like chrome and the blues were like the side of a freshly painted car. But they all had a fisheye perspective, centered on

Charlotte's face. Gary shrugged.

"That was my special lens. A fisheye lens. I hadn't used one in years and thought this would be a good chance."

"Great," Jake said. "We need to find a clue and we have a fisheye."

"You can still see the room."

He could. In all the photographs, everything in the room seemed to converge on Charlotte's pale face. She had no expression. Her mouth was flat. Not smiling. Not frowning. She was frozen there, inside the fisheye, and Jake didn't know how to thaw her out.

"Now, honestly, I have no idea how to go about this."

"What do you want to find?"

"I want something that tells us what happened."

"How much do you need?"

"Not much. We just have to have something. Something that shows that Charlotte didn't die of natural causes."

"Something."

"If we don't, I'll just decide that she was just crazy, that it was just her time. Unless…"

He stared into the photograph and started making a list. Her hair, her eyes, the fabric of her purple dress. Nothing. He didn't know what she'd looked like when she died, so he couldn't infer anything from that. He tried indexing each item in the room, but it all seemed obvious and plain.

"What about this?" Gary asked. He held Jake's digital camera, which was showing the pictures of the beach.

"It's the beach. Where she was found. I took a picture of the footprints, but it's not like we know anything about Charlotte's brand of shoes. And they didn't find anything else on the beach."

"I see why they have me do your photography." He let out a whistle. "Even if we knew her shoes, we wouldn't be able to tell which ones were hers. All these footprints are the same…"

Jake looked back at the fisheye picture again. There she was, in the center, her old life spiraling around her. The duck her husband made her. The coffee table where she read. The blinds she'd been afraid to open. The pills she always took. And then he saw it.

"Gary."

"Yes?"

"You're right. The footprints do all look the same."

"So?"

"That's the problem."

He ran his finger along the trail of color in the fisheye photograph. Away from Charlotte's purple dress and around her body. He pointed.

"Now look at the tracks."

"I see them."

"So, everyone says that Charlotte just went on a walk. She went for one last stroll on the beach because she knew it was her time. Well, Gary, these tracks show a lot of people walking on the beach."

"So?"

"Right here," Jake said and tapped the picture. "You saw her go from the living room to the kitchen. If Charlotte took a walk on the beach, how did she do it without making tracks? The tracks she would have to make?"

"But we can't tell which shoes are hers."

"No," Jake said. "Where are the tracks from this? They didn't find it on the beach."

Swirled in color, next to Charlotte's head, Jake held his finger still. He was pointing at Charlotte's walker.

CHAPTER 19:

"We solved it!" Gary shouted.

"Not exactly. All we know is that Charlotte was taken to the beach to die. Or she'd been killed already. We don't know what actually happened."

"Once we have that, we'll be finished. We'll be heroes!"

"We don't know how it happened, either."

"And then, a front page story!"

"Not quite. We also don't know why it happened."

Gary looked at the picture again, Charlotte still sitting in the swirl. He turned it over.

"Then how do you begin?"

"First, we have to find out Charlotte's name."

"You mean you think she has an alias?"

"I wish. I just realized I don't know her last name."

"Neither do I." Gary frowned and silently picked up his cane. Febreeze and garlic wafted into the room. He came back and dropped the Yellow Pages on the table.

"We'll call."

"It's not that easy. We can't let anyone know that we're looking into this case."

"I know." Gary winked. "I have a plan."

He turned through the phone book and found the entry for "Sunset Cove." He started dialing on a cordless phone.

"Gary, wait! We can't do that."

"No no. It's cordless. It works without a wire. It's amazing!"

"I mean we can't call without knowing what we'll say."

"Jacob?"

"Yes Gary?"

"I forgot my plan."

The phone was already ringing. Jake ripped the phone away from Gary and put it to his ear. It was Mel's voice on the other end of the line.

"Hello, Sunset Cove. How may I help you?"

95

"Yes, hello." He paused and made his voice deep, flattening any trace of a New York accent. He was Nebraska now. He looked at Gary, who shrugged and reached for the phone. Jake held on to it.

"I was calling about…my aunt Charlotte. I heard that there was bad news."

"I'm sorry," Mel said. Her professional voice sounded smoother. Colder. "She passed away two nights ago."

"Do you know what happened?"

"I'm afraid I cannot release personal information over the phone, sir. But the designee is visiting sometime this week. She will be able to pass any information on to you."

"I see." He waited. "I…just want to make sure. I haven't heard from my cousin in a while. I can't believe that it's the same Charlotte. My aunt Charlotte. She seemed so well when I last spoke with her."

"I can't release specifics, I'm afraid. Her medical condition has to remain private."

He knew her medical condition: bad. Gary was pulling at his hair, trying to listen. Jake ignored him.

"Sir, is there anything else I can help you with?"

"I just can't believe it's really my aunt."

"I know these are trying times."

"I just don't believe it's her. That it's Aunt Charlotte." Then he got it. "It must be a different one. It can't be my Charlotte."

"Your aunt is Charlotte Ward, correct?"

He wrote it down in the notebook and circled her name.

"I'm just ashamed I didn't know already."

It was true.

"I understand." Her voice got warmer.

"I have to go." He hung up before she could reply. He handed Gary the phone and looked at the name in his notebook.

"We got it. We got her name."

He breathed out and brushed back his hair. Gary laid the

phone down on the table and looked at the notebook.

"Charlotte Ward is her name. Will that help you?"

"It should." His heart was still beating quickly. Mel couldn't have known. Gary arched his eyebrows.

"That made my nerves tingle."

"Mine too." This was what being aggressive was like.

"What will her name help with?"

"I don't think it will give us a lot. I'll search for her on the internet, but I didn't even see a computer in Charlotte's room."

"Then what will it do?"

"Not much. I don't think we can use it with her pharmacist. Or the hospital either. I'd like to find out why she died, or what medications she was on. But I don't think a fake voice will work as well for more official matters."

"You at least have it for your story."

"And it's something," he said and sighed. "She deserves a starting point. It makes me realize what we need to do next."

Gary closed the Yellow Pages and rested his hand on the cover.

"Jacob, do you think it matters?"

"That what matters? The name?"

"I just don't know if anyone will think something happened. I know we discovered about her walker, that she couldn't have gone out to the beach alone. But do you think that they will investigate?"

"Who? The police?"

"Anyone."

"Well, we care about what happened, right?"

"Yes. I do."

"Then we'll investigate."

Gary pushed up his glasses and coughed.

"So what do we do now?"

"Now? We make a trip to Sunset Cove and see what we can find. If we get anything good, we'll be able to take it from there. That community may be large, but it's tightly knit. We'll be able to find out something. And I know just the person to ask first."

Gary looked tired already, with bags under his eyes. His hair frizzed out and he reached up and patted it all down. Then he frowned.

"There's one thing I want to ask you."

"What?"

"Why didn't you just call Melissa and ask her yourself? She would have told you Charlotte's last name, wouldn't she?"

"Part of the reason I didn't ask is that you handed me the phone mid-call."

"Jacob, that cannot be the real reason."

He didn't know, at first. He saw the pictures of Charlotte on the desk. He took his own camera and looked at the viewfinder. All those feet. All those steps. The prints on the beach were already gone. The prints in the picture had erased other prints, and there had been prints before them. On the small screen, they were just splotches of black. A code he couldn't read.

"Really, that's the only reason I didn't ask Mel. I was caught off guard."

"I don't think so."

"You don't?"

"I don't think that Charlotte Ward would say you are telling the truth."

He sighed.

"I don't think so either."

They looked at each other. Jake put down the camera and picked up the photo. Charlotte, her dress shining purple. She'd been so afraid. She'd been right.

"The real reason," Jake said, "is that I think we have to start believing Charlotte. Ms. Charlotte Ward. I thought that she was crazy. But she didn't know who to trust."

Gary finished the thought. It was obvious.

"We don't know who to trust either."

CHAPTER 20:

They were walking to the common building at Sunset Cove when Gary got cold feet. He tapped his cane on the ground once and waited for Jake to look back. It took him a few steps to notice. He turned back to Gary and asked him what was wrong.

"Jacob, I just don't know if it is the right thing to do."

"What?"

"I know you say this woman, Sheryl, she has some sort of information about Charlotte."

"Right—she may even know what happened. Or worse. She might be a part of it."

Gary swallowed. He tapped his cane on the sidewalk again.

"Jacob, I don't feel right seducing this strange woman, even if it is for a good cause."

Jake put his hand to his head.

"What? Gary, when did I say you had to seduce her?"

"You've met my wife Meryl. She is a wonderful woman. Very understanding. She understands much more than I do. I know we are trying to discover what happened to Ms. Ward, but I fear that this might be acrossing the line."

"Crossing the line, you mean?"

"However you want to put it, it is wrong."

He looked around. It was late afternoon and the sun had started to set. Few people were walking around. When they'd found Sheryl Goldfein's condo, they'd been told she was in the common building, planning for a bridge game that night. It wasn't the normal night. He looked back at Gary, who was struggling with his short sleeve shirt. He was trying to wipe the sweat off his forehead while still holding his cane. It wasn't working.

"Gary, all I said was that I wanted you to come along so she'd be more comfortable. I don't think she likes me. Did I ever say that you needed to seduce her? Or flirt with her? Even talk with her?"

"Jacob, please. It was obvious. I could guess at why you'd want me there. She is a woman and I am a man."

He dropped his cane and looked at Jake. Jake bent down and handed it back to him. He nodded stoically.

"Meryl and I, Jacob, we have a bond. A wedding ring. All these things. You wouldn't understand. Your generation. You kiss and hug strange girls, willy nilly. Love is just a joke for you."

"Gary, I don't want you to seduce Sheryl."

"Does she like a man with a sense of humor? Or the strong silent type?"

"I don't know. You don't have to do anything at all, if you're worried."

"Meryl will have to understand," Gary said and sighed. "It's for our friend Charlotte."

"Wait, I thought you didn't want to seduce her."

"Our search for the truth requires bravery. Sacrifice. Seduction."

He led the way to the building and Jake just followed. Slowly.

"Just remember it's all informal. We can't let her know what we figured out. She probably thinks I gave up on the idea that Charlotte didn't die naturally."

They went into the building. There was a miniature movie theatre in the center—the one they'd passed over for the picture of Palmstead's more impressive one. Tables were pushed against the wall, three covered with aqua tablecloths and three bare. A handicapped rail clung to the side-wall—he thought about Charlotte and her walker, rolling down the ramp. Then Sheryl came out from behind an open closet door.

"Slow news day?" She held a tablecloth in her hand, folded into a square. "Or slow news year?"

"How are you?"

"Who's your friend?"

Gary was walking down the stairs, one foot at a time. He had a grin on his face as he lowered his cane onto each step.

"Hello, a pleasure to meet you." At first it sounded like he was trying to hide his accent. He gave up quickly. Sheryl started unfolding the tablecloth.

"This is Gary Novak," Jake said. "He's my photographer. We've been working together today, so I thought I'd bring him along to Sunset Cove."

"Fine. Can you get that vase in the corner and put it on this table?"

Gary started to walk forward, but Jake cut him off and got the vase first.

"What are you preparing for?"

"A bridge game. I'm sure you heard."

"I did."

Gary coughed suddenly and started speaking loudly.

"You may have heard about me," he said, his chest pushed forward. "I am a photographer. Some say I have my own unique way of seeing the world. I say, perhaps this is so. Some people have prescriptions for their blood pressure or their eyes. I medicate the soul."

She didn't look up.

"What time is your game?" Jake asked.

"A half hour. I can't talk for a long time."

"Sheryl," Gary said dramatically.

"Yes?"

"I love to photograph beautiful things."

Jake pinched the bridge of his nose. It almost made the pain go away.

"Sheryl," Gary repeated. She flapped the tablecloth up and over. It covered the wood in a wave of blue. "Do you normally play bridge tonight?"

"No," she said. "We were going to dedicate it to Charlotte." She crossed to the closet and got another tablecloth out.

"Did you tell anyone that?"

"Ech."

"Sometimes," Gary volunteered, "I cannot bear to look at the images I've made. Such beauty causes me great pain."

Jake sat down at one of the chairs and rested his head against the hard wood table. Sheryl walked out from behind the closet and then she looked up slowly. She spoke in a softer voice.

"Why can't you bear to look at the beautiful images, Mr. Novak?"

Jake looked up. Her accent seemed washed out. It was somewhere under the tablecloth, for a second at least. Gary walked across the room, his chest puffed out.

"I cannot speak of it." He sat down and let his cane drop. "I don't talk about my work. The images, they are a part of me. A secret part."

"Sheryl," Jake said. "Don't mind him. I'm trying to learn more about things at Sunset Cove. Everyday things."

She ignored him and walked over to Gary. He had his eyes closed. She stayed a foot away.

"Why can't you talk about your work?"

"Words. They are blunt tools."

"They are?"

"Like using a baguette to hammer a nail."

She didn't flinch, so he continued.

"Can you describe an open beach? A last birthday? Only my photographs can do that."

"Sheryl," Jake said. "Who will be playing bridge tonight?"

"Ech." Her accent returned. "Didn't anyone teach you manners?"

"What?"

"Rude, inconsiderate. You really are a reporter."

She turned back to Gary and her face softened.

"I was a nurse. I always found it hard to talk about my work."

Gary opened his eyes wide.

"We see the things that other people look away from."

They both looked at Jake.

"What?" he said. "I see things too. I am a reporter."

"Well," Sheryl said, "you think you see things."

"I do."

"Did you see the soul of the city?"

"I have no idea what you're talking about."

"Exactly, my reporter friend."

"I don't talk about it."

Jake bit his lip. Sheryl wasn't even looking at him. She was watching Gary, her eyes sparkling. He started again.

"When I photograph a setting sun, it is poetry. But only because the night is drawing near."

Jake sat down and put his face in his hands as Sheryl leaned toward Gary.

"Do you photograph the beach?"

She was close. The frizz of her gray hair almost touched his.

"The beach? I see it constantly. Waves. Sand. Birds. Waves."

Jake sat up.

"Gary, you said 'waves' twice."

They both shook their heads at him, their hair almost becoming entangled. Gary looked in Sheryl's eyes.

"In fact, a friend of mine just passed away. She took a long walk on the beach and then..."

He turned his head down toward the floor. Then he looked up at Jake so Sheryl couldn't see. He winked. Or tried to. It looked like he was wincing. But Jake knew what it was supposed to be. Sheryl sounded cleaner and calmer.

"Mr. Novak, you knew Charlotte Ward?"

"I did. Jacob and I both knew her."

"I'm sorry. I miss her." She coughed.

"Do you?"

"I'm used to it." The accent was back. She sat up straight and took the edge of the aqua tablecloth in her hands. She rubbed it against her eyes and the corners turned darker.

"No," Gary said. "You don't have to be saying that."

She looked up. Stood up. Then she sat down again.

"It's fine."

"I just wish there were a way," Gary said. "A way that I could find out what she was thinking that last night."

"I can help you." Her voice hardened a little. "I know the last man to see her."

"I photographed her, you know."

"The last man," she said, "was Abram Samuels."

Jake wrote it in his notebook and interrupted.

"When did Abram Samuels see her?"

Sheryl rolled her eyes.

"Excuse me, reporter, we were having a conversation."

Gary nodded his head gently.

"Sheryl, please."

"Abram saw Charlotte at dinner that night. From 4:30 to 5:00, right before her death. Then he probably went on one of his night walks."

"Night walks?"

"You see him every night. He walks the sidewalk trail before going to sleep."

"Gary, I've got to run. I'm going to find him."

"Jacob, wait!"

He ran up the stairs. When Gary tried to follow, Sheryl took his cane and moved it across the room. She smiled at him, showing her teeth.

"You have to stay a little longer and tell me more about your passions."

He shouted from his chair.

"Get my cane! Please!"

"Gary, a struggling artist like you could use a little rest."

As he went out the door he looked back. Gary was staring at his cane and Sheryl was leaning forward, her chin resting on her hands, waiting to hear more.

CHAPTER 21:

It was dark out already, but Jake knew where he was going. A few women passed as they walked to the common building. He waved and started walking faster down the hill. The wind blew the palm tree leaves around in circles, and he could hear the water crashing on the beach. The first day he'd seen Abram Samuels and his red-brimmed hat, he'd been walking out of Building B. Jake bet that he lived in the building too.

He went down the hill and made sure he had his notebook with him. He almost felt cold in the t-shirt he was wearing. It clung to him in the wind and stuck against his stomach. He glanced at the open page of his notebook—only "Charlotte Ward" was written there. Then he looked down the hill. It couldn't be happening, not again. But he'd seen it all before—the door to Building B was open.

He started running. It didn't make sense that something would happen again, this soon. It couldn't have happened. And with Charlotte already gone, who else could anyone want? Unless someone wanted to find Abram. The door was swinging in the wind. He could see it flashing underneath the lights that lit the path. He ran to the door and jumped into the hallway.

"Jake? What are you doing?"

Mel had a camera in her hands and was standing in front of Charlotte's room. Jake rubbed his hands on his knees and pushed back his hair. He tucked in his shirt, hoping she wouldn't notice his exhaustion.

"Oh, Mel. Hi. I was just coming down this way."

She walked closer toward him and he stood still, breathing heavily. Her hair was down and ran to her collarbone. She was wearing a dress with blue flowers, and when she got closer she smelled like them too. She twisted the lens cap on her camera.

"You look like you were in a hurry."

"Uh, I was."

"I can tell."

"Do I look that tired?"

"A little," she said and started laughing. "Actually, a lot."

"Sorry. I ran down here. I saw the door open and I just got worried."

"Worried? About what?"

She looked him in the eye. Even in the soft light of the hallway, her eyes were bright. Mel was still holding the camera, and he looked down the hallway at Charlotte's room.

"What were you doing here?"

"Oh, I was taking pictures. Charlotte's daughter—sorry, designee—is coming down soon. And usually they resell. So…"

She gestured to the camera and shrugged her shoulders. The flowers were an even brighter blue against her tan arms.

"I see. The process happens quickly."

"It does. Lots of paperwork."

They stood there for a moment. He put his notebook in his back pocket and made sure not to let her see the page with Charlotte's name. It had happened a little too quickly. Before either of them said anything, a middle aged man appeared next to Jake.

"Oh," Mel said. "Hi Javier."

The man walked forward. He was wearing a light blue jumpsuit that looked too tight at the chest and too big at the legs, like they'd come from separate uniforms. Jake moved to the side and Mel introduced them.

"Javier, this is Jake."

The man nodded and walked past. He had a paint can in his hand.

"What's he doing?"

"He's just touching up the door. There was some damage on the side, and since we can't go in, we do what we can now to make things nice."

"There was damage?"

"Yes. Charlotte always ran her walker into the frame."

Her walker. He didn't know if he should say anything. He

didn't want to hear what Mel would say back. She spoke first.

"So wait—what were you doing down here?"

At the end of the hall, Javier leaned down and started painting.

"I just..." he started. Then he stopped. Nothing. He was bad at excuses.

"You said you were worried?"

"Yes."

"What were you worried about?"

She brushed her hair back with one finger. A flick.

"I thought...I thought I would miss seeing you before the day ended."

"You did?"

She smiled. Even tan skin could blush.

"I heard you were down here, and I wanted to make sure I didn't miss seeing you."

Javier painted the door and erased the damage. The traces.

"Who told you I was down here?"

"Someone." He couldn't think up a name. "An elderly woman."

"Who?"

He was sweating again.

"She had white hair." Like that narrowed it down.

"Mrs. Costello?" Apparently that did narrow it down.

"Maybe it was her."

"She's a sweetheart."

Mel looked good. No bags under her eyes. Just a smile. She parted her lips barely, then thought of something to say.

"So, your meeting with fate is coming soon, right?"

"Meeting with fate?"

"Mr. Rothschild. Aren't you two having lunch?"

"Oh. That's right. I didn't know he was fate."

"Then you don't know him very well."

Javier walked past them, the weight of the paint can causing him to lean slightly to the left. He took the rock out from where it propped open the door and let it close. They

107

were alone now. No one would know what Mel told him. No one would know what he asked her about Charlotte.

"So the designee is coming soon?"

"Yes. Then it's her property. We don't normally go inside until then. It's just policy. I haven't met her before. She sounded like she would be OK."

"That's something."

"That doesn't mean it won't be a hard conversation."

"Right." He had a hard conversation to start: why had Charlotte died? He couldn't be that direct.

"Mel, did the doctors say why she passed?"

"She had to take her medication regularly. I shouldn't say what she took. I suppose it doesn't matter. The doctors think that since she skipped her meds that night, that did it."

"Right." Try another angle. "Is the community OK?"

"Some are. I think Charlotte had a falling out with some people."

"You even knew about it?"

"I hear too much gossip."

She smoothed out her dress and he looked her in the eye.

"Was Sheryl Goldfein one of them?"

She grabbed his hand.

"We're off the record, right?"

He just laughed, hoping it would be enough.

"Sheryl gets upset easily. But it's understandable."

"Why?"

"She misses her husband. She misses New York. She's a strong personality without a focus. But I don't think that she would have stayed upset. She is a grown woman."

They both laughed, more quietly. He looked down the hallway past her. Empty. No one. She stepped closer. He took his hands out of his pockets. Be aggressive. Ask her. Tell her about the walker. Find out how the side of Charlotte's door was really damaged. Get closer to it, whatever it was. It was time to do something. Mel waited.

Instead he leaned forward and kissed her on the lips. Long,

soft. He felt her warm skin under his hands. She rested her hands on his arms and kept them there. She didn't push away and he pressed in closer.

"Jake, wait."

"What?"

"You're pressing the camera into me."

He took the camera in his hands and gently pushed it around to her side.

"There."

Then he leaned forward and kissed her again.

CHAPTER 22:

Each time they broke the kiss, they started it again. They said it was too unprofessional, too public, too soon. It didn't matter. He pressed her softly against the wall and felt the imprint of the wallpaper brush against his hands. He traced the blue flowers on her dress with his index finger. Then he started vibrating. Mel's voice was a whisper.

"What is it?"

"Ignore it." He kissed her cheek. "It's just my phone."

It stopped. A second later it started again. She moved back to let him answer it.

"No," he said and kissed her again.

It rang another time. He took it out and looked at the screen. He didn't know the number. It was someone from a Sarasota area code. But he didn't know who.

"Do you have to get it?"

"I don't know why they keep calling."

It stopped. They smiled and looked at each other. She pulled his hair forward and he brushed it back.

"Did I mess up your hair?"

"You did." Then it vibrated again.

"Damn it."

"You can get it."

"I better."

He pressed the send button and listened.

"Hello?" a voice whispered. "Is this seventy one ate rake?"

"What?"

"718, umm, 7253?"

"Yes."

"Hurry!"

"Gary? Is that you?"

"Hurry Jacob, I don't have much time."

"Why are you whispering?"

"No time."

Mel looked up and Jake shook his head.

"Gary, what's seventy one ate rake?"

"It's how I remember your number. It's a pneumatic device."

"Do you mean a pneumonic device?"

"I imagine that the number seventy one ate you. Your number spells out your name."

"But my name isn't 'rake.'"

"I get around it," he said a little louder. "I don't have time to explain. I stole Sheryl's telephone."

"You stole her phone?"

"She's playing bridge on the other side of the room. You have to rescue me from her. A good man leaves no soldier behind."

He sighed. Mel was pulling chapstick from her purse and running it over her lips.

"OK Gary, I'll be there soon."

He hung up the phone and Mel nodded. He reached forward and grabbed the hand holding the chapstick.

"Wait." He kissed her again.

"Hi."

"I have to go do this."

"I know."

"But I'll call."

As he walked out the hallway, he still didn't know what had happened. He ran up the path as quickly as he'd come down. He remembered why he'd come in the first place. Abram. Then he realized it was night. If Abram still walked every night after dinner, he'd find him on the sidewalk, not in the building. Maybe on the same route Charlotte had taken to the beach.

When he went in the common room, all the women looked in his direction and then immediately looked back to their cards. He quietly picked up Gary's cane and crossed the room to hand it to him.

"Are you OK?"

"Jacob," he whispered, "thank you."

"What happened?"

"She wouldn't release me!"

"Stay quiet, we don't want them to hear you."

"Let's go, now."

He got up and started moving toward the door. He looked exhausted.

"I talked so much. I don't know what I meant or didn't mean."

"I can't believe it, but you seduced her."

"I wish you hadn't made me do it."

"No time to argue. We've got to find Abram Samuels."

"What did you find out about him?" They looked back. Sheryl was staring at her cards. For now.

"I didn't find out anything. But I think I know where he is."

"Let's go."

"We have to tell them. It would look weird if we snuck out."

Jake yelled.

"Sheryl, we have to run. There's a news emergency. We have to take a picture of some beaches."

She yelled across the room.

"Will you be capturing the eternal sunsets on film?"

Gary hit his free hand against his forehead.

"Jacob, don't ask."

They emerged into the night and started walking down the main path.

"It's a long shot, but we might run into Abram."

"Do you think we will find him?"

"Maybe not. But we have to try."

They walked along the path, their route lit alternately by overhead lights and small ones half buried in the ground. No one else was out. Gary tapped his cane on one of the lights.

"He walks every night?"

"Yes."

"That means that the night that Charlotte went to the beach…"

"I know. He was out here. Or maybe he was there on the beach too, with her."

They scanned down the path but couldn't see anything more than a few feet in front of them. Suddenly, Gary grabbed Jake's arm. Jake turned to him and saw that he was shaking.

"What's wrong?"

"Jacob, I would never betray Meryl. That woman Sheryl. She listened to everything I said. That hasn't happened in years."

"Right."

"It scares me." He let go. "I wanted you to know."

They continued down the path, Gary's cane tapping the concrete lightly every step. They could see the beach on the left and hear the water spitting on the sand. Jake pointed.

"Right here, this must have been the way Charlotte got here."

"But how did she get here without her walker?"

"Somebody took her."

Then they both fell silent. Standing on the beach, looking outward, was a man wearing a brimmed hat. Jake couldn't see the color, but he guessed that it was red.

"I think that's him."

"Abram?"

"Abram Samuels. And see that concrete building right there? The concession building?"

"Jacob," Gary whispered, "now might not be the best time for snacks."

"I don't want snacks, Gary. That's where they found Charlotte."

"Oh. Of course. They probably aren't open anyway."

"They found her there, in back of the building."

"So they aren't open?"

"Gary."

"I'm sorry. I got hungry in that room, talking so much. It takes a lot of energy to say those things. Have you ever had a pretzel with chocolate on it? They are surprisingly good!"

"I'm sure. Wait, what's he doing?"

Abram was walking closer to the water, to the wet foot of the beach. He took off his shoes and sat down on the sand. He looked out at the water and sat very still.

"I want to go up to him."

"Should we disturb him?"

"Who knows when I'll get another chance? And we've met before. I can make it seem like a coincidence."

"There are no coincidences."

"Is that one of your lines for Sheryl?"

He just lifted his cane and pointed it toward Abram. He had already gotten up and was walking the other way. Jake headed down the stairs to the beach and motioned for Gary to stay in place. Abram turned around when Jake was about twenty feet away, but then he kept walking.

"Mr. Samuels, please wait just a second."

Abram looked back, the hat casting a shadow over his face. He kept his hands in his pockets. Jake wouldn't have been sure it was Abram if he hadn't recognized the red brim on his hat.

"Hello. Usually I don't see anyone on these late night walks."

Jake looked at his watch.

"Mr. Samuels, it's 7:30 PM."

"I know. I cannot change the fact that I am a nocturnal creature."

"Do you always walk here?"

"Not always. I changed my route recently."

Jake moved closer, but he still couldn't see Abram's face. It was just a shadow under the hat. Jake's notebook was still in his pocket, turned to the same page. He looked back but couldn't see Gary.

"Mr. Samuels, I was wondering—did you see Charlotte Ward the night she passed?"

The hat tipped down and his hands came out of his pockets. Jake tensed. He noticed the sound of the waves again, crashing louder than before.

"I don't want to talk about it."

"Did you see her?"

"Was I unclear?" He started walking again, more quickly. Jake followed, his feet mashing down the sand.

"I just want to get an idea. It's not a big thing. I need to know more about her."

"Why should I talk to you about that?"

"Why shouldn't you?"

"It's personal. So good night."

"Wait—"

He kept walking away and Jake let him go. He watched him go up the other set of steps and back to Sunset Cove. Gary was still waiting at the beginning of the path, and Jake shook his head.

"Something's wrong."

"What happened? I stayed up here like you wanted."

"I know. Thanks."

"So what happened? I saw him look at you and then walk away. Did you fight?"

"Yeah, he walked out on me. Wouldn't answer any questions."

They walked back to Jake's car. Gary led.

"So what do you think it means? Why did he walk away from you?"

Jake looked back at the beach one last time.

"Because he's running from something else."

CHAPTER 23:

The next day, his phone call with Thompson made him want to keep trying. Not that Thompson would care about Sheryl Goldfein or Abram Samuels. But Jake knew they'd be talking that day. And he knew that he had to be aggressive to learn why Charlotte Ward died. He'd gotten Abram's phone number from the community's directory. Once he finished with Thompson, he'd start asking Abram the real questions. But first, the phone rang.

"Russo!" Same old Thompson. He still sounded like he had a frog in his throat. Or something larger. "I got the article about the banquet spaces."

"Did you like it?"

"Definitely good enough. Very good enough. I bet you loved writing that one, didn't you?"

"Why?"

"The food, Russo! You could gobble it up. It's a free pass. You're welcome."

Better to ignore him.

"How are things going up there?"

"The usual. Terribly. You won't believe it. We're in a newsstand war again. We pushed down our prices to a quarter. But we gave away half...half the issues yesterday. We still lost."

"How?"

"We lowered prices, they added 'features.' Features—seriously. One day it was coupons. A lottery. Then...then the other day they had a great one."

"What?"

"They gave away 3-D glasses! Like the kids used to have in the fifties. They sold out. We had to give papers away just to hold even. Brutal...just brutal!"

He heard Thompson laughing with someone. Probably Carla. Then he heard him breathing in the receiver again.

"They are evil geniuses. We've got good competition."

"They really put in 3-D glasses?"

"Geniuses!"

Jake looked at his desk and picked up the ones Gary had given him. He took out his wallet and slid them in. Genius worked in mysterious ways.

"But enough of the competition, Russo. You need to get back to your meal. And your other hobby. What was it? What was that internet site you spent all your time on?"

"I stopped going on that site."

"What was it called?"

"I'm not going to tell you, sir."

Thompson would forget. He'd have to forget.

"I remember," Thompson said. "That TV show, Buffy! Message boards. You were always there! I look at your screen—there he is. Presto. Buffy!"

"I stopped that, I'm telling you."

"You gave so much time to that cute little vampire."

"Actually, she wasn't a vampire."

"Oh really? What...what was she?"

He sighed.

"She was a vampire slayer, sir."

"Fantastic. Hell of a fact checker."

"You asked."

"Of course."

"It's in the name of the show that she's a slayer. Everyone knows that."

"Russo—remember, you're the one who goes to the site. Not me. Let's keep it that way."

"I just told you because you asked—"

"OK." Thompson cut in when he wanted. "Let's hear what's on the agenda."

"Well, you saw in the banquet space piece that I had a few quotes from Jerry Rubenstein, the owner of Palmstead."

"Was he the fat guy in those pictures?"

"Well, I suppose you could say that."

"I wasn't sure if it was him or...or you, Russo. You're like twins."

"I already told you—"

"Right, right, I know. Go ahead with your pitch."

"So I talked to Rubenstein. Tomorrow I'm talking to another developer, Simeon Rothschild. I'm going to ask him some important questions."

"Let's hear it."

"First, I'm going to ask him about the environmentalists. I told you how one protestor interrupted the banquet because of the upcoming vote on the Development Proposition. And there's also been a suspicious death at one of his properties. I don't want to sling mud, but I think one of his residents may have conspired in it."

"OK—part of it's good."

"The environmentalists? Or the death?"

"The guy. Rothschild. People like profiles. Like…like celebrities."

"But I really wanted to explore the development issues—"

"Russo—here's what you do. You know Gillian Handle?"

"What?"

"Gillian Handle."

"Isn't she one of our gossip columnists?"

Thompson coughed and laughed.

"One of them? The best…best in the city Russo! You know the questionnaire she has?"

"Handling Handle?"

"It's perfect. Write your story off that."

He sighed. Doing "Handling Handle" with Rothschild didn't seem like a good idea.

"Sir, I don't know if that's the best plan. He's a businessman, not a celebrity."

"We have to make do. I like that you came up with it. Now stop complaining and get to work."

It wasn't worth fighting. He just didn't want to have to read "Handling Handle" for research. Or repeat any of it out loud.

"All right. Fine. Is that all? I have some other calls I should make."

"No, wait." Thompson yelled across the room. Someone laughed. Then Carla was on the phone.

"Jake," she said in a sultry voice. Thompson was laughing. "Thompson wants me to ask you if Buffy is a vampire or a zombie."

He hadn't been on those message boards in months, except for his one moment of weakness. It wasn't fair.

"Thanks Carla. Thanks a lot. She's a slayer. Buffy the Vampire Slayer."

He could hear the whole room laughing. It was loud enough that they wouldn't notice when he hung up. It didn't matter. He had more important calls to make, even if Thompson didn't know about them. He opened the phone again and started dialing Abram Samuels' number. It only rang once.

"Hello Mr. Russo."

"How did you know it was me?"

"Have you heard of Caller Identification?"

"Yes. It's just that when I call…"

"People my age don't use caller ID?"

"Yes."

"I know how to use the things I buy."

"I'm sorry."

"It's fine." His voice sounded less harsh, like he wanted to apologize to Jake. Instead he just waited for him to speak next.

"Listen." He had his notebook out. "On the beach the other night, I didn't mean to creep up on you. And I'm sorry if I scared you or offended you or whatever. I'm a reporter. I have to do it."

"Have to?" Abram asked. "Let me quote from your last article. I found it on the internet. You say that the Palmstead 'has a stage fit for a queen and a menu fit for a king.' Whom did you have to harass for that quote, Mr. Russo?"

"Fine. That's fair. But I don't just write puff pieces. And now I'm trying to learn about what really goes on at Sunset Cove. I think that there are some things about the community that people should know about."

"I see."

"Does that seem reasonable?"

"I'm not your boss." He was angry or resigned. Jake couldn't tell which.

"I know you aren't my boss. But you seem upset."

"You followed me."

"There was a reason."

"What?"

He tapped his pen against the open page in his notebook. A scared woman with a walker was the reason. And he had to say it. To tell him right now.

"The reason is that I heard you were the last person to see Charlotte Ward."

The phone went silent. No dial tone. He was still on the line, just not talking. Then he did.

"Who told you that?"

"I can't say."

"Sheryl Goldfein? She's always been a gossip."

"Abram." He waited. "Is it true?"

"Ask yourself why she would tell you that."

"What do you mean?"

"She has motives."

"Maybe." He didn't know what they were. It was best to play along. "But we can talk about those later. Right now I want to know—were you the last one to see her?"

"It's private."

"Why?"

Silence again. He didn't expect him to answer. But for him to be like this... Secretive. Defensive. He refused to even review the basics.

"Mr. Russo, it's private because it is."

"Were you the last to see her?"

"I'm the only one who will admit it."

"What does that mean?"

"It means I'm the only one who will go on the record."

"Who do you think saw her?"

"I have to go." Closing the conversation. It was now or never. Be aggressive, or lose the chance to learn more. The man knew something.

"I think you know why she died. You know why Charlotte Ward died on the beach that night. But you don't want to tell me the truth."

Silence.

"I think you don't want to tell me because you were part of it."

Silence again. He pressed.

"Are you there?"

"Meet me tonight where you found me. On the beach. Don't tell anyone you are coming out there. And don't let anyone see you go. If you do, I'll leave."

"The same time?"

"No. Late, very late tonight."

"Tonight? OK. How late?"

"Very late." His voice turned serious. "Make it 8:15. PM."

He hung up the phone. Jake held his in his hand and looked at the log. They'd only talked a few minutes. But Abram knew something. The only problem was the condition Abram had set. At night and alone on the beach—it sounded a lot like what had happened to Charlotte Ward.

CHAPTER 24:

When he left to interview Simeon Rothschild that afternoon, Kaylie was waiting outside his door. She sat in front of her own, her shorts sliding up her legs. The tan didn't stop. He didn't have time to banter with her now, but she didn't want to banter. She wanted to make plans.

"We're supposed to go out." She was still sitting down, chewing on a piece of grass. He looked down and closed his door.

"I'm sorry, I just made an appointment for tonight."

"When?"

"Around eight."

"What's your appointment? Are you ditching us? You agreed to have drinks."

"I'm not ditching." He put his keys back in his pocket. "I'm just saying that I have plans."

"When will you be back?"

"I'm not sure. I'm going for a long walk on the beach."

"Romantic," she said and tilted her head. "We'll go out when you get back."

"Will your friends wait?"

"They can handle it." She reached up for him to help her stand. He grabbed her hand and pulled her up. Close to him. Then she turned and opened the door to her apartment. It was unlocked.

He didn't like going out with big groups and playing the memory game with names and faces. He hated trying to get in a word before splitting up the check. But he was still looking forward to it. After meeting with Simeon Rothschild and Abram Samuels in one day, he guessed he was going to need a drink.

Rothschild's secretary made Jake wait ten minutes. She didn't bother smiling. He sat in a chair and settled in. Not that the waiting room wasn't impressive. The building was small, but even the fourth floor had an unobstructed water view.

From the couch it looked like a painting on the wall. Jake was staring at it when the secretary said he could go in and see Rothschild.

He was sitting at a perfectly clean desk, wearing a white shirt with the top two buttons undone. The sleeves were rolled up. He might have cleaned the desk, but he was staying loose. He thrust up his chin and stared at Jake. His light clothes made his black eyes look even darker.

"Let's start things off right. How do you like your steak?"

Jake sat down in front of the desk and got out his notebook. Leather-bound books in back. Another view of the beach to the side. And abstract art posing on every wall. The man knew how to make an office, and probably a lunch, too. But he couldn't start eating steak again.

"I'd love a salad."

"A salad? For a guy like you?"

"I had a big breakfast."

"Understood."

Rothschild pressed a button on the desk and started speaking.

"Tell Jean-Gil to bring us two steaks, medium. And a salad. I'll have water. Mr. Russo?"

"Actually, just a salad is fine—"

"What will you have to drink?"

"I really don't need the steak."

"To drink?"

"Water."

"Two waters," Rothschild said and tapped the button again. "If you don't want our steak, we can let it sit. It's very good."

"I see."

"Jean-Gil studied in France. I keep him here and cycle him through some of our communities. He's got a great touch. A real sense of food."

"I see." He looked at his notebook and Rothschild laughed.

"You use a notebook. How quaint. Do you need me to spell Jean-Gil's name? If not, then shoot."

He didn't want to. He had two sets of questions written in. The real ones and "Handling Handle's" gossip inquisition. He decided to start with his own.

"So, Mr. Rothschild—"

"Simeon."

"Simeon," he said. "Thanks again for your time. Are you sure you want to photograph on a separate day? You seem fine now."

"Absolutely. I only do photographs in suits. Our residents expect a professional, not a casual supervisor. You can quote me on that. I'm merely dressed like this today due to a prior engagement."

"What's that?"

"I have kite-sailing later."

"I see." He wrote it down. His readers wouldn't know what kite-sailing was. But whatever they imagined would probably be as glamorous.

"Simeon, I wanted to start with the environmentalists I saw at your banquet. Has that type of protest happened before?"

"I'm glad you asked." He glanced down at his desk and pressed another button. "They are true radicals. Have you seen this?"

Jake looked right as a projector screen descended in front of a well-stocked bar. Rothschild shook his head.

"I had my secretary record this for me. It's simply absurd."

He pressed another button and a bearded man appeared on the screen. It was the man from the banquet. He was flanked by a woman wearing overalls. Images of trees moved in the background, and the woman shouted while the man shook his head in silence.

"Vote No on the Development Proposition! We cannot allow development on our wetlands."

Jake wrote it down.

"Keep watching."

"Our wetlands have been here for centuries," the woman cried. "But man has not! We must respect the native environment. We never should have come here. And we never should have interfered with nature. You all have blood on your hands."

The bearded man showed his hands, painted red. The woman seemed to do the talking.

"We hope you are all destroyed if the wetlands are." Rothschild raised his eyebrows. "It's only fair. Someone will do to you what you have done to our environment. Don't let this Development Proposition hasten nature's revenge."

The bearded man clapped his red hands together. The screen flashed a screaming face and a fallen tree, and then showed "Paid for by the Saving Tomorrow Initiative" before turning black. Rothschild rested his hands on his perfectly clean desk.

"Do you know where they aired that advertisement, Mr. Russo?"

"No."

"Everywhere. They showed it on all the morning shows locally. On the talk shows. On some of the soaps. Every channel that most local residents watch."

"It's very…dogmatic."

Rothschild laughed.

"That's one word for it. I have a few more."

"What?"

"Insane," he said sharply. "Outrageous. Threatening. Cruel. They are willing to do anything for their cause. And you saw it. I'd say that the entire thing is, frankly, anti-human. It doesn't even give people an opportunity to weigh the issues involved."

Jake wrote and underlined the group's name: Saving Tomorrow Initiative. He'd check on them later. He looked at the next line in his notebook—all "Handling Handle" questions. Rothschild's face was red with anger—it wasn't the right time. It would never be the right time.

"Has this been going on long?"

"They've ramped up for the Development Proposition. The

vote is coming soon, and they know they have to resort to this kind of fear mongering. Forgive me, but I believe that people don't have to apologize for building homes. And you can quote me."

He was quoting him when someone knocked at the door. A man wheeled in a cart with their food on it. He set a steak and salad in front of Jake, the white plate tinged pink with juice. He could smell the smoke and steam mingling. He imagined how it would feel, the knife slicing through with just a touch. Like the old days. He blinked and looked at Rothschild.

"How did it get here so quickly? That took less than ten minutes."

"Simple." Rothschild started cutting. "I ordered before you got here."

"But how did you know what I'd order?"

"What you ordered didn't stop me." He stabbed a large chunk of beef. "Did it?"

Jake picked up a fork and looked at the salad. He pushed the steak aside, only touching the plate with his pinky finger.

"Mr. Rothschild, I'm sorry, but—"

"Simeon. Please."

"Simeon, I have to ask you another question."

Rothschild stopped chewing.

"Is it about the recent tax code changes? I think you'll find that we have an interesting position. Some of my critics—Jerry Rubenstein—might tell you differently, but it's really a more nuanced issue than that."

"No, I wish it were something like that."

"Well, spit it out."

He had to ask the question. After all, this is what he'd come to do. Whether Rothschild liked it or not.

CHAPTER 25:

"If you could be on a desert island with any celebrity, who would it be?"

The half eaten piece of meat dangled from Rothschild's mouth.

"What the hell are you talking about?"

Jake looked up from the notebook. "Handling Handle," question number one. Rothschild didn't chew. He just swallowed.

"If I could be on a desert island with a celebrity? Do you mean a celebrity developer? Like the Toll Brothers or something? Or Donald Trump?"

"No. I mean a celebrity. Like a movie star. Or a singer."

Rothschild started chewing another piece, and he didn't talk until he was finished.

"Are these actually your questions? I would never develop on a desert island."

"No, I know you wouldn't develop there. It's like a game, where you pick a celebrity you'd like to be stranded with."

"Right. You chose this question for our time together?"

"No." He sighed. "I just have to ask these. But I want to do more. The rogue environmentalist angle, it has a lot going for it."

Rothschild mumbled.

"Katharine Hepburn."

"What's that?"

"Katharine Hepburn," he said again. "She's my choice."

"Why is she your choice?"

"Because of her humor. Also—don't print this—my managers have told me she consistently wins polls at community movie nights."

"Have you seen her movies?"

"I don't have time for things like that. Just like I don't have time to develop on desert islands."

Jake looked at the next question. The steak bled on his

plate. He didn't know if he'd feel worse about eating the steak or asking Gillian Handle's next question.

"OK. What's your middle name and the street you grew up on?"

"What?"

"Your middle name and the street you grew up on."

"What is this for?"

Jake rubbed his temples. He should have eaten the steak.

"It's a question to figure out…your porn star name."

"Really?"

"Yes."

"Well," he said and paused. "I guess I'm Harold Longwood."

They were both silent. Rothschild ate more steak. Jake's leaked. Harold Longwood.

"Have the environmentalists ever threatened you?"

"I can't talk about it extensively." He didn't miss a beat. "The police won't let me. But let's suffice it to say that they are dangerous people."

"How dangerous?"

Rothschild dropped his knife on the plate.

"Very dangerous."

"I see. Did you press charges against the group for what happened at the banquet?"

"I can't say."

"I understand. On a related note," Jake started, "I have another question."

It was next on the list. He just had to get through a few more.

"Let's hear it." Rothschild wiped the corners of his mouth with a napkin, raised his chin, and stared at Jake without blinking. His eyes were black as stones. Jake sighed.

"Simeon, are you a player?"

"What?"

"A player. You know, someone promiscuous."

"I know you aren't this type of reporter. I know you do real work. You are playing games with me."

"I have to."

They got through the rest of the questions. The favorite foods and colors, vacation homes, and first loves. Rothschild complied. When it was over, Jake merely nodded and left. His plate of steak was still sitting on the desk, uneaten in a pool of blood.

He made the long drive home. Pulled up a chair and sat at the desk. He wrote up his notes and went through the old ones. He wished he'd paid more attention to Charlotte. What should he have asked her? How could he have helped? He thought of her voice shaking while she talked. Confused. Frightened. She had reason to be both. Then he noticed a name in his old notes.

The Saving Tomorrow Initiative. The environmentalists were part of that group. The bearded man with blood on his hands. The shouting woman. They were all involved. And, somehow, they tied back to Charlotte and Sheryl Goldfein. He looked back through everything he'd transcribed.

Charlotte started investigating the group after Sheryl kicked her out of bridge. For Charlotte, it was just revenge on a personal grudge. But all their charitable money went to the Saving Tomorrow Initiative. Sheryl knew that Charlotte Ward was conducting her own investigation. And from the sound of it, Abram Samuels knew about it too.

He tried not to think about the connection during the car ride to Sunset Cove that night. He let his brain line up with the hum of the car. Blank out. But he couldn't stop wondering. As he looked along the side of the highway, he thought about the bearded man clapping his hands. Red. All red. What had Charlotte found about the Saving Tomorrow Initiative? And who wanted to stop her from getting further? The man had red hands. Like the brim of Abram's hat.

At Sunset Cove, he parked in the back of the large lot. As he shut the car door, he heard it echo in the empty night. 8:00 PM. He was early for his meeting. He'd thought about bringing something with him—a witness or a camera. He locked the door. He'd come with his notebook and nothing else. If Abram Samuels was going to do anything, or say anything, he'd have to do it with Jake's knowledge.

The palm trees barely moved. Their trunks seemed too firm to sway, and the leaves sank in the dark. Lights flickered on and off in the residences of Sunset Cove. TV screens clapped on and clapped off. Jake heard his footsteps pad on the path. It was empty when he reached the beach.

The concession building where they found her was just a slab of shadow. A man was standing at the edge of the beach, hunched over. He looked like he was wearing a long coat. And, as usual, he was wearing a hat. Jake let his shoes sink into the sand. The white sea-foam blurred on the dark waves. He approached the hulking body on the beach. It didn't turn.

Jake walked closer and started to slow down. His steps were silent in the damp sand. The form ahead of him seemed surprisingly large. It was a big trench coat, as still as a scarecrow stuffed with straw. But he could eventually see it breathing, then turning left and right. The collar was starched up. It covered everything. All Jake could see was the black water in the distance and the person ahead of him. He hadn't realized Abram was so tall.

He stopped and looked at his hands, shaking. He cursed himself. Be aggressive. What could Abram Samuels do? He might be smart. And angry. But there was nothing Abram could do to him. If Abram had something to hide, he'd already gone too far. Now he'd have to show his cards or hold back again. Jake guessed it was too late to hide again.

He got closer and started to get confused. The body was still too big. And then he saw the hat. It was a dark brown hat, with a thick band of leather circling around the base. No red brim. He decided to stop sneaking up. And his breathing seemed to be getting heavier.

"Hey," Jake said. "I'm here."

He saw the left shoulder twitch. Then the right curved around in a blur, big and loose. He saw the elbow of the trench coat, right before it hit him in the jaw. Then it hit. Everything became brighter. Then the other side was smacked by something solid. Jake heard a crack and started to stumble. He had to catch himself with his hands as sand and gravel dug beneath his fingernails. He felt like he was breathing it.

Next a black stamp. Kicked in the face, faster than he could see. He felt the sand flow in his ear. He was an hourglass, passing time too quickly. He could barely speak when he was kicked again.

"Abram, stop." He wheezed. "It's me, Jake."

His head was flat on the beach. It sounded like he was pressing his ear against a seashell. Or was inside of one. Then he saw the trench coat rise and flap in the wind as the man sprinted in the other direction. Jake's head lay sideways on the ground and he watched the man run away, each crash of the waves making his body tremble. Then he looked out at the water, his eyeballs rolling back into his head. He stared at the white scrapes on the waves. The water and his eyelids were the same color.

Black.

CHAPTER 26:

"Can you hear me? Hello? Are you awake?"

The voice echoed in his ears. Everything was still black. Then he tasted salt at the corners of his lips, seeping in. Each second he felt a little more of the world, that painless place outside his head. There was cold on his face and salty liquid seeping in his eyes. Was it blood? He hoped it wasn't—there was too much of it. He felt his jaw and opened it. Slowly. Then he let his head roll to the right and looked down at the beach. Abram Samuels was cupping his hands and running back to Jake. He got a foot away and Jake realized he could talk.

"Abram," he whispered, "I'm awake."

Too late. Abram splashed more water on his face.

"Can you hear me?"

"I'm awake," he whispered again.

"You're awake?"

He tried to sit up but it didn't go well. He'd try again later.

He could see Abram looking down at him. His frame was smaller than the man in the trench coat, and he was only wearing a light jacket. And there was the hat—the red brim looked dark at night, but it was definitely there.

"It wasn't you," Jake whispered. "It wasn't..."

"I got here at 8:15." He sounded scared. "When we set our appointment. And I looked out onto the beach. At first I thought the man in the trench coat was you, but then I saw that it was one person fighting with another."

"Fighting's one word for it," Jake coughed out. He blinked and opened his eyes again. A little more focus. But it still sounded like he was inside a seashell.

"He was beating you up. As soon as he saw me, he ran away. He was covering his face up with his trench coat. I couldn't see anything."

"I can't..."

"What?"

Jake started to feel it coming back. He closed his eyes and

realized he'd seen the man in the trench coat before. The night that Charlotte died. The man had been watching the concession building from a distance. The only problem was that both times, Jake didn't know who the man was.

"Can you hear me?"

Abram looked worried—Jake didn't see that one coming. He sat up and wiped the sand off his hands. No blood. He felt his face. No blood, but all bruises.

"What happened?" He felt back for his notebook. It was there and he strained to pull it out. Somehow he'd hurt his back too. It ached to stretch. He opened the pad and wrote what Abram said.

"I got here at 8:15. And I saw that man beating you up. I ran a little closer and then I yelled out."

"You yelled?"

"Yes," he said. "I forgot to mention that before. I yelled out 'Stop' and I saw his head turn back toward me."

"Could you see the face?"

"No. Did you?"

"I barely saw the fists."

"After he heard me yell, he looked down at you and kicked you again."

Jake felt his jaw—he believed it.

"Then, after he kicked you, he ran off. I saw he was wearing a hat and a trench coat. But that was all I could see."

Jake looked at his handwriting in the notebook. Nothing better than scribbles. He'd try to decipher it later. Reading anything seemed about as hard as writing. He was scared to touch his face again. He knew that would make it worse. It was like the water in hurricane season. Everything swelled. He finally formed a thought.

"That hurt."

Abram almost laughed.

"I would guess that. Did he say anything? The man who assaulted you?"

"No." That seashell sound got old fast. He hit his ear. Sand came off his hair in clumps as thick as cookie dough. "I just said hello, and then he turned around and hit me."

"I see."

"What?"

"Well, it leads to interesting conclusions." He lowered himself onto the sand. Jake breathed in deep for the first time, starting to recover.

"What conclusions does it lead to?"

"Did the man know who you were?"

"I don't know. He must have, I guess."

"Why?"

"Because he hit me."

"Did he see you though?"

"I guess not. But he must have seen me while I was walking up the beach, right?"

Abram paused.

"Well, do you have a cellular phone?"

"Why?"

"We need to call the police."

Jake stopped leaning on his hands and let his elbows bear his weight. It hurt a little less. Police. He'd hardly worked that beat, let alone been a featured story.

"I don't know about that Abram."

"What? You don't have a phone on you? I do, just in case."

He pulled it out and started dialing. Jake reached forward. He wanted to grab it, but he couldn't make his body move quickly enough. Abram stopped anyway.

"Why don't you want me to call?"

"What would we say?"

"That you were attacked on the beach. We have to report it."

"No." He exhaled. "We can't. Then we'd have to get into everything. Why we were meeting here at night. What we were doing. It would get complicated."

"We could say that we're old friends."

"Sure. Then I'd also have to give up trying to find out what happened to Charlotte Ward."

Abram looked out at the beach and then back at Jake.

"Didn't you accuse me of being involved in her death?"

"That was before."

"Before what?"

"This," he said and pointed to a bruise. "And this…and this…and this."

"I see."

"And if you'd been behind it, I don't think you would have bothered showing up and saving me."

"I wish I could tell you…" He crossed his arms and held them tightly.

"Abram, you wish what?"

"I wish I could trust you."

"I wish I could trust you," Jake repeated.

They looked out at the beach together. Jake's vision was clearing up a little. He could see the place where the beach and water met. Abram gestured back to the path.

"Sheryl Goldfein knows that I take walks late at night. She knows that I take this route. The route Charlotte took."

"What are you saying?"

Conclusions were as difficult as steps, right now. He didn't have the energy for either of them.

"I'm saying that she knew I'd be out on the beach tonight. And the man who hit you didn't know that it was you."

"So?"

"I think they would have attacked me, too."

He didn't want to believe that anyone would hit a man Abram's age that hard. But if he could find out who Abram thought was targeting him, maybe he could find out why anyone had resorted to violence on a deserted beach.

"Can we talk about this?"

"Yes."

"Let's get up and go somewhere."

Abram extended his arm to Jake. Both their hands were wet and cold with sand. He couldn't balance at first, but then he caught himself. Barely.

"God. Can't believe this."

"Haven't you been in a fight before?"

Had he ever been aggressive?

"No, I haven't."

"You'll have some bruises."

"I just didn't even see it coming. I wish it hadn't happened."

"It might be selfish for me to say this, but you should be glad."

"Why?"

Abram touched the brim of his hat and led them down the beach.

"You got some bruises. But I might not have made it off this beach."

"What do you mean?"

"You might have saved my life. I couldn't have taken those hits."

They walked along the shore at the same speed—Jake slowed down by a long night, Abram slowed down by a long life.

"We need to trust each other," Jake said. "If we want to figure out who that person was. If we want to figure out who they meant to attack and why they did it."

"I want to learn more than that."

"What?"

"I want to find out what happened to Charlotte."

"Then we're agreed?"

"Agreed," Abram said.

They went up the stairs together, back to Sunset Cove.

CHAPTER 27:

They were at Building B by a quarter to nine. Abram did live there. With each step, Jake looked both ways for the man who had attacked him. No one. There wasn't even a shadow now. This late at night, the paths were all empty—he'd already run into the two exceptions.

Abram's living room was filled with maps. Maps on the walls, atlases stacked on shelves, and papers spread out on a large oak table. Jake rested his arm on a furled corner. He yelled to Abram, who was in the small kitchen.

"These maps—are they for researching what happened to Charlotte?"

"It didn't happen in Europe, did it?"

Abram brought in a bag of ice for Jake and water for both of them.

"These maps are territorial alignments during World War II. I research them in my free time."

"I see. Sorry."

"Put the ice on your face."

It felt like he was being kicked again. Then it started to turn numb. But Abram didn't waste time on sympathy.

"Jake, do you know why I was shocked? Why I was shocked when you suggested that I knew what happened to Charlotte?"

"No, I don't know why you were shocked." When he moved his mouth it hurt. But he had to say something.

"I was shocked because, when she died, Charlotte Ward and I were in love."

Jake dropped the ice on the table and flecks of water splattered onto the map. He brushed them off and looked up. Abram's expression didn't change. He finally took off the red-brimmed hat and set it down on a green patch of Europe.

"Do you understand why I was upset? I was so upset that you could accuse me of hurting her. Of trying to harm her. This woman…"

He stopped and stared down at the covered table, tracing an attack route with the tip of his finger.

"Abram, I had no idea you loved her. Did she know?"

He laughed and then snorted.

"Of course she knew. We were having an affair."

Jake picked the ice back up and pressed it against his cheek. It was better to be numb for news like this. The bag sweat down his arm and on the wooden table's edge.

"You were having an affair?"

"For a year. We kept it secret, or at least tried to. But Sheryl knew. All the other ladies at bridge knew."

"I just can't believe that Charlotte…"

"She was a very delicate lover," Abram started. Jake pressed the ice compact against his face. Hard. "Always very unselfish."

"OK. I get the idea."

"Sometimes, we even took photographs. Nothing in flagrante delicto, of course. Merely tasteful nudes. Black and white."

"I see." He saw it all too clearly.

"She had one outfit. A combination of fur and nylon that—"

"Abram, it's OK."

"If you like, I can even show you some shots—"

"Good lord—that's fine. I believe you."

They both looked back at the maps. The colors had faded out. Jake slowly recovered the ability to speak.

"If you were having a…relationship, then why didn't you notice her when you were walking on the beach?"

"After dinner that night…" He paused to sigh. "After dinner that night, I went back to my room, and then I took my walk. By the time I returned, it had already happened."

"But why didn't you see her when you were on the beach?"

"Don't you understand?"

"What?"

"I never walked on the beach before. I don't like the sand in my shoes, or stepping on seashells."

"Then why did I find you there the other night?"

"Because." He sighed again. "I was going to see where she had died."

They looked at the maps again, but all the countries in Europe weren't enough of a distraction. Jake looked up first.

"I'm sorry I accused you of doing anything to harm Charlotte. It's just that once I knew something suspicious had happened, I listened to Sheryl. And I saw you leaving Charlotte's room."

"Yes. Your photographer disturbed us during a particularly frisky—"

"Enough. I really don't want to hear it."

Abram changed direction.

"Why do you think there's anything suspicious about Charlotte's death?"

"The walker. She never could have gone anywhere without it, but they didn't find it on the beach."

"Of course. I thought of that too. But I kept my mouth shut."

"Why?"

"Why? Do you want to go to the bathroom?"

"What? What do you mean?"

"Go ahead. You'll find a mirror in the bathroom. Look at the bruises on your face, and you can see why I didn't tell anyone."

"Were you really that afraid?"

"They kept Charlotte off her medication. They killed her. If they were willing to do that, they could do worse. I know that we're dealing with something bigger than us…"

"But Abram, who is behind this?"

"I don't know. I think two people do know."

"Who?"

"Charlotte is one of them."

Or was.

"Who is the other one?"

"I have to think that Sheryl knows why this is happening."

"Her?"

"She banned Charlotte from bridge. Bridge grudges run deep."

Jake pressed the ice a little harder. After all this, he was back where he'd started. Murder over a bridge game. And Abram believed it too.

"Do you feel safe now?"

"I keep a low profile. I'm used to it."

"I see."

Abram took Jake's water glass and refilled it. He didn't realize he'd finished it. It tasted clean, since he still had the trace of saltwater on his lips.

"Your bruises don't look that bad."

"Good."

"I understand, you know."

"Understand what?"

"If you quit looking into this. I know that I should move on. I lost a wife before this. I've lost a lot of friends. Charlotte and I weren't young adults."

Abram flicked his hand in the air, like he was shooing away a fly. Jake took the ice pack off. Numb. He dropped his free fist on the table.

"How can you say that? How can you say that you loved her, and then say that?"

Abram nodded and whispered back.

"I'm sorry you got hurt over this."

"I don't care. We'll get this figured out."

"Good. We have to."

"Then what do we do now?"

He kept his notebook open and listened. Abram had a way of waiting before he spoke.

"The way I see it, there are two things we can do. We can find out what happened from two people. Sheryl and Charlotte."

"Well, let's start with Sheryl."

"I believe Sheryl knows something. She knows everything

that happens here. Even if she wasn't directly involved, she's connected. And she had a grudge against Charlotte."

"Why does she have a grudge? Charlotte said it was because she'd gotten too good at bridge. Is that it?"

"Are you a fool?" Abram shook his head. "Obviously it was about me."

"You?"

"Sheryl wanted me for herself. When she finally found out about Charlotte, she punished her."

"Then why didn't Charlotte realize that was the reason?"

Abram closed his eyes and sighed.

"She was so naïve. She never knew Sheryl wanted me. And I couldn't tell her."

Jake wrote it all down.

"So Sheryl punished Charlotte. And to retaliate, Charlotte started investigating her and the Saving Tomorrow Initiative?"

"Exactly. And that made things worse. Regardless, Sheryl knows everything that happens in this community."

He could tell Abram was holding back. As Jake closed his eyes to think, he saw the bearded man with the red hands. The man from the commercial. He opened his eyes quickly and Abram continued.

"The only problem is that Sheryl is a wall. No one can get through to her, not even me anymore. She won't tell you what's for dinner, let alone what she knew about Charlotte. Or what she did."

Unless she was talking to Gary Novak. Jake would have to confiscate Gary's wedding ring the next time he saw him. It sent the wrong message. Jake reached out to Abram and, even though it hurt to stretch, patted him on the shoulder.

"I may have a way around that problem. Sheryl will talk for us."

"Why?"

"I have absolutely no idea why. But she will."

Abram rose and got Jake another glass of water. When he came back, he was yawning. Jake started to get up.

"It's late. After nine."

"No, it's fine. I'm a night owl. I stay up until nine often."

"I see."

"Occasionally 9:15."

He yawned again.

"I should go home."

"You don't have to."

"I'm supposed to meet someone for drinks. Though since I look like this…"

"You'll be fine. But we didn't finish."

"What do you mean?"

"I said you could find out more from Charlotte as well."

"But how?"

"Simple." He walked over to his bookshelf and moved an atlas. He drew an envelope out from inside the cover.

"I can't go there. And I don't want you to go yet. But Charlotte's daughter hasn't been inside her apartment yet. No one has."

"Right."

"Tonight showed us how big this is. You have to go to Charlotte's apartment and discover what she found."

"How can I do that?"

"With this." Abram tore the envelope open. "I haven't been inside. But I know it works. We used it for late night visits. Special interludes."

He extended his palm toward Jake. He had a key.

"This is your search warrant for Room 112, Building B."

CHAPTER 28:

Jake was trying to figure out a way to cancel when Kaylie started knocking. There was no point in trying to stop her. He went to the door and opened it. She just put her hands on her hips and stared.

"What the hell happened to you?"

"I got in a fight."

"You?"

"Yeah, me. Who else?"

"The other guy."

"No, he didn't get into a fight. He's fine."

"Were you overcompensating?"

"For what?"

She walked in the apartment. She was wearing a short black dress. It looked a little cheap. It looked good.

"Overcompensating for your obese past."

"You got all that from finding one Hershey wrapper in my trash?"

"Sorry." She sat on the bed and crossed her legs. "It looks like it was a bad fight. Are you OK?"

"I'm fine."

"Let's get you some ice."

"I don't need it. We have to go, right?"

"You can't go like that."

"What about your friends? I thought we were having drinks with your friends. Won't they be upset?"

"Jake, I decided it was going to just be you and me."

She tilted her head and laughed. Her short hair fell in front of her face and back to the side. She went into the kitchen and he heard her open the refrigerator. More drawers opened and shut.

"What are you doing?"

"I need a bag for the ice."

"I told you, I'm fine. Bags are in the bottom right."

"Got it. No junk food. I'm impressed."

"Thanks."

She came back with a bag of ice in her hands.

"Here."

She took the cold plastic and held it up against his cheek. He wasn't feeling numb.

"I can get it."

"You relax." She rubbed his shoulder with her free hand as they sat down on the bed. "Now tell me what happened. Did you have a rough game of shuffleboard?"

He moved to the left and she dropped her hand.

"Sorry, I'm sore. And no, it wasn't shuffleboard."

"Then what did this to you?"

"I don't really know."

"Mysterious."

"I know. Too mysterious."

"And look at this." She put a finger to his eye and lightly traced a bruise. "You'll have a black eye."

"I've never had one."

"Really?"

"No."

"It toughens you up."

"I see."

They sat in silence for a moment while she held the ice to his face. She leaned in a little closer and his phone rang. He jumped when it happened. It was Mel. He got up and walked to the other side of the room. Kaylie turned on the TV and voices chattered in the background. He spoke just above a whisper.

"Mel. Hi."

"Hello," she said. "I can barely hear you."

He looked over at Kaylie. She smiled and reclined on the bed.

"Sorry—bad reception."

"How are you?"

"Good. I had a long day."

"So did I. A little too long." He imagined her smiling and

remembered the hallway and the dress. Then he looked at the woman on his bed. He was bad at lying.

"Sorry, I'm supposed to call Gary in a second."

"What about?"

"Photographing. We're supposed to photograph Rothschild."

"Oh, that's actually what I was calling about."

"It is?"

"Yes. He wants to do it here, at Sunset Cove. He just had his secretary call to tell me."

"This late?"

"The man doesn't keep normal hours. Does tomorrow work?"

"Sure, that works for us."

"So tomorrow morning? He thought around ten?"

"That sounds good."

They were silent. Kaylie watched the TV and gestured to Jake. He ignored her and she shouted at him.

"Come here, look, there's a show on."

"Who's that?" Mel asked.

"Just the TV." It was good she couldn't see him blushing. But he doubted anyone could through all the bruises.

"OK." She sighed. "I'll see you tomorrow, I guess. I'm excited."

"So am I."

He was. Then he hung up and sat back on the bed. Kaylie patted his leg.

"Who was that?" She tilted her head and stretched. Cheap fabric stretched well.

"Mel, from this community. Sunset Cove."

"I see. What did she want?"

"Nothing. Wait. How did you know Mel was a she?"

She grabbed his arm and pulled him toward the TV.

"Have you seen these crazies?"

He had. It was the bearded man and the woman wearing overalls. The Saving Tomorrow Initiative. This time they were standing underneath a large tree. The color and quality weren't professional, but they made up for it with their intensity. Just as in the other commercial, the woman spoke while the man remained silent.

"We are here to talk about the Development Proposition. Voting day is coming soon. If you vote for this act, this sickening act, you will be continuing the human genocide of nature."

Kaylie looked at Jake and grimaced. They continued watching.

"What are your priorities? They should belong with nature, not with man. Everything that you see now will go back to the earth. Respect it."

Then the man spoke. His voice was a controlled mumble, as drunken as when he'd jumped on the table at Rothschild's banquet.

"Respect it or pay the price!" The same end sequence played: a screaming face, a fallen tree, and credit to the Saving Tomorrow Initiative. Then black. Kaylie picked up the remote and turned off the TV.

"They're completely insane. I can't believe the networks are letting them air this."

"It's pretty shocking."

"I'm an environmentalist." She rubbed her arms with her hands. "But this is frightening. Those people are extremists."

"I've been seeing them a lot lately."

"Have you?"

"Too much."

"I just don't understand it."

"I was at a banquet and one of them jumped on a table in protest. We thought he might hurt someone."

"They're crazy. You should write an article about them."

"I might."

"Let me know if you do."

"I will."

She nodded and put her small hand on his cheek, slowly.

"How does it feel?"

"I can't feel it because of the ice."

He could see where she put the tip of her finger. It started where he'd held the ice against his left eye. Then at the bridge of his nose and down. Slowly. To his cheek. The lobe of his ear. He could feel it now. Tracing down to his neck, his chin, the bottom of his swollen lip.

He jerked away.

"I'm feeling better. But this is dripping."

He took the bag of ice into the kitchen and dumped out the shrunken cubes. They caromed around the sink and landed in the drain. He went back into the living room and she was still there, leaning back on the bed and looking at his ceiling. He noticed for the first time that she wasn't wearing shoes. He sat down at his desk and she coughed to get his attention.

"So why do you do this?"

"What?"

"This type of reporting. Don't you just write about old people playing backgammon and golf?"

"No. These people are too old for golf."

"I'm serious."

"It's a hostile question."

"I'm a hostile person."

He didn't laugh.

"I do other things."

"Like what?"

"I'm working on something. A big article."

"What?"

"It probably won't get published."

"Now I'm curious."

"Good. That means it's a good story."

"Can you give me a hint?"

"There's not enough for a hint yet."

"Then why bother?"

"Because it's important."

"I don't understand you." She got up and stood close to his

chair, her stomach in front of his face. She was backlit. He could see the outline where her dress stopped and her body started.

"I'm getting somewhere. The article's nothing now. But I just feel that since I have the time to look into other things, I should. I'll always have enough time to write puff pieces about banquet halls or cheap flights to New York."

She leaned closer and he pushed the chair back. He wasn't sure if he wanted to. But he did. She leaned back and sighed. Her hair blew up in front of her face.

"That's good to hear. Please…be careful."

"Why?"

She stopped and looked around the room. She put her hand on a bruise.

"I'm just kidding." She smiled weakly. "I should go."

And like that, she did. He watched her walk out the room. Even though she wasn't wearing shoes, she still swung her hips like she was wearing heels. The door shut and he was left alone with his bruises.

CHAPTER 29:

"My God, Jacob, we have to take you to a hospital!"

"Gary, it happened last night. I'm fine."

Gary's hair frizzed out like it was reacting to Jake's face. It didn't look happy. He leaned in close and examined Jake's bruises, the black eye and jaw level swells. His skin looked like a rotten banana.

"How did this happen?"

"I was attacked when I went to see Abram Samuels."

"Who did this?"

"That's the problem. I don't know. But we should go. We have to be at Sunset Cove before ten. I'm glad Rothschild's being photographed instead of me."

They walked to the car and got in. Then Gary reminded Jake that he needed to get his gear. Jake opened the garage door—pulling it up reminded him of everywhere he ached. He got the lenses, the tripod, the case, and the camera. He put it all in the trunk and sat in the driver's seat again. Gary nodded.

"The doctor says that in a few months, I can carry some of my equipment. None of the heavy things, of course."

They started down the road—they were already running late. Gary stared at Jake's face in horror. At least he was able to ask questions.

"What did Abram Samuels tell you?"

"Well, a lot. That's why I'm glad we're going to Sunset Cove today. He basically gave me two leads."

"Where do they lead to?"

They got onto the highway and sped up. Gary closed the window and listened.

"Well, the leads are Sheryl Goldfein and Charlotte Ward. I can handle Charlotte. I'm going to investigate her place."

"How will you get in?"

"Abram gave me the key. He and Charlotte were, uh, in a relationship."

"They were?"

"Yes."

"Amazing! I never would have known. Although Meryl always says that love is a powerful thing. I certainly agree."

"Right. Funny you should mention that."

"It was funny?"

"Uh, sure. It reminds me of the other lead Abram gave us. I think you're familiar with Sheryl Goldfein. Abram insists that she knows what's going on, or at least has some connection to what happened to Charlotte."

"That woman—she called my house!"

"She did what?"

"She must have found one of my photography credits in the paper and then looked me up in the phone book. She called my house and Meryl answered."

"What happened?"

"Meryl hung up. She didn't know it was Sheryl who was calling, but I knew it was her."

"How did you know?"

"Meryl said that the caller asked to speak to 'her poet of light.' And Meryl said 'He sure as heck doesn't live here.' Then she hung up."

"Well, you certainly convinced Sheryl you're the real deal."

"I know."

They were close to Sunset Cove. The water was shining in the distance and the angle of the sun threw off light in their direction. Jake sighed.

"How about doing it again?"

"Doing what again?"

"Seducing Sheryl."

"I can't!"

"You have to. You're the only person who can break through to her. If we can just find out a little more about what Charlotte might have found, we'll be so much closer than we are now."

"Jacob, she called my house."

"I know."

"She could endanger my marriage."

They descended the highway ramp and reached the main road. Jake turned.

"I'll be breaking and entering to see what Charlotte investigated. You can at least use your charm to chase down a lead."

He sighed. He ran his hands through his hair and flipped down the passenger side mirror. Then he wet his fingers with spit and brushed it back in place.

"For Charlotte."

"Thatta boy."

They pulled into Sunset Cove and found a spot in the lot. Jake lugged the gear up while Gary straightened his posture and tested out romantic lines on Jake.

"I don't see objects, I see shapes."

"That's a good one."

"There's something about the way the clouds move. It reminds me of Venice in springtime."

"That could work. Any others?"

Gary paused to think.

"When I was twelve, I tied a cherry stem with my tongue!"

"You may want to save that one for a rainy day."

Rothschild and Mel were standing at the top of the hill, near the office. A third man stood beside them. Jake recognized him from the banquet. He had long red hair that ran past his shoulders, and he was wearing all black. At the banquet, he'd subdued the bearded man, and now he seemed just as serious. Mel and Rothschild waved, but the red-haired man kept his arms crossed. They got to the top of the hill and Mel gasped.

"Jake, what happened to you?"

"Long story."

"Bar fight, Mr. Russo?" Rothschild asked. He smiled and shook Gary's hand. They introduced themselves to each other and then Rothschild gestured to the red-haired man.

"You've met Conrad before, right?"

"I think so."

It was good he had. Conrad didn't bother with a handshake. He kept staring at the bottom of the hill where the cars were parked. Rothschild laughed.

"He's pensive this morning, aren't you, Conrad?"

"Sir," he said and nodded. Mel walked closer to Jake, but stayed far enough away to appear professional.

"Are you OK?"

"I'm fine."

"I'm worried. When did this happen?"

"Last night."

"Why didn't you tell me when I called?"

"I didn't want you to worry." She looked at Rothschild anxiously. He guessed that his time with Mel was a professional secret, so he covered for her. "I mean, I didn't want you to worry about rescheduling the appointment."

"We still can."

Rothschild frowned and Jake pointed to Gary.

"No, no, I don't even need to be here. Gary's the one doing the work. I just tag along."

Gary set up the gear. They'd be shooting at the top of the hill, with the water and beach serving as Rothschild's background panorama. Gary squinted and leaned in to look in the viewfinder. Rothschild held his hands at his side the entire time, posing. He was wearing a black suit with a white shirt and maroon tie. The wind didn't move his short white hair or disturb his suit, which was carefully tailored. He seemed content to wait hours for Gary to set up the shot.

"Can you back up a step or two?"

"Wait," Mel said. She checked if Gary was going to send Rothschild backward into a ditch. It was clear. "Go ahead."

"What was that about?" Rothschild asked.

"Oh, I just wanted to make sure that you had a clear path."

"I hardly noticed you limping," Gary told Mel.

"Thanks. I don't need the ankle brace. Not every day, at least."

"That's wonderful!"

Gary looked through the viewfinder a little longer and gestured to Rothschild.

"How about you put out your arms out to the side? Like it's all yours."

"It is all mine."

As he took the photographs, Gary shifted his feet side to side anxiously, like his position would change the shots. Rothschild didn't move. He stood totally still, the same smile frozen on his face. His mouth never twitched and he never blinked. Conrad stared silently and Mel pulled Jake a foot to the side.

"How did it happen?" she whispered. "Your face."

"I was attacked on the beach."

"Attacked?"

"Not so loudly."

"Who attacked you?"

"No idea."

"Why did they do it?"

"Same answer as before."

"No idea?"

"None."

Rothschild coughed and yelled to Gary.

"Do you want any serious photographs?"

"Sure, we can try that."

Now, instead of gesturing, Rothschild crossed his arms and flattened his smile into a line. He looked more comfortable when he was stiffer. His black eyes gleamed. Jake guessed it was the picture that they'd use. It made the landscape behind him look grander. It made him look grander too.

"These are very nice," Gary said. "Good lighting."

"Fine." Rothschild stayed still.

Mel reached over to Jake again and tapped his arm.

"You said you were on the beach. What beach were you on?"

He shouldn't have said it. Now he had a choice to make:

how involved would she be?

"It was one around here."

"What?"

"I can't say much more, right now."

Rothschild started to squint while Gary took photos.

"I think I'm done here. The sun is getting in my eyes."

"Just a few more."

Conrad walked over to Gary and grabbed him at the shoulder.

"He's very busy today."

"Just a few more." Conrad looked up at Rothschild. He nodded.

"Certainly." Conrad backed away and let Gary click.

Gary took a few more shots. It wasn't hard to make Rothschild look good, or to make Sunset Cove look beautiful. When it was over, Jake pulled Gary aside and they started dismantling all of the gear. Gary was excited after taking his photos. He always was.

"Jacob, these will look very nice. We can do some slight color correction on the serious shots and they will look great."

"Right. Well, that was the easy part."

"What do you mean?"

"Getting photographs is easy." They looked down the hill. "Now we have to get information. That's a little harder."

CHAPTER 30:

Jake was getting better at explaining his bruises. Practice made perfect. If only it made his wounds heal more quickly.

"I fell down."

"Ech. I've heard that one before. My husband was a cop, you know."

Sheryl Goldfein leaned against her doorframe. Jake had called her before to tell her that Gary would be visiting. She was ready. She had on a long black dress and her hair looked silver instead of gray. When they walked into her apartment, they saw why she'd been leaning. She could barely balance in her heels.

"I've just been spending a quiet day around the house. Would either of you like hors d'oeuvres?"

She hobbled into the kitchen and Jake grinned at Gary.

"Just a quiet Sunday. Apparently she makes hors d'oeuvres on a quiet Sunday."

"What? I can't hear you."

"You don't want me to repeat it."

Jake got up and hurried to the door.

"Where are you going? You can't leave!"

"You're solo. I have to investigate our other lead."

"Jacob, please!"

Sheryl emerged from the kitchen with a tray in her hands. A thick coat of dark plum lipstick seemed to seal her lips together. Jake took the tray from her and set it on the coffee table. She limped to the chair next to Gary and removed her heels with a sigh. Jake rushed out before Gary could stop him.

Sheryl's building was a short walk from Building B. He shifted Charlotte's key in his hand and felt its sharp edges scrape against his knuckles. If no one had been inside Charlotte's apartment, then no one would be able to tell the difference if he searched it. He'd uncover what Charlotte had found, and hopefully he'd continue what she'd been investigating. He was wearing shoes that clicked on the

155

sidewalk, and his steps were as steady as a ticking clock.

People were outside this early in the day. A man with large shades stared at the ground as he walked. Beside him, a man wearing shorts and high socks carried a bundled newspaper. Two women sat on a wide bench, one of them reading and the other with her head down, but no book in her hands. He hurried through the active pathways, knowing he couldn't be seen entering Charlotte's apartment. He almost wished it were night. Now he couldn't hide behind a shadow.

He got to the building and used the key on the outer door. A quick scan around. No one was there. It was better to commit and hurry than look around too much. He went in and shut the door behind him. He continued down the hallway, past where he and Mel had kissed. It seemed like years since it had happened. He traced his hand along the wallpaper as he walked. He was almost at Room 112.

He got to the door and faced it. Be aggressive. Do it quick. He'd get in, look for what Charlotte had found, and then get out. No one would ever know. He pressed the key hard against his palm and prepared to draw it from his pocket.

"Mr. Russo. Have you lost your way?"

He turned and saw red hair and broad shoulders. Conrad. The building door was open. Light flooded in, backlighting the man as he spoke. He stepped forward. He took each step slowly, and he held his arms out like he was confused.

"I thought you were done photographing Simeon."

"I was. I am, I mean." He pressed the key so hard it cut into his palm. "I just wanted to find out a little more about an average hall."

He waited. Conrad bit his lip and looked down at his knuckles.

"I'm sure that Melissa would offer to show you around the residences."

Conrad spoke like he was holding his breath. He didn't exhale.

"Right. I thought Mel might be busy."

"Do you know her well?"

"Not really."

"You don't?"

"No."

He looked at the wallpaper. Now it seemed like it was peeling.

"Is there anything else that I can show you, Mr. Russo?"

"I'm fine." He let the key fall deep into his pocket.

"Then let me escort you out."

The man held his arms out and directed Jake toward the hallway door. He had no choice but to go. He walked outside and heard Conrad following behind him, blocking him so he couldn't get back in. Conrad's next question came from behind and floated over Jake's head.

"How did you even enter the hallway? Our outer doors are all locked."

"This one was open."

"I doubt that Mr. Russo."

"Someone propped it open. Forgetful minds, I guess."

They entered into the light and Conrad shut the door behind him. He pressed forward on the handle and shook the door slightly.

"The locking mechanism seems to work."

"Someone had propped it open."

"I see."

"In the future, Melissa will show you around. Won't you, Melissa?"

She was walking down the path with a binder in her hands.

"Jake? Conrad? What are you two doing here?"

Jake felt one of his bruises deepen as Conrad grabbed him at the shoulder.

"I found him inside of Building B."

"Building B? That's where Charlotte's room was. What were you doing there?"

Jake stared at her and Conrad tightened his grip. He kept squeezing.

"Melissa, who is Charlotte? What is the significance of her room?"

Jake looked at her. If he could just make eye contact with her for a second, he knew it would be OK. He wondered what color his shoulder was turning under the pressure of Conrad's hand. They waited. Then Mel broke her stare at Conrad and looked at Jake. He shook his head, a millimeter each direction. He didn't know if it would be enough.

"Oh." She brushed her hair and put her hand to her chin. "I just thought of Charlotte because I'm going to her room. I have to finish the handover documentation. Her daughter is coming down in a couple of days, so we need to have all the reports finished by then."

"I see." Conrad barely moved when he spoke.

"Just a funny coincidence."

"Very well." He nodded and let go of Jake's shoulder. Jake felt his muscles loosen again. "Perhaps you can show Mr. Russo a residence hall in the future. We wouldn't want him getting lost, would we?"

"No, of course not."

"Of course not." Conrad smiled, keeping his lips pressed tight together. "I have to find Mr. Rothschild."

"Good seeing you."

Conrad walked up the hill without responding.

Mel approached Jake tentatively and waited until Conrad turned the corner before she started talking.

"The beach." She was almost whispering. "It was our beach, wasn't it? That's the beach where you were attacked."

"Yes. But wait."

"What?"

"I don't want to start saying too much. I don't want you to get in the middle of things."

"It's too late for that."

She looked around. At the top of the hill, a child pushed a woman in her wheelchair. Both of them were laughing. They seemed happy and far away.

"What really happened to your face?"

"I was approaching someone on the beach and they turned around and hit me. Again and again. And then they kicked me while I was down."

"I can't believe it."

She touched his face and brushed the black spots under his eyes. Her hands were warm and he couldn't feel her fingernails. He wanted to lean forward and kiss her but was afraid she wouldn't want it.

He didn't have to wait. She touched the back of his neck and pulled him down to her. For the first time since he'd seen Conrad, he felt relaxed again. She was warm and tasted like orange. She spoke softly like she'd just woken up.

"I'm glad you're OK. But I don't understand."

"I don't know if you should."

"It's already too late. I lied and said you didn't know Charlotte."

He looked back up the hill.

"They wouldn't know you lied."

She grabbed his hand and pressed her thumb against his palm.

"That's over now. But whatever happened isn't."

"What do you want me to do?"

"If you want me to cover for you, you have to do one thing."

"What?"

"Explain it to me. Explain what you are looking for."

She looked up at him and waited for him to answer. He looked down. She didn't need to know about Charlotte. She shouldn't. He didn't know what he'd say until he said it.

CHAPTER 31:

The beach was relatively crowded. Members of the community, visitors, and even a few children were enjoying the sunny day. That was good. The more crowds the better.

"This is where it happened. This is where I was attacked."

"And you were going to see Abram Samuels?"

"He's the one who saved me."

He'd asked her one last time if she was sure she could handle it. All the complications, the conflicts, the risks of losing her job or worse. She just touched his face and nodded silently. They walked away from Sunset Cove and to the beach. They might be seen, but at least they wouldn't be heard.

"And why were you meeting Abram?"

"Because we think Charlotte Ward was murdered."

She looked out to the water and then around again. An elderly man dipped a toe in the water and stepped back with a frown on his face.

"Jake, how could someone have killed her?"

"Simple. They just kept her away from her meds. They pulled her out to the beach and left her. Without her walker, she couldn't get back. That's all they had to do."

"Oh God. But who would do that? And why?"

"We think Sheryl Goldfein knows something about it. Before she was killed, Charlotte had bad blood with Sheryl."

"You think Sheryl killed Charlotte?"

"I don't know." He sighed. He wanted to hold her close, but they were sitting a few feet apart. They'd have to face it separately. For now.

"For a while I thought it was Sheryl. Then Abram. The other complication is that, in order to spite Sheryl, Charlotte was investigating a radical environmental group. The Saving Tomorrow Initiative."

"Who are they?"

"Remember the banquet? Remember the bearded man?"

"That's them?"

"Yes."

She put her hands over her face.

"This is too much. We have to tell the police."

"We can't yet." He touched her arm. He didn't care about appearances. "I think we can figure it out. Sheryl shifted the community's charity funding to this group. What's suspicious is that the group also had every reason to stop Charlotte from finding out about them."

"I suppose so. It just seems…"

"What?"

"I don't think Sheryl would do it."

"You never know."

He could tell it hadn't sunk in. He rubbed her forearm between his fingers. She shook her head.

"That kind of thing doesn't happen here. It shouldn't happen here. These people are family. Why am I doing this if they aren't like that?"

"I know."

"Why do I stick around and bother?"

"I know."

They looked out at the beach. The concession building was open now, they could tell from the line in front of it. People walked away with overfilled ice cream cones and sweating soda cans. And smiles. Big, open smiles.

"I have this." He took the key out of his pocket and showed it to Mel. He dropped it in her hand.

"What is it?"

"It's the key to Charlotte's room. I was going to look inside her apartment. Then Conrad showed up."

"How did you get it?"

"Abram gave me the key."

"Of course."

"You knew?"

"I think most of us did."

"Why didn't you tell me?"

"It was idle gossip. Not life and death."

She sighed. She leaned forward and started spreading sand across her feet. They were already half buried.

"You know that's why Sheryl kicked Charlotte out of bridge."

"Abram hinted at that. I thought he was just arrogant."

"Sheryl wanted him for herself."

"And Charlotte thought it was all about bridge."

"I think so. Sheryl knew it would hurt her."

"And then Charlotte retaliated by investigating this group. That's when the real trouble started."

She didn't seem interested in talking about it anymore. He wrapped his arm around her and pulled her against his body. Her feet emerged from the sand, the grains slowly falling to the sides.

"I'm sorry you're a part of this."

"There's a problem."

"What?"

"The key." She handed it back to him. "Once Charlotte's daughter comes, she'll have keys. She can change the locks, stay there, or do whatever she wants. If you use the key, you'll have to do it before she arrives."

"When is she supposed to get here?"

"A couple of days. Obviously you can't go right away, since you almost got caught today. But you should have time."

"Great." He squeezed her upper arm. "That helps a lot."

They sat on the beach a little longer and he held her to his chest. When she spoke, he felt her voice vibrating her back.

"How are you going to find out if Sheryl knows what happened?"

"I have an inside man."

"Abram?"

"Better than Abram."

"Who?"

"Gary Novak. Right now, he's busy charming her. And hopefully he'll learn something."

"Gary?"

"That's right."

He felt her ribs shaking as she laughed.

"How does Gary Novak pull that off?"

"I don't know what to tell you. He's a natural Don Juan. And they are both romantics."

She took his hand in hers. Someone's grandson dropped a hot dog and seagulls dove for the bun. Instead of crying, the child laughed and clapped. Mel looked up.

"This is nice. Despite the circumstances."

"Yeah. It is."

"Can you tell me why I didn't hear from you before all this?"

"What do you mean?"

"Why didn't you call?"

"I've been really busy. Just putting this together. Between work and everything."

"I can imagine, now that I know what's happening."

"And it wasn't that long, was it?"

"A few days."

"Right."

He looked at her and shook his head.

"I just didn't want to scare you off."

She laughed.

"You know I like you, right?"

"Do you?"

"Yes." She kissed him on the cheek.

"I just have a problem with taking charge. Putting myself out there, it's scary. And with you…"

"With me what?"

"With someone like you, it just seems improbable."

"Why?"

"Just look at you."

She kissed him again and stopped.

"Déjà vu. You're vibrating again."

He picked it up. It was déjà vu.

"Hi Gary."

"Jacob! I'm calling you on a cellular phone."

"I know."

"Where are you? Are you in Charlotte's apartment?"

"I got caught too early. But I'm going soon."

"Did you find anything?"

Mel leaned in and listened. He let her. She deserved it.

"I found some things," Gary shouted. "I'm so tired of talking about light. It gets boring after a few times!"

"I'm sure. But what about with Charlotte?"

"What do you mean?"

"Did you find out anything about Sheryl and the Saving Tomorrow Initiative? Did she say anything else?"

"I didn't ask directly."

Jake heard a click.

"Are you there?"

He heard Gary yell to Sheryl.

"I'm just seeing when he will give me a ride back."

"Gary?"

"I am sorry. I had to answer her. She made me a carrot cake."

"A cake?"

"Yes. I'm taking it to go."

"You can't take Sheryl's cake to go. What will Meryl say?"

"She wouldn't want me wasting good food. And did you know carrots are good for your eyes?"

"Gary."

"Your generation, it just throws away everything."

"OK." Mel laughed. "We're off track."

"I asked Sheryl what she was doing the night Charlotte died."

"How did she react?"

"Well, I didn't tell her it was the day Charlotte died. I just mentioned the day of the week."

"Did she react?"

"She had forgotten. She had to look it up on her calendar, even though it happened so recently."

Jake turned to Mel.

"If she actually didn't remember, that definitely removes some suspicion. Even if she was lying, you'd think she'd have memorized her alibi."

"And then," Gary continued, "once she looked up the date, she yelled back to me that she'd been busy."

"Doing what?"

"Bridge. It was one of the games that they didn't let Charlotte play."

"But if they were playing bridge, that means there were witnesses. All those people who could testify that Sheryl was with them. A clean alibi."

"Jacob?"

"Yes?"

"I can tell you more, but please pick me up soon. She wants to show me vacation photographs and have me critique them."

"OK, I will. Good work."

Mel seemed confused. He closed the phone and put it in his pocket.

"What are you thinking?"

"I know Sheryl couldn't do it," she said. "I just know it. And if she had an alibi, then that proves it."

"She could have hired someone."

"I guess. But I just don't think she would."

"Why?"

"She's not a bad person."

"I know." He squeezed her arm. "It's clear that this is bigger than Sheryl. I think the Saving Tomorrow Initiative was involved."

Mel brushed her hair back and started to get up. He pulled her down.

"Where are you going?"

"I should get back to work."

"No. Stay here."

"Thank you for telling me what happened."

"I'm sorry I told you. I didn't want to get you involved."

"I'm glad you did."
"To be honest, I am too. We'll figure out what happened."
"It will connect."

He thought of something to say. It was corny. Sappy. It would scare her off. Make her reconsider and see him for what he was. But he still tasted the orange. He still had her in his arms, for now. Why not say it?

"It will connect," he said. "But I'm glad we did already."

She laughed a little and rolled her eyes. But then she put her hand on the back of his neck again. Softly, they kissed in the middle of the beach, in the middle of the day.

CHAPTER 32:

"Coconut! It's our old friend Jacob! Be nice!"

The dog scampered around Jerry Rubenstein, wrapping the leash around his body like string tied around a Christmas tree. He was small at the top and big at the base. He laughed and untangled himself from the leash.

"He loves to put daddy in a leash, don't you Coconut?"

The dog sniffed Jake's feet and barked.

"I guess that's a yes."

"Come inside."

Jerry guided him inside the office. A portrait five feet high and five feet wide was hanging over a large wooden desk. Jake stared until Jerry saw where he was looking.

"Do you like it?"

"I've never seen such a large portrait of a dog."

"That's Coconut I. Coconut II's mommy. Isn't that right, Coconut?"

The dog looked at the portrait and barked a few times. He looked almost identical to the dog in the painting. Jake laughed a little.

"You love dogs, Jerry. Don't you?"

"They love me. I just give it back."

He laughed and clapped Jake on the back. The bruises hurt a little, but they didn't hurt as much as they would have the day before. Jake started walking toward the chair in front of the desk, but Jerry directed him to a couch and chair on the other side of the room.

"We have to be able to relax. We're having a conversation, not making a deal."

They sat down. Jake quickly. Jerry took a little longer. The dog jumped up on the couch and onto Jerry's lap. He started petting it absentmindedly.

"We enjoyed the article about the Palmstead Homes."

"You did?"

"Immensely. Thank you for writing it."

"My editor cut it down a little. But it stayed mostly intact."

"Will you be talking to Simeon?"

"Oh, we already spoke a while ago. I interviewed him over lunch."

"Did it go well?"

He'd told Simeon Rothschild that his new name was Harold Longwood.

"It went well enough."

"That's good." Jerry leaned forward, depressing the cushions on the large couch. "Jake, I don't mean to be impolite. But I can't help but notice your face."

A day later the marks had just started to fade. He knew they wouldn't be gone for a while.

"Right." He touched a bruise. "In some ways, that's what I wanted to speak with you about. I'm trying to get to the bottom of something. It doesn't involve you in any way. But I need someone who's a decent source."

"I see. Is what we say today off the record?"

"Of course."

"Then I'd be happy to tell you anything. What happened?"

Jake touched another one of the bruises. He knew he shouldn't, but he couldn't help himself.

"I'm starting to learn about the Saving Tomorrow Initiative."

"Did they do this to you?"

"I don't know."

"Why not?"

"Because I didn't see who attacked me. Even if I did, I don't think that I'd know what party was responsible."

"They are definitely radical enough."

"Do you know anything about them?"

He stroked his chin and then pet the dog with the same hand. Both of them looked concerned.

"Well, they're new. I'd never heard of them before the past few months, so I don't know much. To be honest, Coconut and I only seem to hear bad things about the group. Every time we walk around one of the Palmstead communities, someone tells us about a new outrageous commercial. Always complaints. Everyone thinks they are overboard in their rhetoric."

"And you don't have an opinion?"

"We're looking at expanding into some new regions outside of Sarasota. So we don't have a dog in the fight, do we Coconut?"

The dog tilted his head and grabbed at the couch's fabric with a paw. Jake followed up.

"So most people don't approve of their message?"

"I think they would approve of the message. Before this group came around, most people wanted to save the wetlands from development. But now I think that those commercials have turned people against the cause. Before them, people were seriously considering what they wanted to do about the wetlands. But this group acts so outlandishly that it's hard for anyone to agree."

"I see."

"I mean, can you take them seriously based on their commercials? Or if they possibly attacked you?"

"No. I can't respect them, that's certain."

"Exactly. Their techniques aren't appropriate to their audience. The people who live here appreciate respect, not dogma. They've got time to think about the issues, and they don't want to be talked down to."

Jake rubbed his shoulders with his hands.

"It's just all so bizarre that any of this is happening."

"It is." The dog began to burrow between two cushions, and Jerry gently pulled him out. "How did you start investigating this group in the first place?"

"Well, I wasn't investigating them. I was investigating the death of a woman."

"The death?"

"The murder." He was probably saying too much. But he didn't have time to hold back. "I think someone was killed."

"And you've traced it to this group?"

"At first I thought it was a personal grudge. But now I'm thinking it had to be something bigger."

Jerry adjusted his body. Couch cushions tipped in different directions.

"I wouldn't underestimate the personal grudge."

"I don't."

"But what happened?"

"Two people had a falling out. So one of them started trying to hurt the other person's reputation, which was tied to the Saving Tomorrow Initiative. I'm not at liberty to tell you why, right now. But I think she got close to some secret about the group. Closer than she ever knew she'd get."

Jerry scratched his forehead and clicked his tongue.

"It sounds like you have a Penicillin situation."

"What do you mean?"

He smiled.

"Do you know how Alexander Fleming discovered Penicillin?"

"It's mold, right?"

"Yes. He was studying bacteria and he just stumbled onto something big. The bacteria didn't matter. He just accidentally found the thing that did."

"And you think this is like Penicillin?"

"It sounds that way." Coconut whimpered and Jerry scratched his head. "Your victim started out thinking she was looking into something small. But she fell into something a lot bigger."

"You think that's really what happened?"

"I don't underestimate personal grudges. But why would someone attack multiple people if they didn't have something big to hide?"

"I don't know."

"It's a good thing you were attacked."

Jake laughed.

"See if you say that after you've been hit."

"I'm serious."

"Fine then. Why is it good that I was attacked?"

"It means you're onto something. It means a little mold is growing. You just have to keep going after it to make sure it develops."

Jake swallowed.

"Then how do I make sure what happened to this person doesn't happen to me?"

Jerry stood up and stretched. The dog jumped off the couch and scampered at his feet.

"That I can't answer for you. You can guess that I don't fight much. Or run much."

"Then what do I do?"

He shrugged.

"You just get to them before they get to you."

"So it's a race against time?"

"At this point, yes."

"Then what do I do?"

Jerry sat down and clicked his tongue another time.

"You start running it."

He was ready to write.

CHAPTER 33:

"I'm telling you, I just don't think that this is how I should be spending my time."

"Damn it," Thompson screamed, "I'm the guy who's paying you. You can't spend all day at the buffet."

He was in the car, driving to Sunset Cove. As soon as he came back from his meeting with Jerry, he'd called Gary and convinced him to set up a meeting with Sheryl. Jake would surprise her by going in Gary's place. He wanted one more interview, even if they had to lie to get it. But his plans didn't matter now. Now he had to deal with Thompson. And Thompson was angry.

"Just…just listen." He sounded worse than usual.

"How's the weather up there?"

"No time for small talk. You are going to drive to Orlando and get this story."

He sighed.

"Fine. What is the story again?"

"What is it? Where's your little notebook?"

"I told you, I'm driving."

"Russo you…you disappoint me so much. I'd demand that you pull over, but you'd just go to a drive-thru. Now listen to me—you're driving to Orlando."

"You know Orlando is far away, don't you? It's not like New York here. This is a big state."

"New York is a big state."

"How many times have you been outside the city though?"

No answer.

"You're driving to Orlando."

"It's a three hour drive."

"I don't care! Do you know how obsessed our readers are with Melinda Ginelli?"

"She's just a celebrity."

"Just a celebrity? She's the biggest thing there is. And now, out of nowhere, Melinda Ginelli has moved to Orlando. Of all places! We'll scoop the competition—they don't have anybody in Florida. We've finally got our celebrity! And they have palm trees there, too!"

Jake sighed. He went down the off-ramp and stopped at a light.

"Don't you think I could spend my time a little better than covering some celebrity? I'm not supposed to bother with movie stars."

"She's got a CD too!"

"I know, I heard. But I'm chasing a really big story."

"What?"

He turned the wheel hard. He was starting to get frustrated.

"I was attacked the other night. For getting too close."

"Attacked?" Thompson started laughing. Not a good sign. "Russo, was it a food fight?"

"Very funny."

"I'm serious. Those...those can get messy! Carla, come here."

"Don't bring Carla in on this."

He heard Thompson laughing and talking to Carla. He was almost at Sunset Cove, but he was stuck wasting his time on this.

"OK," Thompson said. "I'm back. Now, you say you were attacked?"

"Yes." Firmer now. Aggressive. "And I'm going to follow this story through."

"What is it?"

"A woman was murdered here. And I've been trying to find out why."

"Murder? Our readers don't want to hear about that!"

"They have to."

"How many times do I have to tell you? Palm trees, Russo. Palm trees! And now we have a beautiful woman, Melinda Ginelli, waiting for her reporter!"

"I think she was murdered for a reason. There's a radical environmental group. The one I told you about. I know that

173

they were involved somehow. I just can't put together all the pieces. But I'm starting to get close."

"Russo."

"Yes?"

"I didn't listen to a word of that. It doesn't matter. Cover Melinda in Orlando! You should hear some of the news we're getting."

"Like what?"

"It's just a rumor. But...but I heard she died her hair brown. Melinda Ginelli as a brunette! Just imagine! It's front page stuff."

He parked the car and took the key out of the ignition. As he sat in the Sunset Cove lot, he wondered how far he could throw the phone. But he let it stay on the seat.

"Listen, I have to write this story. A woman was killed. Possibly by environmentalists gone wild. That doesn't interest you at all?"

"Do you even know who Melinda is dating? Or the name of her newest movie?"

"A woman is dead. Nothing?"

"You need to get used to it. People die. They're old. Our readers don't want to be reminded of that sort of stuff. They want good news."

"Like some celebrity?"

"Exactly! I didn't think you understood. You know, she might even have a drug problem! Isn't that wonderful?"

"I don't get it."

"Well start getting it. It's not negotiable. I want you to start commuting there. Find out what Orlandonians think about her."

"I don't think they're called Orlandonians."

"Russo. Find out what they're called then. Orlandonians, Orlanders, Orlandish. Just go there."

"Fine. I'll get you an article."

"Not just an article. Be there. Nobody wants to read about murder in Sarasota. It's...it's depressing."

"Sometimes the news is depressing."

"Like when the cafeteria runs out of tater tots?"

Thompson started laughing. Jake heard him calling people over and repeating his joke. He squeezed the rubber of the steering wheel hard and felt it chafe against his palms. Just ignore it. It wasn't worth getting into a fight. Thompson got back on the phone, wheezing.

"By the way, Mr. Newsman, you did a good job asking that developer the 'Handling Handle' questions. Let's get more of that. And more pictures with the palm trees."

"I didn't want to ask those questions."

"But you did." Gruffer now. Not laughing any more. "Do you understand?"

"I understand." He did understand. That didn't mean he'd like it. And it didn't mean that he'd do it.

"Good," Thompson barked.

"Good."

"Now go ahead and take lunch."

"It's 10AM."

"That's right. You've...you've probably already had lunch!"

Thompson kept laughing. Jake took the phone from the passenger seat and flipped it shut. The conversation was over. He wasn't going to keep on debating. It vibrated in his hand a second later, but he didn't answer. He just put it in his pocket and got out of the car. The path in front of him was blocked.

A line of people progressed along the path, led by someone who looked like a nurse. A morning walk. They were moving slowly as they looked attentively at the trees and grass. They looked happy. Some were in wheelchairs and some had canes. One man was leaning into a walker, light blue pants pulled up high on his waist, his socks taut around his ankles. They stopped and the nurse said something Jake couldn't hear. He saw them nod their heads.

Another sunny day in Sarasota. He was used to it by now. Orlando was two and a half hours away. Who knew where this celebrity lived, or what he'd even find? Was he supposed to dig through Melinda Ginelli's trash? If he saw her, was he supposed to ask her "Handling Handle" questions? Or maybe they'd talk about her latest movie—the one he hadn't seen. If he was going to Orlando, he'd have to start driving now.

The last person in the line walked past. She smiled as she walked by. He took out his notebook and opened it to a fresh page. He had a story to write. He wasn't going to Orlando. For once, the story was in Sarasota.

CHAPTER 34:

Sheryl Goldfein wasn't happy when she opened the door.

"Where's Gary? What did you do with Gary?"

She scowled. She was wearing a pink nightgown, and Jake smelled spices. It was either potpourri or her skin. Her hair looked silver again, and he could see where the hairspray had been sprayed, still wet. She had dark red lipstick on, meticulously and thickly applied. Jake sighed.

"I know Gary told you he would be here."

"Of course he did. Do you think I would have done this for you?"

"I hope not."

"Ech. You're right."

She dropped her hand from the doorframe and motioned for him to come in. He walked in carefully and looked to the right. About thirty rose petals were piled in front of a door.

"That's your bedroom, isn't it?"

"None of your business."

"You and Gary haven't…done anything, have you?"

"Today was going to be the day I convinced him."

"Oh. I see."

"A poet," she said and sighed. Jake looked around the room. No potpourri. The spices were some type of overpowering perfume. Gary Novak was a powerful man.

"So when is Gary coming?"

Better to let her know now.

"It's just me today."

"Ech." She threw her arms down to her side. "I spent so much money. What am I supposed to do with these flowers?"

"I don't know."

"It took me forever to cut through them."

Jake picked up a petal off the floor. It felt wrong.

"Did you use plastic roses?"

"Of course I did." She held up a pair of scissors. "They're reusable. I'm not going to waste perfectly good flowers." She started collecting the petals and putting them into a metal tin. He didn't want to know how many times they'd been reused. She didn't open the bedroom door. Fortunately. She came back and sat down in front of him.

"So why isn't Gary coming?"

"Well." He wouldn't tell her about Gary's wife. Yet. "Gary was busy. And I have some important questions to ask you."

"Ech. I'm sure."

"Do you remember when we talked about Charlotte?"

"I remember."

"Well, I'm still looking into it. I'm going to try one more time. I need to know what happened."

"I told you. She was old. That's it."

She started to pick at the lipstick on the corners of her lips. Jake drew closer.

"I don't think you did it." It was true. "But I do think that you can help me."

"How am I supposed to help you?"

He sighed and drew a line in the notebook. It started now.

"I need to know about the Saving Tomorrow Initiative."

"What?"

She clamped the lid on the tin. One plastic rose petal was trapped between the edges.

"The Saving Tomorrow Initiative. I think they're the ones who attacked me."

He pointed to his bruises and she stepped back.

"I thought you said you fell."

"You believed that?"

"Ech."

"Anyway," he continued, "I think they attacked me. I admit that I thought you were involved before. But now I realize that this is bigger than you."

He believed it more now. It was hard to suspect a woman wearing a pink nightgown. Her hair started to droop as it dried.

"Why would I know anything about them?"

"Because this year you gave them the community's

charitable donations. That's why Charlotte started investigating them."

"She had a silly grudge about bridge."

"And you had a silly grudge about Abram. Right? That's why you kicked her out, isn't it? You found out they were together and decided to make her life a little worse."

He felt bad after he said it. Her face began to sag.

"Maybe. But that doesn't matter."

"She just wanted to find out something to retaliate. But the Initiative—the group you gave money to—was more than she bargained for."

"I don't know what she found. But she was old."

"No." Firmer. "It wasn't old age that killed her."

"It was because she forgot her medication."

"She forgot it? You don't really believe that, do you? It's a great excuse. But it isn't true."

"It could be."

He stared at her, seeing past the makeup and mascara. She stared right back. She wasn't the type of woman who could be easily intimidated. He kept talking.

"What do you know about the group? Why did you switch?"

"I don't know much about them. It's not important."

"Have you seen their commercials?"

She swallowed and pulled her nightgown tighter around her.

"I have heard about them."

"They're total radicals."

"I've heard that."

"Charlotte must have found something. Do you know what it was?"

"You're just looking for a story."

"No. I'm looking for the truth."

"I don't know anything about them." She sighed. "We decided to switch to them because they supported the wetlands. And that's important. We didn't know what they would be like."

"But didn't you already help a charity that did that?"

"It's good to pass the money around."

"It just seems a little unusual."

"It was one decision. Charlotte was just angry about bridge."

"Well, whoever killed her was mad about something else."

"I'm telling you." She stopped a little, caught her breath, and spoke more loudly. "You don't really think they did something, do you?"

"I do. I can't prove it yet, but I do."

"Ech. You're just a paranoid reporter."

"I wish."

"Well, we just gave them money. I don't talk to them or anything like that."

"I just don't understand why you switched. And why you chose the Saving Tomorrow Initiative."

"That's why it's our decision."

They were both silent. He'd written down her answers. He looked at them—scribbled lines, shorthand without a translation. His handwriting looked as angry as he was.

"What argument did you give when the rest of the community voted for it?"

"I don't give arguments. I tell them what we should do. They follow."

"So you admit you made the decision yourself?"

She stopped. Then she gave in.

"Yes, I made the decision. But we all had input. We give this money out. It's only fair to give it to more than one group."

"You know that the Saving Tomorrow Initiative has supported some outrageous positions. They've said nature is more important than humans. That all development should stop."

"I'm not responsible for that."

"Your money couldn't have hurt their efforts. How do you think they got the money for TV commercials?"

"I don't know."

"I've never even seen TV commercials for a group like that. Don't you think that's a little odd, Sheryl?"

"I'm not their treasurer and I'm not their leader. All we did was give them money, and I don't see why that means Charlotte was killed. She was just mad that she couldn't play in our bridge games."

"You know something? These hurt." He touched the bruises. "They're a dangerous group."

"Listen. We talked about this before. I guess you weren't convinced. But I was a nurse. Now I'm just an old woman who plays bridge two days a week. I don't spend my time getting involved in things like this."

Sitting there, she started to look a little sadder in her pink nightgown. It folded into smooth shadows, places where the pink darkened to red. She'd peeled the lipstick off at the corners, and her lips floated crimson in the center of her face. Then she seemed to wake up again. She scowled at Jake.

"Are we done? I don't want to waste any more of my day."

"Sure." He closed the notebook and put his pen in his pocket. "We're done."

He started walking toward the door. He stepped on a petal that she'd missed and looked back.

"I'm sorry we tricked you."

"Did I do all this for nothing? Is Gary coming?"

"Not today. I'm really sorry. I just care about Charlotte."

She nodded her head and stood up slowly.

"If you really think these people attacked you and hurt Charlotte, then I have a little advice."

"What?"

"Know when to draw the line."

"I do."

"And be careful."

As he closed the door, he saw her staring out at him, waiting for it to shut.

CHAPTER 35:

He was getting slower. He tapped his stopwatch as he went up the stairs to his apartment. He'd only run five miles. Charlotte Ward hadn't left him much time for running. But he felt relaxed, calm even, until he got to the top of the stairs.

"Out for a jog?"

He thought he'd seen a lot of Kaylie before, when she wore tight t-shirts and cut off shorts. It was nothing. She was wearing her swimming suit. That was how she'd gotten her tan. Her tan lines really were lines. Her suit wasn't any thicker than a centimeter. He collected his breath and wiped the sweat off his forehead.

"I was out for a run. I don't jog."

"Well well."

She sat down in front of his door while he stood above her.

"Excuse me."

"Do you need to get in?"

"Yes." She didn't move and he sat down beside her.

"Going to the beach?"

"I just got back from the pool."

"Do you swim?"

"I sunbathe. Does that count?"

"You must work out a lot."

"Oh really?" She tilted her head and looked at him. "How do you know I work out a lot?"

"Because you make fun of me so much. For having been a little overweight."

"Right, that's how you know." She hit his shoulder.

"That hurt."

"Did it?"

"You forget, I'm sore."

"You're starting to heal."

"I think I'm almost better."

"No." She shook her head. "Looking at your face, you've got a way to go."

"Thanks. I should probably get to work."

He started to get up. He took his key out of his pocket and put it in the door. She sat there, letting her legs stretch.

"Tell me what you've been working on. Where have you been? You still owe me a drink."

"When did we agree on that?"

"You have to agree." She stood up beside him and pointed at the dark stain on his t-shirt.

"I sweat a lot."

"I bet you do."

"Right."

"Where have you gone today?"

"I was out doing some research."

"About what?"

"You wouldn't care."

"I wouldn't ask if I didn't care." She tilted her head. "Would I?"

"I guess not."

"Good. You understand. Were you with your girlfriend?"

He'd been with Gary's girlfriend.

"I don't have one yet."

"Yet?"

"Yet."

"Then tell me why we can't have a drink? You can finally tell me about your story."

She leaned in close. He started to lean back, but he caught himself.

"You did go to the beach. Not the pool."

"What?"

"I can smell it on your hair. I can smell the water."

"Oh." She backed away and crossed her arms. "It's the same thing as the pool, really. I take a five second dip to cool off. Then I go back and lie down. I could be on the roof and take a shower. It would be the same thing."

"I see."

He opened the lock and she moved aside. Then she

followed him in and shut the door. Her swimsuit looked darker. She smiled.

"Do you like it?"

"What's that?"

"This." She took a strap and pulled it up. She snapped it.

"I guess that's a bikini, isn't it?"

"I guess it is."

"It's good for this weather."

She nodded her head and slid over to his desk. He had pages from his notebook arranged side by side. She looked down at them.

"What's all this?"

He ran over and stood between her and the desk. There wasn't much space between her and the desk. Now there was even less between her body and his.

"You're a little nosy."

"Am I?"

"You are."

"I'm sorry, Jake."

She sat back on the bed and stretched her arm out toward him.

"Come here."

He sat down beside her and she flexed her arm.

"I've been lifting weights. Do I seem strong to you?"

He felt it. Soft skin over her muscle. The rope of her tricep.

"You're doing OK."

"Good."

They both stared ahead and he remembered to let go of her arm. She pointed to the TV.

"Have you seen any other commercials like that one? The crazy one?"

"No. Not recently."

"I saw one the other night." She laid back on the bed. She looked comfortable. "They were screaming the whole time. Chanting, almost."

"Wow."

"You should write about them."

"We'll see," he said and started to get up. "I should get showered."

"Can I take a shower too?"

"What?"

"You said I smelled like the beach."

He sat back on the bed.

"You're very strange."

"That's not a nice thing to say."

"Did you get a job?"

"That's not very nice either. Now, young man, why don't you try being nice?"

She leaned in and took his face in her hands. She rested her fingers on the naked bruises. He felt her warm breath on his face and they got closer. He broke away.

"I don't understand. Why do you come on so strong?"

"Is it so hard to believe that I like you?"

"Yes," he said. "It is."

"You're an attractive man. You're used to the way people treated the old you. But you're a new man now. You should act like it."

"I don't know if I want to act like that."

"Why?"

"I don't know."

"Is there someone else?"

He stopped. He wondered how pale her skin was where the tan stopped. Then he looked at his desk. He did have work to do.

"I just think it's all so sudden."

"I'm not apologizing. I don't like to wait around."

She leaned against him and rested her head on his shoulder. He could smell the seawater in her hair. A little salty. A little sour. He brushed it with his free hand.

"There you go," she whispered. "Now, you said my arms are getting stronger. Let me get another opinion. I've been running a lot recently."

She lifted her leg and stretched it out, her toes pointing at the wall. She waited and looked at him.

"Come on. It's fitness."

The room was dark because the blinds were closed. They hadn't turned on the lights, so only thin yellow bands drew through. It looked like the running had worked out well. Why not? He was better now. He'd just run. This was why he did it all, wasn't it? To do things like this. To be this person. He was supposed to be aggressive.

While she waited, she turned her head and started to kiss his neck. He should let it happen. He deserved to let it happen. He started to turn his head and move his hand toward her outstretched leg.

The desk vibrated.

"What's that?"

"My phone."

He got up quick and shook his head side to side. He felt like he was waking up. He smelled the sweat stain on his t-shirt and the beach on her. She reached for his hand but he twisted his fingers out.

"Just give me a second."

It was Mel. Perfect timing, as always. He motioned to Kaylie to be quiet and answered the phone.

"Jake. I'm so glad you answered."

"Why? What's wrong?"

"You have to hurry. Charlotte's daughter just called. I tried to stop her, but I couldn't. I couldn't…"

"What? You couldn't stop her from what?"

"She changed her schedule. She's coming today to get the keys and see Charlotte's apartment."

"Today? When?"

"She said she'd be at my office in fifteen minutes. I can stall her a bit."

"And you have to give her the keys?"

"I can't get out of it. This is your only opportunity to see inside."

"All right, I'll hurry."
"I don't know if you'll have time."
"I'll have to try. Stall if you can."

He closed the phone and grabbed his keys from the desk. He shoved the keys, his wallet, and his phone in the back pocket of his running shorts. Kaylie looked up.

"Your bulge is in the wrong place."
"I don't have time for this."
"What is it?"
"I have to go, now. Hurry."
"Why?"
"My whole story's going to fall apart if I don't go now. Just move."

She got up and walked toward the door.

"Will you be coming back?"
"Sure, just go."

She walked out the door and he locked it and ran past her.

"What just happened?"

"This is more important," he shouted back. He was running again, bounding down the stairs. He didn't have time for pleasantries. This was his last chance to discover what Charlotte Ward had found.

CHAPTER 36:

Everything in the room was in order. Dust floated idly and the air was stale and forgotten. But everything was there, except for Charlotte Ward. And somewhere in the room, he'd find what she had discovered about the Saving Tomorrow Initiative. He just didn't know where. He shoved the key deep in his pocket. He didn't have enough time to look things over any longer. He'd left his notebook in the car—he wasn't there to observe, he was there to act.

He rushed to a secretary and pushed a row of pictures aside. Everything had to look the same when he left. He opened a drawer and looked through it while he got out his phone to call Gary.

"Hello?"

"I don't have much time. I'm in Charlotte's place."

He waited.

"Is this a telemarketer?"

"Please. It's Jake."

"From the newspaper?"

"Yes, I don't have time—"

"Jacob, hello! How are you?"

"Now listen—I'm going back to my place right after this. I want you to meet me there. We have to figure out what we'll do next."

"What have you found?"

"Nothing. Yet. I have to get to work."

He clicked the phone shut and shoved his hand into another drawer. Letters. They could be something. He read the light blue cursive on the first one. A letter from Patrick to Charlotte. Dated 1954. He wanted to read it. But there wasn't time. He put them all back into the drawer and went on to the next one.

Then he noticed the windows. The blinds were closed. He pulled one up and saw the window met the sill. Closed. Either Charlotte had closed the windows when he and Gary left, or someone else had. Maybe to muffle noise. To silence a scream.

He lifted his finger off the window sill and blew away the collected dust.

He looked around the apartment. He had to cover the living room, the bedroom, the bathroom, and the kitchen. He'd never searched a room before. He didn't know how to look. And he didn't know how resourceful Charlotte was. He hadn't brought tools or even a flashlight, but he couldn't see Charlotte lifting furniture or unscrewing a ventilator shaft in order to hide her findings. Not because of her personality, but because of her disability. That might be the best way for him to narrow down the places to look. Charlotte couldn't go too high or work too hard. Whatever she'd found was hidden somewhere in the middle, if someone else hadn't gotten to it first.

He was looking through a drawer of bills when he jumped. His phone was vibrating again. It was Mel. She whispered once he picked up.

"Are you there?"

"I'm inside. I haven't found anything yet."

"Her daughter and son in law are looking around the community right now. They hadn't visited. Typical. But I can only make them sign so much paperwork before I go and show them her residence."

"How much time do I have?"

"Not much."

"Can you warn me?"

"I'll try."

"How should we do it?"

Right after he asked her, he heard the phone click off. They must have come back inside the office. He was on his own for now, and he didn't know how long he had. The sweat stain on his t-shirt had dried, but now it was turning dark again. He had more rooms to search.

He hurried into the bedroom and turned on the light. Purple covers and purple curtains—the woman liked to match. He found an electric blanket under the bed and a TV on the dresser, nothing else. Then he spotted the drawers and stopped for a moment. When she'd come up to him that first day on the path, had she known that he'd be doing this? Searching through her life? Trying to collect a solution through the things she used to own? He started to feel a little sick. He was thirsty after a long run, without anything to drink.

He opened the first drawer and it slipped off the rollers and fell to the floor. Blouses and folded dresses poured out. He ran through them quickly and felt the different textures rub against his hands, the soft scratch of denim and the cool splash of silk. He only went through enough to make sure that there weren't any documents hidden inside, then he refolded them and picked the drawer up off the floor. He might be going through her possessions, but he still wanted to maintain the woman's dignity. And make sure he wasn't caught.

The second drawer was filled with cotton shirts, the third stacked with pants. The fourth had everything else. He sighed and shuffled through the nightgowns and underwear. Then he found something. An envelope. It was thick and labeled "Private" on the front in neat cursive loops. This could be it. He turned away from the drawer and looked inside.

"Good God!" he shouted out loud.

Abram hadn't been lying about the tasteful nudes. Charlotte didn't always need her walker. And Abram never took off his red-brimmed hat.

He left the room and slammed the door. There had been nothing inside, but if there was more, he didn't want to see it. He said "Good God" another time. Once wasn't enough. He did a quick look through the bathroom. Just toiletries and her medication. He wanted to write the medication down but he didn't have his notebook—or time. He did see everything she used to track her doses. All the timers and holders made it clear that she didn't make mistakes. Mistakes had been made for her.

He had to get through the living room, but he didn't have a lot of time to do it. He shoved his hands underneath couch cushions but didn't even find coins. He looked through all the other drawers and behind all the cabinets. Nothing. Where would Charlotte Ward have put the information? He thought for a second. Why didn't Abram know where she had put it?

He looked to the side wall and saw a series of photographs. Pictures of Charlotte's husband and family. The one thing that she and Abram probably hadn't talked about—the one secret. He pulled one down off the wall and looked at the back. Nothing taped there. He looked at the front quickly. He'd been a tall man. Thin. An open smile on his face. Not the way that Jake thought of Abram. Maybe she'd wanted a change. He looked at the man's face again and hung the picture back on its nail.

He went through them all from right to left. It started with the wedding photos, both people impossible to recognize. Nothing on the back. No documents. Then he went on to the honeymoon photograph. A woman with sun shining on her face, her identity only recognizable in the distance between her eyes, or the way they turned down at the corners. She seemed to be laughing while their picture was being taken; her husband seemed to be practicing putting his hand on her bare shoulder. There was nothing on the back.

They had lived somewhere colder. The next picture showed a child celebrating her first Christmas, with Charlotte's hands covering her ears. The back was blank. He ran his hand over her face while she was laughing, somewhere in her thirties, holding a sign that he couldn't read. Her husband was in the background holding another. He could make out the word "election" on the bottom, but the word on top was out of focus. He turned it over. Nothing.

Then he went forward. The daughter graduating from something. High school or college. Then less pictures with her, except for the one of her wedding. She looked like her mother when she wore white. Then the husband getting older. He didn't bother taking the picture down again. There was one last one of Charlotte, behind the sign for Sunset Cove. She was smiling again, leaning over the sign or her walker, looking just to the right of the camera. He took it down. Nothing.

He'd gone through her life, but he hadn't gotten what he needed. He needed to know what she'd found, not how she'd lived. He didn't have time for anything else. Where could he look where Abram hadn't been? What could he find that Abram hadn't seen?

Then he heard it. His time was already up. He heard footsteps coming down the hall and people talking. Mel's voice was the loudest and her voice carried through the thin doors and walls.

"So we'll just go right inside the apartment. We're going inside now."

She was warning him. Did it matter? Maybe there wasn't anything anyway. Charlotte Ward was just a woman who thought she'd found something. Maybe her work was nothing more than a desperate guess. Whatever it was, it didn't matter now. He heard a key jiggle in the lock. Now he had to hide. He hadn't found Charlotte's information, but that didn't mean they wouldn't find him.

CHAPTER 37:

"Did you hear that? I heard something."

A woman's voice, sounding panicked.

"Did I hear what?" Mel asked.

"A door shutting. I could have sworn I heard a slamming sound. Didn't you?"

Jake was breathing heavily inside the small coat closet. He kept his hand on the door knob and felt the metal warm underneath his palm. The daughter had a nasal voice. She was either sophisticated or congested. Then he heard the husband's voice, muffled by the door.

"I didn't hear anything, Claire." Thank God. "You imagine things sometimes."

Jake leaned against a full row of coats. Why had Charlotte brought coats to Florida? It didn't matter now. All he knew was that it was hot. Some of the coats were wool. He started to feel a tingling in his throat. He covered his mouth and listened.

"It's really very nice," the daughter, Claire, said.

"It is."

"It's one of our better units," Mel told her. "And Charlotte, obviously, kept it in very good condition."

Jake wiped his forehead. He was starting to feel itchy. He breathed in but couldn't inhale as deeply as he wanted. All the wool. Who knew how much dust there was in an unused coat closet? He scratched his throat with his thumb and a single finger.

"Mom always came up to see us. And for the funeral, of course, she came to us too. She wanted to be buried next to dad. So we never even got to come down here and learn about what she was like as a Sarasotan. Was she active?"

Once they saw Abram's photographs in the bedroom, they'd find out just how active she was.

"She was just a kind woman," Mel said. Jake smiled, barely. He realized he didn't really know if it was true. She'd shown a flash of every trait when they'd spoke, but he didn't know which one was really her. Now he just knew about the medication, the pictures, and the information that he was missing.

"This is nice," the man said.

"Dad made that. Mom loved it. We had so many of them around the house."

"Were they all ducks?"

Jake nodded. They were talking about the duck Charlotte's husband had made.

"No no," the woman said. "We had all different animals. I designed them and dad made them. But even before she moved here, mom loved water animals. Do you remember when she showed us her photo album?"

"Of course."

"So many pictures."

Jake knew Charlotte had loved animals and the wetlands. Yet she spent her last days alive investigating a group that was trying to save them. It didn't make sense. He shifted his feet and inhaled. Dust. His eyes started to water. He scratched his throat. They were too close for him to even think about coughing. But he wasn't sure if he could hold it in.

"Are you thinking about reselling?" Mel asked.

"Of course. We don't have anyone else who could take it."

"Off the record, I'd encourage you to act soon. The market here is heating up so quickly. Everyone is scrambling to develop."

"Really?"

"Oh yes. Of course, if the Development Proposition vote goes the other way, there won't be a need to hurry."

"What's that?" the woman asked. Her voice seemed softer and more tired.

"It determines whether or not developers can build on some areas that are near or on the wetlands. So if development is allowed, it might drive down prices."

"Would it happen quickly enough to affect us?"

"Mr. Rothschild works very quickly. But I shouldn't even

be saying this. He'd hate for me to talk business."

They all laughed weakly. Jake wanted to cough. Then he breathed in too quickly. His lungs filled with dust, lint, and wool. He was going to sneeze.

"What's over here?" the man said. "Is this another room?"

Step by step, Jake heard the man approach the small coat closet. He pressed his finger under his nose. He had to stop the sneeze. He winced and ducked back into the coats as far as he could, but his body still stuck out. The knob began to turn underneath his hand.

"Look!" Mel shouted.

The knob stopped.

"What's up?" the man said. The knob stayed still.

"Look at that!"

Silence. The man laughed.

"That what? What did you want me to look at?"

"The refrigerator. It...has an icemaker."

"That's very nice," the woman said. Jake heard them walk further away. The voices receded and Jake wiped his sweaty hand onto his pants.

"Can I answer any other questions?"

He lifted his finger from his nose. He was fine. For now. He felt his eyes begin to water. He couldn't stay in the closet much longer. He started to itch everywhere, and he didn't want to guess how he smelled. After a long pause, the woman spoke again.

"Thank you for your help. You've really done more than you need to."

"Well, I miss Charlotte."

"Still. You must be used to this sort of thing." The man, practicing sounding stoic.

"No. I really don't get used to it. Charlotte was a sweet person."

Silence. Jake shifted again. He heard himself wheeze. Hopefully the door was thick enough to muffle it.

"Do you hear something?" the woman asked.

Or it wasn't thick enough. He held his breath again and waited.

"Claire, you're hearing things."

"It's probably the air conditioning."

Jake exhaled, slowly. The air came out silently. He kept his hand on the knob.

"So once we leave, we are going to make it official and change the locks."

"Would you want another day or two?"

She was trying to buy him time.

"No, we'll do it as soon as possible."

She couldn't get it.

"Are you sure?"

"Yes. I have to be back at work tomorrow, so I'm afraid it's a short trip. And Claire is going to come back in a few weeks."

"I see." She'd tried at least. "When we leave, I'll have Javier come and switch the locks."

"Great."

"I have a work thing, but we'd just like to formally take possession." The woman sounded tired again. "I want to get everything cleared up here."

"That's fine," Mel said. He heard her sigh, even through the door. "I'm sorry you have to go through it."

"It's OK. I knew I'd have to."

"Still."

The group was quiet and Jake realized his phone was on. He took it out of the back pocket of his running shorts. Everything else spilled out on the floor. Naturally. He inhaled and tried to hold his breath.

"I heard another noise."

"Chimes." Mel said. "Should I show you the bedroom?"

Saved. This was it. This was his only chance to get out. But he hadn't found what Charlotte had discovered. He exhaled. This was where it ended. Finding nothing. Just breathing in some dust and looking at some pictures. Whatever Charlotte had found about the Saving Tomorrow Initiative, she had hid it too well.

He stooped down and picked up the keys. He put them in his back pocket. Then he picked up his wallet. He didn't understand. What else was there that Abram wouldn't have known about? He'd looked at every picture. Gone through every drawer. There had to be an answer somewhere. But he didn't know how to find it.

Footsteps. The sound of a door opening. He couldn't be sure that they had all entered the room. Then Mel gave him some help.

"Good, we're all in," she shouted. She was a good accomplice.

As he put his wallet back into his pocket, he noticed a piece of cardboard sticking out. In the darkness he couldn't tell what it was, so he drew it out. Cardboard and thin colored plastic. He'd forgotten about them: the 3-D glasses Gary gave him. He put them back in the wallet and shoved it in his pocket. Then he almost screamed.

3-D. Why hadn't he thought of it before? He'd looked at the backs of pictures. But he hadn't thought about looking on the inside. He wiped the sweat from his forehead and stifled one last cough. 3-D. It made perfect sense. He opened the closet door and started running to the hallway.

As he ran, he dropped down his right hand. He opened the doorknob with his left and didn't break his stride. With his right hand he grabbed the neck of Charlotte's wooden duck. He picked the duck up and clutched it close to the sweat stain on his chest. He pulled the door shut behind him and kept running until he reached his car.

CHAPTER 38:

He waited until he was in his apartment building's parking lot before he tried anything, since he couldn't be caught in Sunset Cove handling a former resident's possessions. He drove as quickly as he could, the duck in the passenger seat of the car, wobbling slightly with every turn.

It was painted dark green and had an orange bill. He looked over and saw the long neck teeter under the movement of the head, the duck staying upright thanks to the balance of the wide base. He watched Sunset Cove, then the Palmstead, sink under the horizon as he drove along the highway. He was still breathing deep, even though he'd finished running hours before. He wondered how high his pulse was after a day like this.

He called Mel as he drove. He knew they wouldn't be able to talk long, even though he wanted to. She answered after one ring.

"Did you make it?"

"Yeah. Barely. Thanks to you."

"Did you find anything?"

"I don't know yet. But I think I did."

He was closer to his apartment and pulled down the off-ramp.

"I want to see you next time."

"What about tomorrow? I can show you what I found. If I found anything."

"I can't." She paused. "Oh wait, I can. I thought I had something, but I don't."

"What?"

"We normally have movie night then. But Sheryl is changing her second bridge night this week. So the common room is full."

"Second bridge night?"

"They play twice a week now."

"So you're free?"

"Yes."

"I'll see you then."

"Good luck."

"Thanks. I'll need it."

He got to his building and sped into a parking space. He pulled on the tight neck of his t-shirt and opened the windows as he idled. No one else was in the lot—it was just him and empty cars. He unbuckled himself, then he released the duck and set it on his lap. He turned it over to the bottom. He read the neat loops of cursive, ones that he recognized from the letters he'd found.

"From Patrick to Charlotte, 1974."

He traced over the writing with his hand. Her husband had been able to carve inside of things, he remembered Charlotte telling him. The only problem was figuring out how to open it. He looked around the base of the duck. There weren't any obvious holes or doors. Just the writing. But at the bottom of the neck he noticed a thin black line.

He grabbed the bill on the duck's head and started to jiggle it. When he pulled up and down it didn't give. Then he pushed it right. It twitched. Then left. The neck began to turn all the way around, and the duck's head revolved around its body. He kept turning, and like a screw it unwound from the base.

Papers fell out as he pulled the head away. They were rolled up tight and bound by a thin rubber band. Whatever Charlotte had, he'd found it. He peeled off the rubber band and the sound twanged inside the car. He unrolled the pages and placed them on his lap.

The first one was predictable. A bridge schedule for the past three months. He knew that Charlotte would try to tie it back to bridge. Now that he'd found it, it all seemed a little sadder. He looked. It was a schedule for the week—the days Sheryl had slighted her. Monday and Thursday she played in the common room. Charlotte had marked both of them with an X. Jake didn't want to look at it long. He wanted to get to what she'd found—not what she'd imagined. There was a real conspiracy behind the one she was obsessed with. It was called the Saving Tomorrow Initiative.

He found them on the next page. It was a call log. She'd written down a phone number and a series of times and dates next to it. She'd been calling, trying to find out their agenda. Each time, the log read "no answer," except for the last call.

Reached Initiative. I talked to a man. He said to stop calling. I asked him why. He said he knew who I was. I said I knew who he was too. He hung up on me. Will research more...

She made the call the day before she died. Seeing the three dots in a line chilled him. They were like goose bumps on the page. Why wasn't there more? He turned the paper over.

She'd recorded everything she'd tried to find out about the Initiative. The problem was that she hadn't found much. Apparently, the group was less than a year old. She couldn't get any financial information. The articles of incorporation listed a P.O. Box outside Sarasota as the address. A dead end. They weren't in any charitable directories or listings. All she'd found was that phone number and whoever was on the other end of the line. And then they'd found her.

Jake took out his phone and impulsively turned it on. He saw his thumb shake as he pressed each number. Area code. Then three more. He looked at the paper—Charlotte had last called the day before she died. Four more digits. It started to ring. Again. Then a click. Was that it?

A recording played.

"You have reached the Saving Tomorrow Initiative." It was the voice of the woman from the commercial. "Please vote against the Development Proposition. Humans must learn their place. If they don't, we will show them. This war is just beginning."

A beep. He clamped the phone shut. He wasn't ready to leave a message when it was a matter of life and death. There was only one other page left. He unrolled it and flattened it on his lap. It was just a series of questions. Some had checkmarks

next to them. Some didn't.
Why did Sheryl keep me out of bridge?
She didn't know. But he did. Abram.
How can I get back in?
Checked. He sighed. More bridge.
What is the Saving Tomorrow Initiative?
Checked.
What do they do?
Checked.
How are they funded?
Checked.
How do they connect to Sheryl?

There were wrinkles in the page, but it was checked. She knew a lot more than he did, and she'd even figured out the connection, if there was one. If only she'd written it down. Jake was sweating as he read the last three questions. It was a cold sweat.

Why am I being threatened?
Checked.
What will they do to stop me?
Checked.
He rolled the page up after the last question.
Can I stop them?
It was blank. But he knew the answer.

He bound the pages together and carefully slipped the rubber band around them. He'd gotten a phone number. And now he knew that the Saving Tomorrow Initiative had threatened her. But he had the same questions that Charlotte did. He twisted the neck back onto the base of the duck. How did Sheryl connect? How was the group funded? And what were they trying to do?

He also had a few questions of his own. Who had attacked him? Why had they done it? He wondered if he could escape when Charlotte hadn't.

It was enough for one morning. He wasn't tired, but he didn't want to think about any of it for a while. He decided to go inside the apartment and rest. Maybe he'd even research Thompson's celebrity article. There was nothing wrong with having a diversion. Melinda Ginelli wasn't bad to look at, and he still had a job. If this was all Charlotte had found, he was starting to doubt that he'd have a real story. He screwed the neck of the duck back on and shut the windows.

The exhaustion didn't fully set in until he reached the stairs to his apartment. They seemed to multiply now that he was tired. He took each wide step one at a time, the wallet, keys, and phone in his back pocket bulging like a pulled muscle. He felt hot again. He couldn't wait to go inside and finally take his shower.

He put the key in the lock and turned it. Then he opened the door.

The first thing he felt was something pulling at his shoulder. His t-shirt ripped. Then he tripped on the divider between the door and the living room. Something shoved down his head and pressed a cold boot down on his neck. He dropped the duck and his keys fell from his pocket. He heard the sound of duct tape being pulled out from a roll and ripped. His wrists were pulled tight together and bound and the gray tape covered his mouth. He tasted and smelled fresh glue.

He tried to twist his body up, but the foot on his neck had dragged down to his back. Then he felt the tape start to rip his hair. He closed his eyes. He couldn't open them again. They were taped shut. He tried to scream but he couldn't open his mouth. Then he couldn't even do that. Someone taped his ankles together and he felt another hit to the back of his head.

The last thing he felt was a sense of déjà vu. Once again, everything was black.

CHAPTER 39:

It was the second time that day that Jake was stuck inside a closet, assuming he was inside a closet. He couldn't really know. But when he tried to kick his legs out, he felt something hard stop them. It could have been a car trunk. Or a box. Anything. It didn't really matter since he couldn't get out. Because of the duct tape, he could only breathe through his nose. He was glad he didn't have a cold.

He had time to think about what had happened. He hadn't seen anything, only a blur of shadows and colors. All he could remember was wincing. It was different than on the beach. The hits were lighter and faster. And whoever it was had tried to attack him anywhere they could. It was different in other ways, too—this time he hadn't been rescued. He pushed his legs hard against the wall. Nothing gave. He was too tired to try to kick it open.

Then he heard a voice.

"He's out cold."

He'd recognize it anywhere. Kaylie.

"Do you think I'd even call you if he was conscious? I'm alone now, yeah. But he's locked in the closet. And he won't wake up any time soon."

She was on the phone. Someone else must have knocked him out and left her to finish the job—she was strong, but not that strong. Or that big. She sounded more serious than normal, and definitely more afraid.

"I told you, it's just me. We tied him up."

He tried to sit up and did. He wasn't as sore as when he'd been attacked on the beach. Maybe he hadn't been hit as hard. Or maybe he was used to it. He didn't want to be used to getting attacked. Kaylie spoke again and sounded closer to the closet.

"No. Nothing. We looked through his wallet. Just money and credit cards. The last outgoing call on his phone was to you. Did you get it?"

He nodded. His last outgoing call had been to the Saving Tomorrow Initiative's line. They must have had Caller ID and known not to answer his number.

"Yeah. I'm going to leave the note on the bed."

She was going to leave. Would she let him go?

"I'll call his editor in twenty minutes. Yeah, I'll do it from the payphone. He'll send somebody over."

Jake almost laughed. It might be worth it to make Thompson help him. Then he'd get to write his story, too. When Kaylie spoke again she sounded angrier.

"No. He doesn't have a girlfriend."

A pause.

"No, he doesn't. He liked me."

He could hear her pacing across his carpet.

"Whatever. I'm calling the editor. They should know anyway…Yes, I know you're my boss…Yes, I know. But he doesn't have a girlfriend."

Jake tried to lean closer to the door without letting her know he was awake. He pressed his ear against something. He hoped it was in the right direction.

"I know," she said. "I just would like to tell him."

Tell him what?

"It's fine. He'll figure it out when I'm gone. I already packed everything. I just wish he knew…"

He tasted the glue on the duct tape and tried twisting his hands free, but they were bound too tight. He barely had circulation. He realized his legs were taped at the knees as well.

"I told you, that was all he had. He was carrying an old wooden duck too. But he didn't have any information about you, or anything like that."

If he could breathe he would have sighed. She hadn't figured out how to open the duck. He still had that. At least he could write his story when all of this was over. And he was going to make sure to include her in it.

"OK. I'll leave now…don't worry. I won't."

Silence. He heard her moving around the room and wondered if she wore her bikini for this type of job. Or shoes. Then he heard the closet door open. He slouched back as quickly as possible. Something warm was near his face. A hand. He stayed still so she wouldn't know he was awake. Then her mouth was down at his ear.

"I'm sorry, Jake. I didn't want to, but they made me."

Soft. Her lips against his temple, just for a second. Then she closed the door. He jerked back up to plant his ear against it and heard a knocking sound.

There was another knock. Then another. It started getting faster and faster.

"Damn it," Kaylie said. The knocking continued and he heard a deep voice that sounded garbled.

"Mr. Russo, this is the police! Open up!"

More knocks, then everything happened quickly. He heard the outer door open. Another sound. And then Kaylie screamed as the outer door slammed shut.

"Stop!" she screamed. "Stop, stop."

"Where is my friend Jacob?"

He couldn't believe it, but Gary Novak was in the apartment. Kaylie screamed again.

"He's here. Please, just stop."

"I'll stop, but you show me where he is."

"How am I supposed to show you where he is when I can't see?"

"Where is he?"

"Over there, over there."

Jake heard the closet door open. Then he screamed through the tape. All the hair on his wrists had just been ripped off. Gary grabbed his hands.

"Jacob, I took the tape on your wrists off very quickly. Like you do with a band-aid. Otherwise you'd never get it off."

Before he could stop him, Gary grabbed at his cheek. The tape ripped away from his mouth and he screamed. He wouldn't have to worry about shaving. Maybe ever again.

"How did you get here? What's happening?"
"Just wait. We have to get to your eyes."
"No."
"We have no choice."

Jake lifted his hands to his eyes and blocked Gary, barely in time.

"The tape on my eyes will come off slow. I like having eyebrows."

"Fine." He sounded disappointed.

"Where's Kaylie? Don't let her leave."

"You know this girl?"

"Yes." He ripped the tape off his ankles. "At least I thought I did."

"Well, we're going to learn a lot more."

"How's that?"

"She isn't going anywhere."

"How do you know?"

"Trust me."

"Can you get me a wash cloth and wet it. I need to get this tape off my eyes before she escapes."

"I can just rip it off. I'm strong enough"

"No." He pushed his hands in the direction of Gary's voice.

Gary got him the washcloth and he wet his face. Water leaked in and the tape started to loosen.

"Scissors?"

Gary handed them over. Jake pulled the tape out and cut by his nose. Then he slowly peeled it away. He rubbed his eyes and felt the glue still stuck to his skin in a thin layer.

"All right. Do you see the tape she used?"

Kaylie finally said something.

"I'll just go. I'm sorry."

He looked over. Her eyes were shut and her face was covered in something brown. She was wearing shorts and a t-shirt, just like the first day he saw her.

"Oh no," he said. "You aren't getting off that easy."

He found her purse and grabbed it. A half roll of tape was

inside. She tried to kick when he bound her ankles. She was barefoot, of course. And she was strong, but not strong enough. He leaned over her and grabbed her arms while he pressed down her legs. He taped them tight, but not as tightly as they'd bound him. She couldn't leave now.

"Did you get her, Jacob?"

"I got her."

"Good. I brought another washcloth for your eyes."

He rubbed it against his face. Removing the sticky substance was like cleaning up spilled soda. He rubbed his red hands and ankles. He was still wearing the dirty sweat stained t-shirt. It was ripped now, too. He limped to his desk and got his notebook. Predictably, she'd gone through it. He picked up a pen and started writing. After a few lines, he looked up at Kaylie.

"You're in trouble."

"You don't understand."

"Well, I'm going to," he said. "Gary, sit down. We're going to find out what happened."

CHAPTER 40:

"First, get this mace off of my eyes."

Her eyes were still shut tightly and her hair was stuck to the front of her forehead. A lump pulsed next to her temple. Jake picked her up and set her on the bed. Then he leaned toward Gary.

"What did you do to her? And how did you have mace?"

"I didn't have a mace. Where would I put it?"

"Mace, Gary. You know what mace is, right?"

"I didn't have that. I sprayed her, then I hit her with my cane."

"You hit her with your cane?"

"It's from Ethiopia." He rapped it against the floor. "I'm sure the tribes use it as a spear, on occasion."

"But what did you spray her with?"

"Yeah," Kaylie said. She coughed. Then she licked around her lips. "Wait—is that…"

Gary handed a bottle to Jake and he read the label.

"Please tell me why you have a bottle of Dark Chocolate Body Spray."

Kaylie slowly opened her eyes.

"I thought it was chocolate."

"Yes. I visited Sheryl Goldfein before I came here. I wanted to apologize for misleading her."

"With chocolate body spray?"

"No. Sheryl gave it to me. She said she wouldn't be needing it. And she said I might want to use it with Meryl."

"Oh." Jake wished his eyes were taped shut again. "Will you, uh, use it?"

"I don't understand it. Is it a new type of suntan lotion? Wouldn't it attract flies?"

Jake unscrewed the top of the bottle.

"I'll take that as a no."

He poured the full bottle into his mouth and swished the liquid around. He'd earned it. Trapped twice and knocked out once, he'd burned enough calories for this. It was a rich, almost bitter flavor, and he felt it stick in the back of his cheeks. Thick and full. It was like breathing fresh air. Kaylie tilted her head.

"Don't relapse."

"Don't tell me what to do. You have some explaining ahead of you. And you should enjoy the chocolate you got. I don't know how much they'll give you in prison, but it can't be a lot."

She frowned. Jake saw a trail of water trace a line through the dried chocolate on her cheek. He laughed.

"Like I believe you're actually crying."

"Jake, I'm sorry." She sighed. "I didn't want to do it. I didn't want any of this to happen. But they said I had to."

"Who's they?"

Gary pointed his cane at her.

"Exactly!"

"My employers." She looked at Jake again. "Please believe me."

"Gary, come with me."

Jake pulled Gary into the bathroom and shut the door. He washed the chocolate from the corner of his lips and whispered into Gary's ear.

"Listen. We'll get the information out of her. But we have to do it quickly. We should play good cop, bad cop. Now, I'll be the good cop. She likes me, I think. Gary, you be the bad cop. We'll get the information out of her somehow."

"I'm sorry. I didn't hear any of that."

"You're the bad cop, I'm the good cop."

Gary nodded. They left the bathroom one at a time.

"Here," Jake said and walked over to Kaylie. He dabbed her face with a washcloth and her skin softened to its normal tan.

"We need your help."

"I can't tell you anything."

Jake looked over at Gary. Gary blinked and nodded.

"Miss, you look very nice today. You are not a bad person at all."

"Gary. Really?"

"Oh no!" He hit his head with his hand. "I forgot which cop I was. I'm the good cop, right?"

"Well, it doesn't matter now."

"You don't look nice today!" Gary shouted. "You are a bad person! Very bad!"

"Gary, it won't work now."

"I'm sorry."

Jake sat beside her on the bed. She tried to lean into him, but he pushed her away. Then he noticed the note in the middle of the bed. He picked it up and read it out loud.

"The Saving Tomorrow Initiative was here. For millennia, nature has suffered. This is just the beginning of what we are willing to do."

Kaylie pressed her head into her chest. He grabbed her chin and pushed it up.

"This doesn't make sense. Why would you advertise that you were the ones who kidnapped me? Why would you leave this note?"

"I don't know, I don't know."

"Tell me."

"They don't tell me why." She jerked her head away. "I don't know why they did it. Probably because they are crazy. I didn't know when I started all this. When I started it was…different."

"What was different?"

She looked away.

"A lot."

"You aren't part of their organization?"

Gary rapped his cane on the floor.

"Gary, it's fine. She'll answer."

"I saw an advertisement in the paper. It said they needed an actress or a model. They wanted someone who was dedicated. So I went in for an interview. I'd just lost my job."

She looked down at the duct tape binding together her ankles.

"They said they'd get me an apartment. I needed one. So I took it."

"And what was your job?"

"You were. They said a reporter lived next door. They wanted me to get him to write a story about their group, any story. The rest of the time I could do what I wanted. It was a great job, great pay."

"I pay well, I guess."

"But then they said there was more. I had to start keeping tabs on you. Telling them when you were coming and going. When you left. Who you were hanging out with. Everything about you. I turned into a spy. But they gave me a raise. So it was something."

"How could you do this with a straight face?"

"I had to. It was my job."

"You didn't have to do anything."

"Jacob," Gary interrupted. "Let her speak."

They all waited until she started again.

"When you said you were going to meet someone on the beach, I told them. I didn't think it would matter. I thought they'd just watch for you. I had no idea that they'd attack you. That they'd…"

"Just continue."

She did.

"I had no idea that they would go that far. After that happened, after I saw you, I realized that they must have done it. I told them that I wanted to quit. I couldn't do it any more."

"You did enough."

"I know."

She leaned on him and he let her. Then she sat back up.

"Is he asleep?"

Gary was snoring, lightly.

"Gary, are you awake?"

He jerked up.

"I was working."

"On what?"

"You've never heard of 'good cop, asleep cop?'"

"No Gary, I haven't."

Kaylie tried to fold up her legs, but she couldn't because of the tape.

"I told them I wanted to stop. But they said it was too late. Things had already gone too far. You'd already found out too much. So they decided to change their plan and become more...aggressive."

"I see."

"I didn't do anything. But they had me call as soon as you left. Then he came over."

"Who?"

"Roderick. You've seen him before, haven't you?"

"Is he the bearded man?"

"Yes."

"I've seen him in the commercials. He attacked me?"

"Yes. He saw the same posting in the paper. Apparently he's had experience with this sort of thing."

"And you just stood there?"

"I didn't have a choice. You've seen how dangerous they are."

"I've felt how dangerous they are."

"I know."

She turned to him and leaned into his body. She kicked out her legs, barefoot as always.

"Can you forgive me?"

He laughed out loud for the first time in a while.

"Oh no. You've told me what happened. Now you have to tell us what you know."

CHAPTER 41:

He got a glass of water from the kitchen. He was going to give it to Kaylie, but he ended up drinking it first to wash down the chocolate. It was still thick in his throat, coating it completely. He got ice and put half in the water glass and half in a bag to soothe his fresh wounds. He went back in the room.

Gary was standing guard at the door while Kaylie sat on the bed. Jake gave her the water and Gary started jerking his leg.

"My foot was falling asleep."

He shook his leg out. Jake sat down and looked at him until he finished shaking.

"How did you know that I'd been kidnapped?"

"Because you had duct tape on your eyes and mouth."

"No, I mean when you were outside. You knocked a couple of times. Then you said you were the police. How did you know to say that?"

"I saw your car outside when I arrived. And you've never been late before. I knew that something was wrong."

"I'm impressed."

"I could sense it, Jacob. I could smell the fear, like a sinister bacon."

"OK. Don't ruin it."

They stopped and looked at Kaylie. She sulked like she felt forgotten. Jake sat beside her again.

"We need to know more. Do you know who attacked me on the beach? I don't think it was the bearded man. It felt…different."

"I don't know."

"You don't know?"

"I told you." She breathed in. Calmed down. "They didn't tell me they were going to do anything. They just did it. I didn't know that any of this was going to happen."

"But you know that someone else was involved, right?"

"Yes." She adjusted her body on the bed and sat up straighter. "There was someone who I never met. Normally I worked with Roderick. But whenever I made a phone call, it was another person. That's who I interviewed with, too."

"Male or female?"

"It was a man. He was always very formal. He just gave me directions."

"What did he sound like?"

"I don't remember. His voice wasn't distinctive. Deep, I guess."

"Nothing?"

"No." She bit her lip. "I just remembered. When I called to tell them you were going to the beach, I spoke with him."

"So it was him?"

"I don't know. But he was always the person I talked to."

He turned the page in his notebook. He'd already filled a few pages recording what she said. As he started writing again, Gary rapped his cane on the floor.

"I don't understand this. It doesn't make sense, what you are saying. Why would this group want Jacob to write about them and then do all these terrible things to him? Why would they threaten him?"

She looked up at him.

"I don't know. They wanted publicity?"

"But why would they want that kind of publicity?"

She shook her head and Jake turned to Gary.

"You're right. It just doesn't make sense that they would do this. Why would they draw attention to themselves and to their practices?"

"Do you think they knew you discovered what happened to Charlotte?"

Kaylie tilted her head.

"Who's Charlotte?"

Jake ignored her.

"But they killed Charlotte. Why did they just threaten me? Kidnap me? If they wanted me to stop writing about them, they could have handled it better."

"Maybe they didn't get a chance. They tried to kill you, but you got away."

"But I didn't get away. I was trapped right here. It doesn't make sense."

Kaylie's face had changed from brown to red. They could see the duct tape ripple slightly because her hands were shaking.

"What are you guys talking about? Who is Charlotte?"

"You didn't know?"

"No, who is she? What is this? What happened?"

Jake put his hand on her shoulder.

"I believe the Saving Tomorrow Initiative took her life. She was a resident at Sunset Cove."

Gary stared at Jake.

"Should you be telling her about this?"

"She didn't know."

She plunged her head into Jake's shoulder. He let her. Her hair was soft and he put his arm around her. Slowly, he started to smell chocolate rising from her face. She stopped shaking after a while and lifted her face from his chest. She whispered to him.

"You smell terrible."

"I never got to take a shower."

"I can tell."

She sat back up. She couldn't wipe the tears with her hands, so she waited for them all to fall off of her face.

"That's really all I know. I told you everything. And I didn't know they killed somebody."

Gary coughed.

"Jacob, we can't let her go. She'll tell the group."

"And then what? They'll want me to write another story? They aren't going to kill me. They just want publicity."

"But it will be bad publicity!"

"Maybe they want people to know they're serious. It makes sense—look at their commercials. All bluster. They want to scare people into voting for them, and they don't realize it does more harm than good."

Kaylie sniffled.

"I promise you, I will never talk to them again."

"Where will you go?"

"I'm staying with a friend. They kicked me out of my apartment."

"Do you have money?"

"Enough."

"Are you sure?"

"Sure enough."

Gary nodded and Jake got the scissors. He cut loose her ankles and pulled the tape off for her. He started slow but then decided it would be better to go fast. She breathed in quickly when he did it, but she didn't scream. He wrapped his hands around her wrists and cut away the tape. Then he grabbed her legs and cut her knees free. She curled up as soon as he drew the scissors away.

"I'm sorry."

"You should go."

"No." She stood up. "I want to help you. I don't know much, but I can help. I want to. Please, just trust me."

Gary crossed his arms and shrugged. Jake didn't know what to do. She still had red eyes and was rubbing her wrists with her hands. She touched his arm.

"Will you trust me?"

She touched a bruised spot near his ear, from when he'd been attacked. He grabbed her hand and pulled it away.

"There are two things you can do."

"What? Just let me know and I'll do them."

"Don't tell anyone what you told me. Don't tell this guy Roderick, don't tell the woman, and don't tell the man who you spoke to. Whoever he is."

She nodded her head eagerly. He hadn't seen her excited before. It wasn't like her.

"What's the other thing I can do? How else can I help?"

He got up off the bed and looked at her.

"You packed all your stuff?"

"It's already moved to my friend's place."
"Then you can do one thing."
"What?"
He backed away and stood next to Gary.
"You can leave."
She put her hands on her hips and yelled back at him.
"You can't do that. I know that you liked me. And I really liked you."
"When you were getting paid."
She lowered her voice.
"No, not just then. I liked you because you cared. Because you weren't like other guys."
"How?"
She pushed her hair behind her ears and whispered.
"You respected me."
"How?"
"You didn't just come on to me or take advantage of me. You respected me."
She walked closer to him, but he looked at the floor as she came forward. Gary grabbed the back of Jake's shirt.
"I don't want to interfere."
"What is it?"
"But you need somebody who respects you. Anyone who would let this happen to you is somebody you can't trust."
She walked closer to him and grabbed his belt by the buckle.
"I mean it. I can stay here, with you. We'll work together."
Gary coughed and tugged at Jake's shirt again.
"Jacob, I know somebody who's always worked with you. Who took risks before she got fired, not after."
She pressed her body close to his. He put his hands around her waist and touched the skin between her t-shirt and her shorts. He looked at that pixie haircut and then in her eyes again.
"I believe you. But that's going to have to be enough for you. If we had anything, at all, then there's only one thing you can do."

"Leave," she said and tilted her head. "I guessed it. Didn't I?"

He nodded. She backed away from him and stepped to his side. He watched her go by one last time as she walked to the door. She still swung her hips like she was testing to see if they worked.

They did.

Just not well enough.

CHAPTER 42:

When he was alone, he called the number. What he didn't expect was an answer.

Gary left a few minutes after Kaylie did. Then Jake got out the duck. He unscrewed the neck from the base and unrolled all the papers, including the phone log of Charlotte's calls to the Saving Tomorrow Initiative. Calling again was worth a try, even if he got a machine. He still had work to do.

His story should have been wrapped up. He had a note, plans, and a veritable confession. He didn't know how much of it he could print without risking libel. He could at least tell the story truthfully. But he knew it wasn't finished. He dialed the seven numbers and waited to hear the answering machine. Except he didn't.

"Hello, friend. It's a surprise to hear from you again."

The voice laughed. It was unnaturally deep—it sounded like someone had placed a filter on the receiver. Jake pressed the tip of his pen hard against the paper.

"Who are you? What's your agenda?"

"Do you want my Social Security number too?"

The voice laughed.

"Who are you?"

"I am a representative of the Saving Tomorrow Initiative."

"I'm looking at the closet where I was tied up, and I'm not happy. Why did you answer?"

"Because I wanted to." The voice laughed again. For being anonymous, it was confident. "You can't scare us away. You can write whatever story you want. But we will still let the voters know that if they choose to strike at nature, they will suffer the consequences."

"Who are you? I asked you once."

"You know who we are and what we have done. Even a reporter like you can figure that out."

It laughed again. Jake bit his pen and decided to say it. He had to. The voice was still laughing when he spoke.

"If you think you'll get away with what you did to Charlotte Ward, you're wrong."

The laughter stopped.

"What?"

"You heard me. Beating up a reporter may not get you in trouble. But I'm telling the police what happened to Charlotte."

Silence.

"What do you know?"

This time Jake didn't talk. He realized that he'd said too much. They thought that he only knew about their scare tactics. Not that Charlotte had been murdered.

"What do you know?" the voice repeated.

"Nothing."

It was too late.

"Let's meet," the voice said. "We can discuss this. You said you were at your apartment? Stay right where you are."

"Why?"

"Just stay there."

Jake hung up the phone. This time they wouldn't let him live to write a story. He turned off his laptop and put it in a bag. Then he got out his phone to call Gary. He didn't wait to say hello.

"Listen. I have to come and stay with you. The Saving Tomorrow Initiative is coming for me. They didn't realize I knew about Charlotte's murder."

"What do you think will happen?"

"Now the publicity is too bad. I think they want to do to me what they did to her."

"Hurry, Jacob!"

His phone rang again. It was the number of the group. He answered and the voice spoke.

"If you want your story, stay there Mr. Russo. We just want to talk."

He hung up. He grabbed his bag and ran outside to the parking lot, bounding down the stairs as quickly as he could.

He jumped the last three. Then he reached his car and started driving. He was halfway down the block when he looked over to the empty passenger seat.

He'd forgotten Charlotte's duck.

He had to go back. He parked the car and got out. It was starting to get darker, and he could hardly see his apartment building in the dusk. He walked quickly and reached the stairs, ran up, and unlocked his door. He shut and locked it quickly. The duck was still on his desk. He picked it up and stepped forward.

Then he heard the lock on his door start to click. The handle began to turn.

He gasped and ducked behind the door. He was breathing deep. He could feel himself sweating again as the door opened. He grabbed the duck close to his body and felt the wood splinter against his hands.

"Mr. Russo…"

A higher voice than the phone, but still deep enough to chill him. He couldn't place it. The door opened further and started to press against him. He watched a hulking shadow flatten out onto the bed. Jake's arm shook. Wedged in the spot between the door and the wall, he wouldn't stay hidden long.

The body walked toward the bathroom. A man wearing a ski mask and dark knit cap came into view. And he wore a trench coat, just like at the beach. Tall and slow moving, he lumbered forward and extended his neck in the direction of the bathroom and kitchen. Any moment he'd look back and see Jake. He had to make a break for it before it was too late.

He jumped out from behind the door and tripped before he could run outside. He got up and heard the man shout at him. Then he felt a hand grabbing on the back of his shirt. But he could run fast enough. He kept going and pulled the door handle behind him. He slammed the door and heard a scream and the sound of fingers crunching. He opened the door and slammed it shut. Then he tried to move forward. He couldn't. The back of his t-shirt was stuck inside the door.

He jiggled the knob and heard a click. Locked. He couldn't reopen the door. He was trapped with the duck in his hands. He just had to wait.

Unless he didn't. He dropped the duck and pulled his arms inside the sleeves. He got the right one in and then fit the left, his arms pressing against the sides of the shirt. He shrank down and began to slip out of the shirt as the man in the apartment yelled. He pulled his arms out and let the shirt drop as he picked up the duck and started running.

When he reached the bottom of the stairs, the door opened and the shirt fell down. Jake stopped looking back and ran forward, sprinting as fast as he could to the car. He held the duck close to his body and pulled his keys from his shorts pocket. He fumbled to fit them into the door lock and then he looked back. The black shape was running toward him. He heard the trench coat flapping in the wind.

He threw the duck in the passenger seat and felt the splinters scrape off of his bare chest. He slammed the door and turned the key in the ignition. The man grabbed the side mirror with gloved hands and tried to stop him. Jake accelerated and the mirror ripped off with a crack. He looked back. The man was left there holding it in his hand, shaking his head. He tied the trench coat around his waist as the car pulled away. Jake had time to breathe again. He ran a red light and drove up the on-ramp to the highway.

Ahead of him, the road was long and dark. He'd gotten everything out. He stopped shaking and started focusing on the road. That was it. His apartment was gone. He'd made it out. The only problem was that he couldn't go back.

CHAPTER 43:

"Jacob, when you said you wanted to stay here—"
"You assumed I'd be wearing a shirt?"
"Yes."
"You were wrong."

He was standing in front of Gary Novak's door, shirtless, with a wooden duck clutched to his chest. The scent of Febreeze and garlic wafted out the doorway and onto his body. He let it soak in. He was glad Sarasota was warm. It might have been the first time. He started to explain why he was shirtless, but Gary waved him off.

"Hurry—Meryl can't find out that you're here."
"Why not?"
"I'll get in trouble."
"Did you tell her I was staying here?"

Gary shrugged and pointed his cane at the garage.

"I'm staying in your photo lab?"
"She never comes in there. I set up one of our nicest cots."

He went into the garage and set the duck down on the floor. It would be good enough. He stared at the cameras hanging on the wall and all the brightly colored prints. At least he was safe. He explained to Gary what had happened—the man, the pursuit, how he had barely escaped capture. Gary shook his head.

"They didn't realize you'd discovered about Charlotte's murder?"
"No. Like an idiot, I tipped them off."
"What do we do now?"
"We just try to get the story out as quickly as possible. Then something will change. After that, I'll call the cops and we'll be done."
"You can work here as long as you want."

He set up his laptop on a metal desk. Gary closed the door and Jake spread everything out. It was just like at home. Except for the disinfectant and development fluid.

He called Thompson. It was worth bothering him this time.

"Who is it?" Thompson growled. "I'm about to go have my steak."

"It's Jake."

"Russo? Did you take my steak?"

A long laugh, as usual. Jake waited a few seconds.

"Listen. The story is bigger than I ever thought it would be."

"She dyed her hair red?"

"What?"

"Melinda! Melinda Ginelli. Do you have a...a scoop for us?"

"I haven't started your celebrity piece."

"Russo! I need something soon."

"I have something much bigger. Someone is out for my life, Thompson. I have the story on these environmentalists nailed down and ready to go. Tonight they tried to kill me, so I'm going to make sure they don't get away with it. I'll write it tonight. It's huge news."

"Russo, I want Melinda Ginelli." He paused and laughed. "I want a story about her too!"

"I know, but this is more important."

"No it's not. Do you understand?"

"Thompson, listen. Will you do this?"

"You get me my story about Melinda Ginelli and I'll be a happy man."

"But will you print mine? About the group? The Saving Tomorrow Initiative?"

"We'll talk about it when I see it."

"Great."

"And Russo, remember."

"Remember what? To be careful? Make sure to document my sources?"

"Remember to...to ask Melinda about her favorite type of guy! You always forget the good stuff."

"All right."

It wasn't perfect, but he had the go ahead. He opened his notebook and had started looking through his notes when Gary came in.

"Jacob, you can use this."

He laid a shirt out on the desk. It was light blue and two sizes too small. Gary looked up and Jake held the shirt in front of him.

"Won't this be a little…tight?"

"It won't be tight. It's fitted."

"But you're at least a foot shorter than I am."

"I stoop. I have a cane."

"Gary, come on."

"Jacob, I'm surprised."

"About what?"

"You have hair on your chest."

"You didn't think I'd have hair on my chest?"

"I don't know, I just…"

"That's enough. If this shirt rips, I'm not responsible."

He grabbed the shirt and put it on. It wouldn't rip in the back. But he had to leave the top two buttons undone. The collar flared out like he was going to a disco. If he'd worn his shirts like this before, Gary wouldn't have been surprised that he had chest hair. Half his chest was still showing.

"Can I get you anything else?"

"Maybe tomorrow we could go back to my apartment. Would you mind coming with me? I'd just like to get some things."

"Like what?"

"Clothes."

"You can have as many as you want. I have many different styles."

"Right." The shirt sleeves pinched his arms. "Thank you."

"Is there anything else?"

"No, I'm good. Thank you for taking me in. I know it seems sudden, but my rear view mirror was literally ripped off. I could have died."

"Ah." Gary sighed. "Street gangs."

"No Gary, it wasn't 'street gangs.' Remember, the Initiative chased me."

"Oh, right." He started to go walk the door then turned back to Jake. "I still don't understand all of it."

"He broke in to my place. And once they realized I'd figured out what happened to Charlotte, they wanted to kill me."

"Right. But I don't understand. Why didn't they kill you before then?"

Jake laughed.

"Thanks."

"But, Jacob, am I right in saying it does not make sense?"

"What doesn't?"

"Why would they let you write a story that would ruin their group? A story that would ruin their reputation in the community?"

"I just think they are so delusional, they didn't realize how bad they looked."

Gary clicked his tongue against his teeth and shook his head again. He patted down his frizzed hair and looked like he was concentrating.

"Something doesn't fit."

Jake sighed.

"I know. But once we put the story out there, we'll be fine."

"Is that how you are supposed to do it?"

"In this case, we have to have the police do more. And with the Development Proposition vote so soon, they'll be motivated to act quickly."

"I just don't know."

"I know. It's fine. Don't worry about it."

He started typing, drafting the outline of his story. He hadn't written anything so serious in a long time. He felt his fingers tingle as he began to type, but Gary still stood at the doorway with his arms crossed.

"Just be careful Jacob. Make sure all the pieces come together."

"I will."

He still didn't leave the garage.

"What about Sheryl?"

"What about her?"

"Why did Charlotte suspect her in all of this? And why did she give money to the Initiative?"

"I hate to say it, but Charlotte was wrong. She was obsessed with her silly bridge game."

Gary shrugged, bringing his cane up two inches off the ground along with his shoulders.

"She wasn't wrong before."

"Well, she lost control. She became biased. Besides, you talked to Sheryl, right?"

Gary raised his fingers to his lips.

"Not so loud Jacob! Meryl has ears like a hawk!"

"Ears like a....never mind. Where is she?"

"Asleep."

"Well anyway, you met with Sheryl, right?"

"I did. I think she's a good person. But there must be some sort of reason Charlotte suspected her of being involved. And a reason she donated the money."

"I think Charlotte just didn't know." He didn't want it to be true. "She got involved with a group bigger and crazier than her. Something modern. Something she couldn't understand."

Gary finally went up the stairs. But before he closed the door, he turned back again.

"I think you'd be surprised what we people know."

Jake was left alone in the room. He turned on the light. The red bulbs would have to do. The collage of Polaroids on the wall seemed to glow at their white bases. He looked at his laptop screen pulsing in the darkness and started to transcribe his notes from his notebook into the computer.

It didn't come as easily as he'd thought it would. He blamed the light, but he couldn't just punch the story out. Something seemed wrong. Unfinished. He stared at the red glow coming from the ceiling. He'd had a long day. It was time to call it a night. He'd go to his apartment the next day and then he'd be done. Things were as clear as they could be. He switched off the red light.

As he fell asleep on the cot, he noticed the white bottoms of the Polaroid pictures in the collage, and then he looked at Charlotte's duck, which he'd set beneath them. He could barely make out the orange bill in the light. It was silly, he knew. But as he shut his eyes, he couldn't help but think that the duck was frowning.

CHAPTER 44:

Gary liked to ride with the windows down.

"I like how it feels!" he shouted over the noise of the highway wind. His hair frizzed out around his head and Jake had to keep brushing his own hair back. It was a short drive to his apartment, and he had to admit the rush of air felt good. He was wearing another one of Gary's shirts and had two buttons undone, the wind flapping against the wide collar. Gary was playing with the duck, unscrewing the neck and then screwing it back in.

"It's genius!" he shouted.

"It is clever."

"What?"

"It's clever."

"What?"

"You can't hear me over the wind."

"It's clever!" Gary shouted back.

They'd go to the apartment and get a few shirts and some pants. Then he'd go back to Gary's garage and finish up his story. He'd be done by the middle of the day. They'd figure out what to do next, once he contacted the police. He probably had more driving ahead.

"Just so you know, after this, Thompson wants me to drive to Orlando."

"What?"

He closed Gary's window.

"Thompson wants me to drive to Orlando to write about Melinda Ginelli."

"Who's she?"

"I'm glad I'm not the only one who doesn't know her. She's a celebrity, apparently. She just moved down here, so I'm the only one here who could cover her."

"They probably want pictures."

"I guess so." He hadn't thought of that. They passed Sunset Cove beneath the highway. "I'll ask Thompson when I get back. I'll see if he wants you to come along."

"Good."

"It's funny, Gary."

"What?"

"I'll be glad to work on a normal story. But after this…"

"It seems a little boring to write about."

"Exactly."

"I still haven't taken any exciting photographs."

"That's true—Melinda Ginelli might be more interesting for you."

"I can be a paparazzo!"

Jake laughed as the Palmstead whizzed by beneath them. Maybe it wouldn't be so bad—writing about famous people instead of trying to make news. Then he looked over at Gary. He was frowning.

"I hope it turns out OK."

"So do I."

They continued down the highway. It was a beautiful day at least. The sun was high in the sky and there weren't any clouds. He could let himself enjoy it this time. He opened the windows again, now that he and Gary were done talking. Gary's hair frizzed out immediately. Jake's blew back, then to the side, and then in front of his face. He grabbed the wheel with both hands and watched the road. The sleeves on the borrowed shirt crept up past his elbows.

He turned on the windshield wipers. It was all there. Palm trees to the side. Heat blasting in. And giant bugs on the windshield. The water shot out and the wipers started pushing the bugs away. They'd all be washed off by the water and the wind. As he did it, he thought about his story. All this was being wiped away. Abram Samuels, Sheryl Goldfein, the Saving Tomorrow Initiative. Charlotte Ward, too.

They descended the ramp and after a few minutes pulled up to his apartment building's lot. It seemed calm. Empty. He still asked Gary to come with him. They crept up the apartment stairs, Jake moving slowly so Gary could follow with his cane.

The sound of the cane tapping on the stairs echoed over and over as they climbed to the second floor.

First, Jake stepped past his apartment and stood in front of Kaylie's. The blinds were gone. He realized he'd never seen inside. Of course, its current condition didn't give him any clues. The walls were empty and only a bare bed and dresser remained. He pressed his face against the window while Gary waited.

"Jacob, she's gone."

"I know. Let's go inside and get my stuff."

As he started to turn away from Kaylie's apartment, he saw something move. A flash of blue. He looked back. Someone was inside.

"Stay right there."

He knocked on the apartment door and waited outside. He braced himself for another attack. He looked at Gary, who had his cane pointing toward the door. He should have prepared better. They waited for the door to open.

But he didn't need to worry.

The door opened and a man walked forward. He was wearing a light blue jumpsuit, too tight at the chest and too big at the legs. He looked up at Jake and started speaking in broken English.

"Hello, I help you?"

"Wait." Jake stepped back. "I've met you before."

"I am sorry?"

"Your name is Javier, isn't it?"

"Yes, hello. What is your name?"

"What are you doing here?"

Gary rested his cane and Jake got out his notebook.

"I'm cleaning the apartment. Another person come in soon."

"But why are you here? I met you at Sunset Cove."

"I work here too."

"A second job?"

"This is same job. I am maintenance for three different

buildings for Mr. Rothschild."

Jake put the notebook away and pulled at Gary's arm. He followed Javier and asked another question.

"So all these buildings—they're all owned by Mr. Rothschild?"

"Of course."

"Is he on the lease?"

"Different name for the company. But it is his."

Javier smiled and went back inside. Jake's lease was inside his apartment, but he wasn't going to risk getting it. He led Gary down the stairs with one hand and put his other hand on the rail. He realized he was sweating.

"Jacob, why are we going? Don't you want your clothing?"

"Let's hurry."

They got in the car and Jake locked the doors. He brushed his hair back. Gary's shirt felt even tighter.

"Jacob, I don't understand. We should get your materials."

"Don't you see? Rothschild owns all the buildings."

"He is very rich."

"Can you hand me the duck?"

Gary took the duck and passed it over to Jake. He pressed his hands against the base and slowly unscrewed the top. The duck's head twisted around and around and the neck came unscrewed. He looked in the remaining rear view mirror. No one was coming. He rolled the papers out on his lap and Gary craned his neck.

"What are you looking for?"

"Just a second."

He'd been looking at the wrong pages all along. The call log, the journal—they were irrelevant. He held the final piece in his hand, the thing that made it all make sense. Gary held his glasses and leaned in.

"Are you looking at the bridge schedule?"

He was. He read each line, every day and week meticulously recorded on the page. He turned to Gary and shook his head.

"I can't believe I didn't realize."

"Realize what?"

"Charlotte Ward was right. It all makes sense." He turned the key in the ignition, shifted gears, and pressed his foot on the gas. "It was all about bridge."

CHAPTER 45:

"I'm very busy," Sheryl Goldfein said. She unfurled an aqua tablecloth and placed it on the table. "I have an important bridge game tonight."

Jake got out his notebook.

"Oh, we know you have a game tonight."

They'd driven to Sunset Cove as quickly as they could. Jake explained what he thought had happened and Gary nodded in agreement, offering the occasional refinement to the theory. As they pulled in the lot, they made sure nobody was watching. Even Melissa. They had to be secretive—they were on enemy territory in Sunset Cove. They looked at every passing walker with suspicion. When they entered the common room to see Sheryl, she glared at them.

Gary walked down the handicapped ramp, holding the rail with one hand and letting his cane tap out on the hollow sounding floor. Sheryl finished placing the tablecloths and put her hands on her hips.

"Ech, what is it? What do you want?"

"This is very serious. We want to confirm what happened to Charlotte. We think we finally understand."

She looked confused.

"Have you gained weight?"

Jake looked down at his shirt. At the chest, it looked like it was about to rip apart. The tails furled out, nearly splitting.

"No, I haven't gained weight. Now Sheryl, we need to talk about this immediately."

"It looks like you've gained weight."

"It's the shirt."

"It's a tight shirt."

"It's not mine. I borrowed it."

Gary nodded.

"It's not his!"

"Then whose is it?"

"It's mine," Gary said. "I let him borrow it."

Sheryl leaned to the side and arched her eyebrows. She walked over to Gary and patted him on the shoulder.

"Now I understand. When you said you told me you had a 'wife,' I didn't know this is what you meant. You know, you could have just told me. I'm a modern woman."

"Jacob, what is she talking about?"

Sheryl laughed.

"Always traveling together, borrowing clothing. It finally makes sense. You two are cute together."

Jake stepped to the side.

"Don't listen to her. Sheryl, we're not…that."

Gary appeared outraged.

"Jacob, is she implying we own our own clothing company?"

"No, no. I'm afraid that's not what she's implying."

They stood in a circle, silent. Then Jake coughed.

"We have real work to do."

But before he could go on, he heard a sound come from the corner of the room.

"Are we alone here?"

"Well…"

Abram Samuels walked out from behind the corner.

"Abram? What are you doing here?"

"Hi Jake." He tipped his red-brimmed hat. "I should have told you. Today, Sheryl and I finally…"

"Finally what?"

"Made love, Jake. We consummated our relationship and made love."

Jake sighed and touched his fingers to his temples.

"You give me so much unnecessary detail, Abram. So much."

"You can't stand in the way of love. Or love-making."

Jake looked over at Gary. His head was down and he looked a little disappointed. But he quickly recovered and gestured to both of them.

"I'm happy for you. But we need you to sit down,

considering what we've found out."

"I told you," Sheryl said, "I have a bridge game."

Abram walked forward to Jake. Jake tried to prevent a mental image from popping up.

"Abram, how did this happen? How did you and Sheryl..."

"Make love? Well Jake, it's very simple. First, we—"

"No." Jake put his hand up. "I don't want to know...that. But how did you...start seeing one another."

He walked over to Sheryl and stroked her neck with his hand.

"Yesterday, she came into my room in tears. She said a true romantic had broken her heart. And so we sat on the couch."

Gary blushed as Abram spoke.

"We started to realize how much we had in common. We'd both lost the people we loved. And so I sat closer next to her and placed my arm on her thigh. Then—"

"OK, I get it." Jake raised his hand again. "Unfortunately, we have more important things to talk about."

Abram dropped his arm and frowned.

"Now Jake, what's the meaning of this?"

"We know what happened to Charlotte."

"What do you mean?"

"We know who killed her."

"Was it the environmentalists?"

"Sort of." He clutched the duck close to his chest. "But it's more complicated than that."

"I don't understand."

"You will."

Sheryl started to turn and walk toward the table. Her purse was at the far end. Jake grabbed her arm gently.

"Where are you going?"

"I just need a Kleenex."

"Or are you trying to get your phone?"

"Abram, make him let go of me."

Abram walked up to Jake and grabbed his arm.

"Let her go."

"Listen, we can't let her call anyone. They've already tried to kill me."

He winced.

"She just needs a tissue."

"Abram, help us. For Charlotte's sake."

Sheryl reached out and grabbed Abram's arm. The three of them were linked together in a triangle. Abram grabbed Sheryl's hand with the tips of his fingers. They all waited to see what he would say.

"Sheryl, I know you didn't do anything wrong. But let's at least hear what the man has to say."

"I didn't do anything at all!"

"That's what we'll figure out," Gary said. He sat down at the table first. Jake sat next, then Abram. Sheryl looked at her purse at the far end. It was unzipped and open. But she didn't walk to it. She sat down beside Abram and leaned into his shoulder. Then Gary shouted.

"So, you made love?"

Abram nodded.

"Enough," Jake said. "No more information."

"Then what is this about?" Sheryl asked. She tried to sound angry, but they could all tell she was simply scared. Slowly, Jake unscrewed the neck of the duck. He took out all the papers and rolled them flat onto the table. Abram chuckled.

"I was wondering why you had her duck. I didn't know it was hollowed out like that though."

Sheryl stayed silent. She strained to see what was written on the pages, but she didn't seem close enough to make them out.

"What are all those papers?"

"We'll get to them later. First, I want to talk about the changes you made to the community's charitable donations. I finally know why you chose the Saving Tomorrow Initiative."

"I told you, we just chose something at random."

"I don't think that's true."

Jake got out his notebook and double-checked. He was

ready to call her on it. To be aggressive.

"Last year, you advocated the redistribution of a significant amount of money. It went from a lifetime charity to a relative unknown."

"It was for the wetlands."

"So was your old charity. You see, Sheryl, that was always the problem. It never made sense for you to switch all of that money in the first place."

"I told you—"

"Let me finish." He breathed out and calmed down. He'd get through it. But he wouldn't bully her. "It made even less sense when we started seeing the group you chose do terrible things. Airing radical commercials that didn't make sense. Making threats to people who got too close to the truth. Do you see the bruises on my body? Those are fresh."

"I don't know anything about it."

Abram grabbed her arm and brushed it with his hand. She pulled away. Jake continued.

"And I know that the Saving Tomorrow Initiative killed Charlotte Ward. They took her from her home and kept her from her medication. They left her to die. Now, why would you give money to an organization like that, Sheryl?"

"I told you." She was whispering and her accent was gone. He pressed on.

"Here's the difference between when you told me that before, and when you're telling me it now."

"What's the difference?"

He looked at Gary and then at the pages on the table.

"This time, I know why you did it."

CHAPTER 46:

Jake smoothed out every wrinkle and fold on the pages in front of him. He had the most important page laid out. It was the weekly schedule for bridge.

"Sheryl, you like bridge, don't you?"

"I told you, I have a game tonight. I need to get ready."

"You've been playing a lot lately, haven't you?"

"I always do."

"She does," Abram said. "I don't understand."

Before Jake could continue, Gary shouted.

"The jig is up!"

Jake sighed.

"They don't know what the jig is yet. Let me tell them."

"It's up! That's what the jig is!"

"Gary," he said and waited. Gary stood up and left the room. Jake went on without him. "Now Sheryl, I noticed that until very recently, you only played bridge once a week in this common room."

"How do you know that?"

"Because Charlotte saved the schedule."

He waved the pages in front of her. She tried to grab them but he didn't let her.

"And the schedule shows that every Monday you played a game here."

"So?"

She was still whispering.

"So, I also know that you don't control the times for the common room. Mel does. She decides who gets the room and when they get it. Apparently you would squabble too much about it."

"Right. And that's the time she gave us."

"I know that. But then you changed the funding for the community's charity."

"Yes, we did."

She was staring at the aqua tablecloth.

"That's interesting. Because at that same time, your bridge schedule changed too."

Abram leaned forward.

"It did?"

"Oh, it did. From one night a week to two. Sheryl got an extra night to do whatever she wanted in the common room. Mel happened to mention to me last week about your switching nights at will, being able to use them whenever you wanted. A surprising amount of power, Sheryl. Now, correct me if I'm wrong. But it sounds like you got paid off for giving the Saving Tomorrow Initiative money."

She didn't even bother whispering this time. She was silent. Abram tried to say something.

"It doesn't make sense..."

Jake continued.

"So the question is, who would be able to trade you more bridge nights for switching the community's donations? Now, it doesn't make sense that an environmental group would have the power to give you time in the common room."

Abram finished the thought, his voice rough as gravel.

"But Rothschild could change the schedule. Mel could."

Sheryl turned her head and spoke.

"I didn't know that anyone would get hurt." Her voice was hard. She wasn't going to cry today. "I didn't know they'd do something to Charlotte. They told me that if I switched the money to this harmless group, I'd get another night for bridge. Everyone wanted it instead of movie night. Everyone. I just made it happen."

She breathed out. Gary came back in the room.

"The jig is up," he whispered.

Jake pulled him down to his seat.

"Sheryl, who told you about the deal? Who presented the offer?" He choked before the next part. "Was it...Mel?"

Sheryl stared at him. She thought for a moment. Then she shook her head.

"A man named Conrad called me. He said that I'd get more

time for bridge if I convinced everyone to donate to the Initiative. All I had to do was keep it secret. He sounded so...harmless."

"Who's Conrad?" Abram asked.

"He's Rothschild's assistant."

"So this was all Rothschild's doing?"

"Yes." Jake tapped his pen on the table quickly. It left dark blue dots on the fabric. "Simeon Rothschild was behind the entire thing. He's the man behind the Saving Tomorrow Initiative."

Just as he said it, Mel opened the door.

"What's happening here?"

Jake turned to Sheryl.

"How did you call her?"

"No Jacob," Gary said. "I did."

"Why?"

Mel sat down beside Jake. He looked at her quickly and covered his notebook. Gary reached out toward Mel.

"Jacob, I know you are trying to be careful. But you have to trust Mel. When I left the room, I found a telephone and called her. She needs to know what happened. You know you can trust her. I'm positive she didn't have a part in any of this."

Jake wasn't so sure. He looked in her eyes as she waited for him to talk. He told her everything that had happened. As she listened, her eyes widened. Then they started to shine, wet with tears.

"I don't understand." She was calm at least. "I'm guilty too, aren't I?"

"How?" Abram asked.

"I gave Sheryl the extra nights. I run the schedules. I'm a part of it."

"Did you know what the extra nights were for?"

"He just told me what to do."

"Who did?"

"Simeon. He just told me to give Sheryl an extra night each week. And I can't argue with him, you know that."

"I know." Jake put his arm around her and held her close. He could feel her heart beating as she shook. It could be an aggressive thing to believe in somebody. As she calmed down, Abram took off his hat.

"But I don't understand. Why would Rothschild help an environmentalist group that was campaigning against the Development Proposition? Why would he kill…"

Jake didn't make him say her name.

"Charlotte was learning too much about the Saving Tomorrow Initiative. She started investigating bridge when Sheryl kicked her out. Then she realized there must be a reason that Sheryl had gotten more days, so she started investigating everything Sheryl had done. Including the group. Eventually, she traced them back to Rothschild. Maybe she had already threatened him. And that would have ruined everything: all the money, all the investment, and all of his plans for the group. She made too many calls and learned too much."

Mel sighed and brushed her hair back. She looked good, despite having cried a few minutes before. Jake wiped a tear off her cheek. She smiled faintly. She was whispering too.

"How did you know? How did you figure it out?"

"I didn't, at first. I had to wait for it to hit me over the head."

"What do you mean?"

"I didn't realize until I found out that Mr. Rothschild owned my apartment building. I saw Javier working there today."

"How did that help?"

"Because there weren't any marks on my door the day I was attacked. That's because they didn't have to break in. They just used their copies of my key."

"And that's why the girl was in your building!" Gary shouted.

Mel looked at Jake sideways. He mumbled an answer.

"They installed someone in the apartment next to me. Since Rothschild owned the building, that was easy. And they paid her to tip them off to my whereabouts. Once I realized that Rothschild was behind that, I knew there had to be a connection to what happened at Sunset Cove."

Sheryl interrupted.

"And then you looked at the bridge schedule."

Her accent was back and she sounded tough. Her fists were on the table, clenched. Abram had his jaw shut tight, and Mel was biting her nails.

"Now," Sheryl said, "I don't know if you can trust me. But I swear I had no idea. I want to get him for this. I don't want him to get away with what he did."

"Oh he won't," Gary said. "The jig—"

"Is up," Jake finished. He had to be aggressive. Firm with her. "Sheryl, you can't be a part of this. You've done enough already."

She put her head in her hands. Abram shouted.

"It still doesn't make sense. Didn't Rothschild want to develop on the wetlands? Why would he support a group that was fighting for people to vote against him on the Development Proposition?"

"I think I know why," Jake said. Mel looked at him, surprised. He continued. "But we have to make sure that anything we accuse him of sticks. I have a plan to catch him on this. He can't get away with it any longer."

"But why did he do it?" Abram asked. Jake clapped his hands together.

"The best way to find out is to ask him in person."

CHAPTER 47:

The next day, the view was still impressive. Rothschild's office was as clean as the first time Jake had visited. The leather-bound books sat in back, drowning in sunlight. The blobs of color on his paintings looked more like stains than art. And then there was Rothschild, meticulous in a black suit, his white hair gently tousled, and his chin raised up.

The plan was set. He'd go in and talk to Rothschild while recording the conversation. Then Mel would rush past the secretary and burst in, leading Gary, who'd be there to photograph everything. They'd have a fully documented confession. Jake smiled when he entered the room. Rothschild didn't.

"Mr. Russo. I've been expecting you."

Jake looked in his eyes. They were darker than his suit. They both stayed standing.

"Good. I've been looking forward to talking to you."

Rothschild leaned back on the desk, barely raising his feet. Then he laughed.

"Mr. Russo, have you gained weight?"

Jake looked down at his shirt. Today it was blue with a Hawaiian print. Gary liked bright colors.

"I haven't been able to get to my apartment. I borrowed this shirt from a friend."

Rothschild nodded and moved on quickly.

"So what are you here to talk about today? My favorite ice cream topping? If it will save you some time, I like vanilla."

"Mr. Rothschild—"

"Simeon."

"Mr. Rothschild." He gritted his teeth. "I'm here to talk about something else. I know you're behind the Saving Tomorrow Initiative. And I know you ordered Charlotte Ward's murder."

Rothschild hardly reacted. His black eyes got wider. Then he snapped his fingers. Slowly, the bookcase behind him opened. A man with long red hair emerged, his teeth bared. Conrad. He wasn't part of the plan. He waved with a bandaged hand. Rothschild flicked his hand forward toward Jake.

"Conrad, will you secure Mr. Russo? I believe you've done this before."

Jake didn't bother resisting. Conrad sat him down in a leather chair and then bound his hands with elastic cord. Jake glared at Rothschild.

"Your other henchman used tape."

Conrad finished binding Jake's hands and secured his legs to the chair. He took his phone and turned it off. No contact with the outside world now. He didn't struggle, but the binding was tight enough. He couldn't have moved if he wanted to. Conrad grabbed Jake's hands and smashed them on the arm of the chair.

"This is for slamming my hand in your apartment door."

Jake bit his lip hard enough to draw blood. Rothschild stood next to him. He brushed Jake's shirt and tapped a flower with his finger. Then he punched it.

"I must say, I'm actually a little surprised. Did you think you could just waltz in here and accuse me of murder? Haven't you concluded by now that I'm a dangerous man?"

He punched again. Not in the shoulder. Jake felt blood trickle from his nose down to his lips. That wasn't part of the plan.

"I know what you did."

"Of course you do," Rothschild said. Conrad went to the back of the room and stood silently. "I know that you've been toying with me from the beginning."

Jake focused on the pain. He didn't want to disagree.

"Do you think I didn't notice, Mr. Russo? Do you think I didn't notice that you were going to my properties twice a week for no reason? There was no conceivable story except for the one that you were working on. The one that you were going to use to take me down."

Twice a week. Apparently, Rothschild didn't know that

Mel had been his reason for visiting Sunset Cove. Jake let him keep talking.

"And then, Mr. Russo, I put someone in the apartment next door to yours. I admit you're quite clever. Telling her nothing. Acting like you're so insecure. It's the type of cunning I'd expect in, well, myself."

He stepped forward. He flicked a bruise with his index finger. Then he hit Jake in the stomach. Something cracked. He tried to release himself but couldn't. Rothschild reached forward and unbuttoned Gary's Hawaiian shirt. The tape recorder was bound around Jake's stomach. He ripped it off and handed it to Conrad.

"I thought you only used a notebook." Rothschild hit him again, before he had time to scream.

"And then I take the time to do an interview with you and you pretend not to know anything. Very cunning of you, Russo. Very cunning. I was impressed. Asking me questions about my favorite colors! You were toying with me. Taunting me. Asking me who I'd marry!"

Jake looked up, his head wobbling.

"I asked you who you'd hook up with. Not who you'd marry."

Rothschild hit him again and Jake grunted. The man brushed his hand on his suit pant.

"No, I knew all along that you were on to us. But it seems that you thought I'd just give up and let you go. You're not so lucky. Not today."

"Wait." Jake strained to raise his head. "The Initiative. Tell me why you created the group."

"Oh, I think you know that."

Rothschild looked at a fingernail and wiped something off. Probably blood. Jake tried to concentrate long enough to talk.

"You did it because you knew you were going to lose on the Development Proposition. You'd never get to develop the wetlands." He spit on the expensive carpet. "You knew that if you made a group crazier than your opponents, people would turn against them. People would vote your way. The only way to convince them was to trick them into thinking wetlands were for extremists."

"And it will work," Rothschild laughed. "I've done polls. No one will vote to save them. They believe the wetlands supporters are insane, thanks to my scrappy and well-funded activists in the Saving Tomorrow Initiative."

"Your company depends on it."

"No, that's not true." His chin seemed to sink a little. He recovered and hit Jake again. Jake felt his teeth shake as he spoke.

"And you thought I'd go along with it. That I'd write your story and hype up your case to the public." More blood leaked out. "But you didn't know that I discovered Charlotte was murdered. Then the stakes became too high to let me live. Just like they were with her."

Rothschild hit him again. This time, Jake didn't raise his head up as quickly. The man hit hard for someone his age. Out of the corner of his eye, Jake saw Conrad, standing quietly with his arms crossed. Rothschild was doing his job for him. When he stopped punching, he walked to the desk and took a sip from a crystal glass.

"Unfortunately, you're correct. You do create a problem with my plan, Mr. Russo. I can only have the Saving Tomorrow Initiative take blame for so much. If they're a radical group, they will only face so much scrutiny. Not many reporters are tenacious, anymore. By the time I have to reveal funding records, everyone will have forgotten about it all."

"And when you do, they'll show that the group got charitable donations."

"Exactly. I didn't send them a dime. But every community I own kicked a little in. And so did my foundation. On their own accord, of course."

He grinned widely. Then he suddenly frowned.

"But there's the unfortunate problem you've created. If people begin to think a woman was murdered, things become…difficult. The police will trace the group to me and start to get suspicious. But you're the only one who thinks that, aren't you?"

Jake stayed quiet. He couldn't speak.

"So I have to kill two birds with one stone. Well, actually, I assume Conrad will be killing you in a different way than he killed Charlotte. He's very creative."

Jake looked up and opened his eyelids. The red hair looked like fire. He could see Conrad was smiling. He still had the strength to speak. He spit blood out on the carpet. If only Mel showed up now.

"You aren't going to get away with this. People won't stand by for what you're doing."

"Ah, you'd think that." He went over to the bar and got out a bottle. "Club soda for the carpet. It's wonderful for unfortunate stains. Like you."

He placed the bottle on the desk and leaned back again.

"You see, I'm going to win. I have you here. And I always win. No one cared about an old woman dying on a beach. And no one will care about a third string reporter, sent to Sarasota because he couldn't cut it in the big city."

Jake spit again. Rothschild didn't bother moving.

"Do you know why nobody will care?"

"Why?"

"Because they are used to it. They are used to old people dying. They are used to crazy environmentalists, and they are used to developers getting what they want."

He laughed a little.

"And most of all, they are used to me winning and you losing."

He stopped laughing. He straightened the collar of his suit and tightened his tie.

"Conrad, I think we've said everything. Tonight, I'd like you to transfer him out of here. For now, make sure he's pacified."

Conrad opened the bookcase and carried Jake's chair in. He

felt something shoved inside his mouth and then elastic cords pinched his neck. He started to feel dizzy, and as he began to faint, he only thought one thing.

So much for the plan.

CHAPTER 48:

A light came in, first a thin line, then a wide band. Suddenly, the whole room was filled with light. He looked up, his neck sore. The bookcase was open and Rothschild was yelling at Conrad.

"Just get in there. And hurry. I'll have her leave in five minutes."

"I'd rather stay outside."

"Get in there. I don't want Mel to know you're here. She might put two and two together."

"If I could stay in here—"

"Do you not understand what I'm saying?"

Jake looked around the small room behind the bookcase. The walls looked like they were a silver color, possibly metal. Filing cabinets were lined up in a row on the left, and a wine refrigerator sat on the right. Conrad yelled to Rothschild.

"Just don't let her in. Lock the doors, sir."

"Who is the boss here? Last time I checked, I was. If I want to meet with her, I will."

Conrad shuffled into the small room. He cursed at Jake as he pulled the door shut.

"Don't think about screaming. I will make it more painful if you do."

He tightened the elastic cords around Jake's neck. Then he planted his hands firmly on the back of the chair. The room was completely dark. Jake tried to shake, but he couldn't move at all. Conrad was too strong. He decided to shove his whole body forward when he had a chance. If he did, they'd hear him slam against the back of the bookcase. It was his only chance.

He couldn't hear the words they were saying on the outside. He heard Rothschild's voice, muffled by the books and the wall. Then he heard Mel's. He tried to scream, but Conrad clamped a hand over his mouth. The man breathed silently. His hand almost covered Jake's entire face. They listened to Mel and Rothschild but understood nothing.

They waited. He could smell his own sweat in the space of the dark room. Or maybe it was his own blood. He started to think. If only they'd planned a little longer. If only he'd been smart enough to hit Rothschild first. He wondered how they would kill him. Where he would die. How long it would take Thompson to even notice. He guessed a week would go by before anyone in New York even realized he was gone.

He hoped Conrad had loosened his grip. It was now or never. With everything in him, he jerked his body forward in the chair and it started to tip forward. His head was only an inch away from the wall. They'd hear him and save him. He'd get to file his story.

He stopped falling. Conrad had caught the chair. The voices outside the wall started to sound fainter. Maybe it was his hearing. Or maybe they were walking away. They must have thought he'd never shown. By the time they realized, he wouldn't be able to be saved.

Then he heard a loud ringing. He looked back. He couldn't see well, but he saw hands moving frantically in the dark. It rang again. It wasn't his phone—it was Conrad's. The ringing stopped, but then the voices got closer and closer and became clearer. He heard a man shout.

"It's in there."

"Open it," Mel said. "Now!"

The thin line of light drew across the floor again. Then it turned into a wide band. Conrad shoved Jake's chair into the corner and leapt out of the room.

"Hold it right there," Sheryl Goldfein shouted.

Someone came over and pulled Jake up. Mel. She untied the cords around his neck, hands, and legs. He rubbed them and then stood up. Conrad was standing with his hands over his head and Jake walked out in front of him. Rothschild had surrendered. Then he saw Sheryl and Abram. Sheryl had a pistol in her right hand and used her left to brace her elbow. Jake wiped the blood from his mouth.

"Sheryl? Abram? Why are you here?"

She shrugged her shoulders and kept the gun steady.

"We had to come. For Charlotte."

"And you own a gun?"

She shrugged again.

"Are you really that surprised?"

He regained his balance.

"Do you mean because your husband was a cop?"

She steadied her grip.

"Ech. I mean because I'm Sheryl Goldfein."

Gary had set up his tripod and was taking photographs of Rothschild and Conrad. He pointed the camera at Jake and the flash went off. He rubbed his eyes and Gary raised a thumb up above the camera.

"You don't look good, but it's a good shot."

He turned to Rothschild.

"Looks like your plan didn't go so well."

"I should have killed you right away."

"Thanks for that quote." He reached for his notebook. "I'll have to get that on paper. Do you have my tape recorder?"

"I destroyed it."

Sheryl pointed the gun directly at Rothschild. He laughed.

"Your gun can't get his tape recorder out of the incinerator."

Conrad was totally silent. Mel grabbed a tissue and wiped Jake's forehead. Rothschild growled.

"Mel, are you and Mr. Russo…together?"

She walked up to him and spit on his face. He didn't bother wiping it off.

"Mel, you're fired."

"I don't care. You won't be behind this company much longer."

"Oh really?" He laughed. "You don't have any evidence. And now you're holding me at gunpoint. My lawyers…"

Jake hobbled over to the bookcase and opened it. He pointed at the filing cabinets.

"Oh we'll have evidence." He hit one on the top and listened as the metal echoed. "We'll get a warrant to look through all of these. Thanks for showing me where everything is."

"A warrant?" For the first time, his chin sank down into his chest. Jake walked in front of him.

"That's right. A warrant. A front page story. This is going to be everywhere."

Jake walked away and Sheryl steadied her gun. They heard knocking at the door.

"Is there a problem here?"

Four policemen stood at the door and Gary motioned them into the room.

"I called them on the telephone before we arrived. I knew that we'd need some backup."

Jake rubbed his wrists and buttoned up his Hawaiian shirt. Abram walked over to the policemen and pointed to the men. They pulled out their handcuffs.

"You are under arrest for attempted kidnapping."

Gary pointed his cane at them and almost hit Conrad.

"And you're going to get a lot more than that! The charges are just starting! Lot's of charges! Like a credit card, but for bad things!"

Rothschild turned to Conrad.

"Stay quiet. The lawyers will take care of this."

As the police read the men their rights, Jake stepped forward. One of the policemen tapped Jake on the shoulder.

"Sir, there's a paramedic outside as well, if you need attention."

"There is?"

"I called him," Gary said. "I thought we might need one."

"Thank God."

They followed the police out of the office and into the hallway. Once they were all outside of the building, they led Conrad and Rothschild to the police cars. Both stayed quiet. Jake could hardly move. But he was strong enough to walk over to Rothschild and get his attention before he entered the car.

"Hey, Mr. Rothschild. You know how you said everyone was used to developers winning? I've got something else you'll need to get used to."

Rothschild turned his head as he was pushed into the car. His eyes were solid black. Jake smiled.

"It's called jail."

The car doors slammed shut and the five of them watched as the police cars drove away.

CHAPTER 49:

"I think you're going to be fine. You don't even need a stitch."

Jake knew the paramedic—it was the Hispanic kid he'd met at Sunset Cove. He gave Jake some bandages and cleaned his wounds. The peroxide almost felt good. A healthy sting. Gary walked over and introduced himself to the kid.

"I remember you. You're the young man who helped me the day I saw the white light."

"You?" the kid said. "You're the guy who choked on his camera strap, aren't you?"

"You remember me?"

"Oh yeah." He smiled. "I see a lot. But how could I forget you?"

When he was finished, Gary waved as the ambulance drove away.

"I'm a celebrity!"

The five of them stood by Jake's car. Abram and Sheryl held hands while Gary watched the ambulance drive away. Jake wanted to hold Mel's hand. But he wasn't strong enough to stand without her support, so he leaned on her instead. She kissed his cheek at the one spot where there wasn't a bruise.

"How many times have you been beaten up?"

"I lost count. But that might be because I have a concussion."

They leaned on the trunk of the car. She was warm and they were both finally safe. Sheryl and Abram looked like they were waiting for him to talk.

"Look, I'm sorry I didn't trust you. Both of you. I should have asked you to come and help me. I think you saved my life today, Sheryl."

"Not just me." She squeezed Abram's hand. "He helped too."

"How?"

"How do you think we knew that there was a room behind the bookcase?"

Abram pulled out a paper from his back pocket. He unfolded it carefully and smoothed out all the creases. It was a dark blue page with white writing.

"I don't just study maps." He held it up. "I have a thing for blueprints, too."

Jake grabbed it. Abram had marked the spot behind the bookcase with a chalky white X. He handed the blueprint back and Abram folded it up.

"Abram, thank you." He meant it. "I'm just glad we got so lucky. What are the odds that someone would call Conrad? If he hadn't been called, you might not have known anybody was in there."

Gary stood up straighter and shook his head.

"The jig was up!"

"Right, Gary, the jig was up."

"No," Mel said. "He's the reason that Conrad got the phone call."

"What do you mean?"

"Before we went inside, Gary looked through all of Charlotte's papers. He found Charlotte's list of calls to the Saving Tomorrow Initiative. So he made me give him my phone."

"And he called the number?"

Gary nodded.

"I called it on my own! And then we heard the ringing behind the bookcase."

"So Conrad was the number all along."

"Yes," Mel said. "At least he carried the phone. They had a different line just for the Saving Tomorrow Initiative."

Gary piped up.

"I left a message."

"Did you?"

"I did." He laughed. "Jacob, I don't think they'll be calling back!"

Jake felt like he was getting his energy back, slowly. He walked forward and hugged Sheryl and Abram. He hoped the stains had dried. They hugged back tightly. It hurt against the bruises, but he didn't mind.

"I'm sorry I didn't trust you. But thank you again, for all you've done."

"You did the right thing," Abram said. "We just had to help."

Gary was still excited.

"So what will happen to the company? To his building?"

"My guess is that the company will be fine. They're not just one man. But I'm betting the vote on the Development Proposition will change. I doubt anyone will be able to develop on the wetlands any time soon. Once this story comes out, that will have changed forever."

He pulled Mel close to his side.

"I have to thank you too. You risked everything for this. I can't believe you did it. You're amazing." He brushed back his hair. "Am I terrible to look at?"

"Why?"

"Because I need to kiss you."

She was blushing already. But she nodded and Jake pulled her lips to his. It was soft—it had to be because of the bruises. But she still felt the way she had before. Except now he didn't have anything to hide. Or anything to be afraid of. It wasn't about being aggressive. It was just about being right. He let her go, gently, and looked to his right.

"Good lord."

Abram was dipping Sheryl halfway to the ground. She moved her hands around the back of his head as she kissed him. His hands shook from the strain of supporting her.

"That's nice," Mel said.

It continued. Abram switched arms and shook out the one he had been using. He seemed to have strength left.

"Very romantic," Gary noted.

They broke. Then Sheryl leaned forward and pushed Abram down. She dipped him back and they continued to kiss. Abram's hat fell off.

"All right!" Jake shouted. "We get it."

They stopped and both of them wiped their mouths on their sleeves. Abram picked up his red-brimmed hat and put it back on.

"It was romantic."

Gary sighed loudly.

"So this is it, I suppose. We've solved everything and figured it out. The criminals are in jail, the evidence is on the way. What do we do now?"

Jake got out his notebook. He still had a list of things to do.

"I'll finish my story tonight. And then we develop the pictures. If we stick to everything, the police should take it from here. I don't think they have a lot to do. And I'm sure they're happy for our help."

"Ah." Gary coughed. "The pictures."

"What? What's wrong?"

"Well Jacob, as you know, due to my accident, I'm not allowed to carry any of my gear around. It could endanger me!"

Jake sighed.

"So the lenses, the tripod, the case, the camera…"

"They are all still upstairs in Mr. Rothschild's office."

He could barely walk.

"I'll get it."

"Thank you."

"You're welcome." He clapped his hands. "So, I guess I'll see you all later. We did it together."

"For Charlotte," Abram said.

"For Charlotte," they all said in unison.

They started walking toward their separate cars and Jake walked toward the building. Before he was out of range, he called to Gary.

"Can I stay on your cot another night? I don't want to go back to my apartment yet."

"Of course you can! We can develop the film together!"

He waved and started walking. Then he felt someone grab

the back of his shirt. He turned around. It was Mel.

"You can get his stuff, but then come right back."

He nodded.

"OK, I will."

"But you'll have to tell Gary you'll see him later."

"Why?"

"Because tonight, you're staying with me."

CHAPTER 50:

The first thing he smelled was waffles. Then the other scents became distinct. Sausage. Syrup. Pancakes. He heard something sizzling on a pan, then crackling after a few minutes. By the time he sat up, Mel had brought a tray back to the bed. She placed it in front of him and joined him under the covers.

"I never cook. But considering all you've gone through, you deserve breakfast in bed."

It smelled too good. He looked down at his stomach, past the bruises.

"Mel, I have something to tell you."

"No, wait." She sat up and grabbed his hand. "I have something to tell you."

"OK. You first."

"Are you sure?"

He stared at the half empty honey bear.

"Yes."

"Last night, while you were writing your story, I got a call from Jerry Rubenstein."

"At the Palmstead?"

"Yes. Have you met his dog?"

"Coconut?" He laughed. "I've met the dog."

"Well…I'm going to meet Coconut too. Jerry offered me a job planning events for residents. No more paperwork, and no more meetings. Just the people."

He hugged her. Even in the morning she smelled good.

"That's amazing. I'm so happy for you."

"I know. So, what did you want to tell me?"

"Well…"

He looked at the waffles on the plate. Waiting.

"The thing is—"

"Your diet?"

"What?"

She pointed at each item on the tray.

"The waffles are low fat. The syrup doesn't have any sugar. The honey is artificial and the sausage is turkey. It's all very healthy."

"How did you know about my diet?"

She grabbed his waist and squeezed.

"Well, I couldn't tell from looking at you. But when we went to dinner I knew something was up. Then Gary told me that you'd lost a lot of weight your first month here."

"Before I met you."

"Right." She started cutting the waffle. "So start eating."

Before he could, his phone rang. He searched through his clothes to find it. Thompson. For once, he wanted to answer.

"Sir! Did you get the story? I stayed up all night writing it."

"Russo." He didn't sound good. "Just wait a minute."

"Gary's going to send the pictures to you tomorrow. The police said that all of what I put in is usable, so that should be great."

Thompson just growled.

"Russo, have you seen the news lately?"

"I told you, I made it. This story's amazing: murder, corruption, politics. I'm begging you."

"I asked you, have you seen the news?"

"Uh, I don't know. I guess I haven't."

"Have you seen the tabloids?"

"I don't know. No. Why?"

Mel looked confused. Jake was too.

"Where did I tell you to...to go Russo?" Thompson coughed loudly. He wasn't laughing.

"Orlando, sir. But we broke this amazing story instead. It's going to change the whole market."

"I told you to go to Orlando, Russo. Do...do you know what happened?"

"No. I guess not. But this story—"

"Melinda. Melinda Ginelli."

"What? Did she dye her hair?"

"Oh no. Bigger." He growled into the phone. "Apparently,

261

she went to a dance club and took some nasty drugs."

"Oh. Well, that's too bad."

"That's not all."

"OK. Well, my story is pretty amazing—"

He interrupted.

"She took these drugs. And then…then she started having hallucinations."

"That's terrible."

"She started having hallucinations. Started thinking she was an animal, or a wild child, or something."

"Well, that's a tragedy."

"Do you know what happened?"

"No, I told you, I don't know."

"Turn on your TV. You'll find it. I guarantee."

He asked Mel for the remote control. She gave it to him and he turned her TV on. He flipped through the channels. Sports. A commercial. Cartoons. Then he saw it.

"Wow. Sir, I had no idea."

Melinda Ginelli was stuck on top of a palm tree.

"Did you see it?" Thompson screamed.

"Yes, I see it."

"Palm trees Russo! And celebrities! It's the greatest picture I've ever seen! And where were you? Sarasota?"

He turned off the TV.

"That's pretty impressive, I admit."

"Palm trees. Palm trees."

Thompson kept repeating the words, getting louder each time. Jake didn't think he'd stop. He pulled the phone away from his ear and handed the remote control back to Mel.

"I think I'm in trouble."

"Why?"

"I just missed the most famous palm tree in the world." He picked up the honey bear. "Let's eat."

"Wait," she said. "I have something else to tell you first."

"What's that?"

He poured some syrup on the waffles and Mel got up from

the bed. He watched her walk over and take something out of a bag. It was Charlotte's wooden duck. The dark green paint glinted in the morning sunlight, and the bill was soft orange. She unscrewed the neck and pulled out a piece of paper. Jake tried to see what it said.

"What's that?"

"Brunfelsia Americana."

"What?"

"The flowers. Remember? I couldn't remember the name of the flowers that we were putting in the new garden."

"You found them?"

"I found the name that night. But I kept the answer to myself."

"Why?"

She smiled and handed him the paper.

"Because I wanted you to keep coming back to see me."

He took the paper and dropped it into the base of the wooden duck. He screwed the neck back in and lifted the tray aside. He took Mel in his arms and kissed her deeply. She touched his face and shoulders.

"The food is getting cold. But I suppose you have to go." She pointed at the TV. "You have to follow up that story, right?"

He tried the waffles for the first time. She was right. They tasted like low fat.

"I could go to Orlando. But I'd rather stay here."

"Can you do that?"

"I think we should go to the beach."

"You do?"

"I have some things I'd like to say while we look out at the water."

"I'd like that. I'd like it a lot."

"Then let's do it."

So later that day, they did.

THE END

BOOKS BY PHIL EDWARDS

Jake Russo Mysteries
Retirement Can Be Murder
Death By Gumbo
Dead Air Can Kill You
The Show Must Go Wrong
Lights! Camera! Murder!

Thrillers
Cloud Crash: A Technothriller

Humor
Fake Science 101: A Less-Than-Factual Guide to Our Amazing World
Dumbemployed: Hilariously Dumb And Sad But True Stories About Jobs Like Yours
Snooki In Wonderland

Learn more and connect with the author at PhilEdwardsInc.com.